Advance Praise for *A Man of His Word*

"A fresh and captivating voice in the Amish genre, Kathleen Fuller weaves a richly patterned story that explores not only the depths of the Amish faith but also the most intimate struggles of the heart."

—Tamera Alexander, best-selling author of *The Inheritance, Beyond This Moment,* and *From a Distance*

"For romance fans, Kathleen Fuller provides a double-dose in *A Man of His Word*. [R]eaders will enjoy the peaceful setting . . . Fuller puts you in the heart of Middlefield, Ohio and her details about this Old Order Amish community left me feeling like I was an onsite spectator among her well-drawn characters. I highly recommend . . ."

—Beth Wiseman, best-selling author of *Plain Perfect*

"*A Man of His Word* by Kathleen Fuller is heartwarming story of how faith and commitment can overcome betrayal. Highly recommended!"

—Colleen Coble, best-selling author of *Cry in the Night* and the Rock Harbor series

"Terrific! I was totally engaged in the characters and the families in this lovely story. With Gabriel as the hero, the title is certainly well chosen. His faith, along with Moriah's, represents a steady, underlying conviction and peacefulness despite the very real struggles they face within the pages. This is a story—and characters—I didn't want to leave."

—Maureen Lang, author of *My Sister Dilly*

A Man of His Word

A Man of His Word

A Hearts of Middlefield Novel

KATHLEEN FULLER

THOMAS NELSON
Since 1798

NASHVILLE DALLAS MEXICO CITY RIO DE JANEIRO BEIJING

To Maria . . . *Danki.*

Published in Nashville, Tennessee, by Thomas Nelson. Thomas Nelson is a registered trademark of Thomas Nelson, Inc.

Thomas Nelson, Inc., titles may be purchased in bulk for educational, business, fund-raising, or sales promotional use. For information, please e-mail SpecialMarkets@ThomasNelson.com.

Scripture quotations are from the King James Version of the Bible.

Library of Congress Cataloging-in-Publication Data

Fuller, Kathleen.
A man of his word : a hearts of Middlefield novel / Kathleen Fuller.
p. cm.
ISBN 978-1-59554-812-2 (softcover)
1. Middlefield (Ohio)—Fiction. 2. Amish Country (Ohio)—Fiction. 3. Amish—Social life and customs—Fiction. I. Title.
PS3606.U553M36 2009
813'.6—dc22

2009020423

Printed in the United States of America

09 10 11 12 13 RRD 6 5 4

A Note from the Author

A Man of His Word is set in the lovely village of Middlefield, Ohio, located in Geauga County in northeast Ohio. About forty minutes east of the city of Cleveland, Middlefield is the fourth largest Amish settlement in the world, making up 12 percent of the county's population. The Amish established themselves here in 1885, when David Miller, in search of cheaper farmland, moved from Holmes County, Ohio, to the Middlefield area.

Middlefield's slogan, "Where Industry Meets Agriculture," neatly describes this pleasant town. Amish buggies share the gently sloping roads with "Yankee" cars and motorcycles. Modest white houses and barns dot the landscape amid large businesses like Middlefield Cheese House and Dillen Products. Shops producing handcrafted Amish goods are as easy to find as the local CVS pharmacy and Wal-Mart.

Many of the Middlefield Amish, like the Lancaster County Amish, are Old Order. While both the Middlefield and Lancaster settlements are divided into districts, each with its own *Ordnung*—an unwritten set of rules members abide by—there are noticeable differences in buggy style, dress, and cultural influence. In Middlefield non-Amish are referred to as Yankees, while in Lancaster they are called *Englischers.* A Lancaster Amishman might drive a gray-colored buggy, while Middlefield buggies are always black. A Middlefield woman's prayer *kapp* at first glance might look the same as a Lancaster *kapp,* yet upon deeper inspection one realizes they are of differing design. There are also varying guidelines for the use of technology. While these superficial differences are evident among all Amish settlements, they do not detract from the main tenets of the Amish faith—a desire to grow closer to God, the importance of family and community, and living a plain and humble lifestyle.

With the help of some extremely generous Amish and Yankee friends, I have tried to portray the Amish in Middlefield as accurately and respectfully as possible. If there are any mistakes or misconceptions in my story, they are of my own making.

I hope you enjoy *A Man of His Word* as much as I enjoyed writing it. If you are ever in the northeast Ohio area, I invite you to visit Middlefield and experience everything this wonderful village has to offer.

Kathleen Fuller

Pennsylvania Dutch Glossary

Ausbund: hymnal
bann: excommunication from the Amish
Biewel: Bible
boppli: baby
braut: bride
bruder: brother
daed: father
dawdi haus: a separate dwelling built for aging parents
danki: thank you
dochder: daughter
dummkopf: dummy
Frau: wife, Mrs.
Fraulein: unmarried woman, Miss
fehlerfrei: perfect
geh: go
grossdochder: granddaughter
gude mariye: good morning
gut: good
Herr: Mr.

kapp: an Amish woman's prayer covering

kind: child

maedel: girl

mei: my

mami: mother

mudder: mother

nee: no

nix: nothing

Ordnung: an unwritten set of rules members abide by

recht: right

reck: coat

rumspringa: the period between ages sixteen and twenty-four, loosely translated as "running around time." For Amish young adults, *rumspringa* ends when they join the church

schwei: sister-in-law

schwester: sister

schwoger: brother-in-law

sehr: very

seltsam: weird

sohn: son

Wie geht's: How are you?

willkum: welcome

wunderbaar: wonderful

ya: yes

Yankee: a non-Amish person

yank over: to leave the Amish faith

He healeth the broken hearted,
and bindeth up their wounds.

Chapter 1

Moriah Byler ran her fingers across the soft fabric of the dress hanging on her closet door. Its powder-blue hue, her favorite color, resembled a clear summer sky. Giddiness coursed through her. In three hours she would don this new dress, and before God and her church, she would become Mrs. Levi Miller.

Closing her eyes, she pictured her handsome husband-to-be, his sandy-brown hair falling across his forehead, his chestnut-colored eyes filled with mischief when he was up to something—which was often. She smiled broadly. Was he experiencing the same excitement she felt? Since he had proposed to her a few months ago, she had dreamed about this day, the day she would marry the man she loved, the man God had set apart especially for her. Memories of his proposal flashed through her mind. He had taken her by surprise that day in the barn, first by asking her to marry him, then by boldly kissing her.

Opening her eyes, she touched her cheeks, flushing at the memory. She had always thought she would experience her first kiss after she married. Then again, Levi had always been unpredictable. Although he had tried to kiss her again, she had stopped him.

Kissing led to other things—things that should occur after marriage, as their faith taught. She had seen the disappointment in his eyes, but he had agreed to her wishes. Since then he had also been on his best behavior.

She took one last look at the dress she and her mother had finished a week ago, then frowned. Was that a hole in the sleeve? She removed the dress from the hanger. Sure enough, a part of the shoulder seam had separated. She retrieved a needle and thread and quickly stitched it up. After knotting the thread, she snipped it close to the stitches with a small pair of scissors. *There. Now it's perfect.* The dress and her wedding day would be *fehlerfrei*.

Moriah hung up the dress and walked to her second-story window, peering into her family's backyard. She gave thanks for their two-acre spread, which included a large clapboard barn and storage shed, both painted in the same shade of white as the house. She spied her father and two of her younger brothers, Lukas and Stephen, bringing inside a long wooden table the family had borrowed several days ago. Behind them followed Gabriel, Levi's identical twin brother, carrying a couple of wooden chairs.

As she watched Gabriel, she recalled the close friendship the three of them had shared as children. Some of her favorite memories revolved around watching Levi and Gabriel try to outdo each other in everything. Gabriel always had the better grades and was physically stronger, as he had proved in third grade when he and Levi had taken turns to see who could lift her up. Gabriel had carried her across the yard as if she weighed no more than a kitten while Levi had carried her only a few feet. But Levi soon proved he could best Gabriel in games of speed and agility, and she smiled as she remembered his determination to climb trees faster and higher than anyone in their school.

She and Levi had begun courting at age sixteen, just after *Frau* Miller had passed away. Gabriel quickly distanced himself, as if they had never been friends at all. At first, she thought Gabriel was grieving the loss of his mother, but he continued to treat her coolly, more so with each passing year. She hoped that would change once she was a part of his family. She missed his friendship.

Moriah started to turn away when she heard a *plink*ing sound against the windowpane. Then another. She gazed at the ground to see Levi standing below. Sans hat and coat, he had on a long-sleeved, white shirt with black suspenders attached to his dark trousers. Oh, how handsome he looked! He was bending down to pick up another pebble when she shoved open the window. The chilly November air rushed into the warm bedroom.

"Levi! What are you doing?"

Levi's boyishly wicked smile spread across his face. "Looking at *mei braut*."

She couldn't help but smile when he called her his bride. "You'll see enough of me at the wedding."

"I can't wait that long." The sunlight glinted off his hair.

Giggling, she said, "You'll have to. I shouldn't even be talking to you."

His shoulders slumped slightly. "Don't you wish we could just run away and get married? Forget all this"—he spread his arms out and gestured to the house and backyard—"and do something different?"

His words shocked the smile from her face. Run away? She knew Yankees sometimes eloped, but she would never consider getting married anywhere but among her family and friends, receiving the full blessing of the church and the Lord. "Levi, why would you even say something like that?"

"I was only kidding," he said, the tone of his voice dropping. Then he straightened his shoulders and grinned again, calming the twinge that had suddenly pinched her heart. He reached for a ladder that had been propped against the house. Her father and several other men from the church had finished reroofing the house last week, and the ladder had been in heavy use. Levi moved the ladder until it clattered against the house, right next to her window.

When he placed his foot on the bottom rung, her jaw dropped. "Levi, you can't come up here."

"Why not?" His hands gripped the side of the ladder and he took a step up. "I have every right to see my bride."

"But not this way." She put her hand to her head. She didn't even have her *kapp* on, nor was her hair brushed and pinned up. He couldn't see her like this, and he definitely couldn't be alone in her bedroom. He knew that. "Levi, if *Daed* sees you—"

He glanced up but kept climbing. "Everyone is inside, Moriah. Don't worry, he won't catch me."

Alarm rose within her. She couldn't be alone with Levi, especially not in her room while both their families were downstairs. Other than a few buggy rides together, they hadn't been by themselves since he had proposed to her, and she had been fine with that. They would spend plenty of time together once they were married. "Levi, *nee*!"

He climbed one more step, then stopped. He was halfway up the ladder now, and it would only take him a few more seconds to reach her bedroom. She froze, wondering what he would do. Meeting his gaze, she saw something in his eyes she had never seen before. Frustration? "You don't want to see me?" he asked, sounding hurt.

She shook her head. "Not right now."

After a fleeting hesitation, he gave her his trademark cocky smirk, and she thought he would respect her wishes. Instead, he continued to climb.

"Levi!" Gabriel's voice startled her. She stepped back from the window, far enough so she wouldn't be seen from the outside, but still within hearing distance of the two brothers.

"What are you doing?" Gabriel asked, his tone hard.

She listened as Levi shimmied back down the ladder, straining to hear his words. "Just having some fun, *bruder*."

"By sneaking into Moriah's bedroom?"

Although she couldn't see Gabriel, she could imagine him standing in front of Levi, his arms crossed, his facial expression set in stone as it often was when he and Levi argued.

"She's *mei braut*, Gabe. Lighten up."

"I'd think you'd have better things to do than goof around on your wedding day."

"That's right," Levi retorted. "*My* wedding day."

Moriah's brow furrowed. What did he mean by that? She leaned forward as much as she dared, but the men's voices grew faint. Peeking outside, she saw them heading toward the barn, still arguing with each other.

Moriah closed the window, wrapping her arms around her body. The cold air had pierced through her cotton nightgown, icing her fingers and toes. What had gotten into Levi? They would be married in such a short time, why would he risk getting both of them into trouble by doing something so reckless? Certainly he wouldn't entertain something that would put not only him, but also her, in the *bann*? While she often found his spontaneity attractive, he had unnerved her this time. Fortunately only Gabriel had spotted him. It would have been much worse if their parents had.

Taking a deep breath, she relaxed and started to dress, putting

Levi's antics out of her mind. He'd done no harm, and she somehow knew Gabriel wouldn't say anything to anyone. A tiny smile played on her lips. One thing she did know, life with Levi would never be boring.

She brushed out her waist-length, blonde hair and wrapped it tightly in a bun before fastening her white prayer *kapp* with two bobby pins. She would later cover the *kapp* with her black bonnet, which would conceal her hair completely. In three hours, the ceremony would begin, and after slipping on her shoes, she went downstairs to the kitchen to help with the preparations.

The thick scent of stuffed roast chicken baking in the oven mingled with the tangy aroma of coleslaw and potato salad. As she entered the kitchen, she also caught a whiff of spicy cinnamon from the apple pies that had been set on the countertop to cool.

Argumentative voices reached her ears—the deep bass of one of her younger brothers, Tobias, mingled with the melodic yet irritated soprano of Rachel Detweiler, one of his former classmates from school and the daughter of one of her mother's dearest friends.

"You don't know what you're talking about," Rachel snapped. The two had turned the kitchen into a battle zone. The petite nineteen-year-old cast a glance toward Moriah, irritation splashed across her delicate features. "Tell your *dummkopf* brother to stay out of the kitchen. He keeps adding more spices to my cauliflower casserole. *Unnecessary* spices."

"That's because it tastes like wet cardboard smeared with moldy cheese." Tobias, who at five feet ten was a good six inches taller than Rachel, reached around her slim body and shook some salt on the steaming casserole.

"You're going to ruin it!" She swirled around until she faced him, then grappled at the salt shaker he held over her head.

"Too late for that." He put the shaker behind his back and taunted her with a mocking look.

Moriah watched the two of them with amusement. Tobias and Rachel had grown up together, just as Moriah had grown up with Levi and Gabriel. But unlike the easy friendship she'd had with the Miller brothers, Tobias and Rachel could barely abide each other's company. Though Moriah thought that lately it seemed her brother enjoyed teasing Rachel a little *too* much and that Rachel didn't seem as put out by him as she had in the past.

"Are you two at it again?" Emma Byler, Tobias and Moriah's mother, entered the kitchen. She readjusted her apron around her trim waist and scowled at Rachel and her son. "We still have much to do, and I can't have you two bickering the whole time. Behave yourselves."

Tobias set the salt shaker back on the table, a lock of dark blond hair slipping across his forehead. He looked appropriately contrite. "Sorry, *Mami.*"

Rachel apologized as well, but Moriah didn't miss the quick, triumphant look the girl shot at Tobias, as if she'd won their little spat.

"Tobias, you shouldn't be in here anyway," Emma added.

"That's what I said," Rachel muttered.

Emma walked over to her son. "I need you to see if we have enough chairs and tables for everyone. Also, help your *daed* and brothers in the barn. He's making sure there's enough hay and feed for the extra horses."

Tobias nodded and headed out the back door of the kitchen and toward the barn, without giving Rachel a second glance. Moriah thought she detected a slight frown on the young woman's face in response to being ignored, but she could have been imagining it.

Turning, Emma gave Moriah a look of surprise, as if she'd just noticed her standing nearby. "What are you doing down here?"

"Offering to help."

"*Nee,*" clucked Emma. "Not on your wedding day. You've done enough this week already. We have everything under control, and there are plenty of people giving a hand. Rachel is finishing up her casserole, and her *mudder* will be here shortly. Now, you go upstairs and relax. You have a big day ahead."

For the first time since Levi had proposed, she felt anxiety seeping into her. Not about marrying Levi, but about the wedding itself. The focus would be on her and Levi, and she wasn't comfortable with that realization. She preferred to be involved, helping with preparations in the background. Somehow she had to keep busy, as she couldn't imagine pacing the floor of her room upstairs for the next couple of hours.

As if sensing her daughter's apprehension, Emma put an arm around Moriah's shoulders and spoke in a soft voice, "Go upstairs and read your *Biewel.* Pray for Levi, for your marriage, and for God to bless you and give you a family. I can think of nothing more worthwhile than spending time with the Lord before your wedding."

Moriah nodded, comforted by her mother's wise suggestion. "*Ya, Mami.* I will do that."

"*Gut.*" Emma kissed her daughter on the temple. "I want this day to be *fehlerfrei* for you."

"It will be, *Mami.* I'm sure of it."

Emma playfully shooed Moriah from the room. "Now, *geh!*"

Just then Joseph, Moriah's father, walked into the door. He took off his hat and ran his hand through his dark-brown hair liberally streaked with silver. He placed his black hat back on his head and eyed Moriah with a slight smile. "What are you doing in here?"

"I already told her she wasn't needed," Emma said, moving to stand by her husband. She glanced up at him. "Have you enough chairs?"

"*Ya,*" Joseph said, looking down at his wife. He leaned down and whispered in her ear. Emma smiled and gave him a lighthearted pat on the arm. "*Geh!* I've enough work to do without you messing about in here."

Joseph chuckled and walked out the kitchen door.

Moriah grinned. For as long as she could remember, her parents had been like that—playful, in perfect partnership, and totally in love. If her marriage was half as wonderful as theirs, she would be a blessed woman indeed. Her thoughts filled with Levi and the love they shared, she turned to go back upstairs, but not before she caught Rachel discreetly adding a dash more salt to her casserole.

Gabriel Miller tugged on the neck of his collarless shirt; the growing warmth of the crowded house grated on him. He could bear the heat if he weren't watching his twin brother, Levi, standing only a few feet away, speak his wedding vows to Moriah Byler. Gabe tried to keep his focus on his brother, but he had never seen Moriah look as lovely as she did today. Her simple sky-blue dress accentuated her round, blue eyes that, as she looked at Levi, shone with evident happiness. She was a beautiful bride. But she wasn't his.

Guilt stabbed at him. Once again, he was coveting his brother's woman, and he didn't know how to stop. When Levi and Moriah had started courting, he fought against his attraction to Moriah, begging God to take it away, to make his heart pure. He'd hoped when he joined the church last fall, months before Levi, he could relinquish his sin forever. Yet since then, his feelings hadn't ebbed. Instead, they had only grown stronger.

It was torture, witnessing Levi marry Moriah. He should be happy for his brother. He *wanted* to be happy for his brother. But his intense jealousy clouded any other emotions. Why Levi and not him? Did Levi know what a precious woman she truly was? Gabriel wondered if he did, especially after catching him trying to sneak into her bedroom right before the wedding, an act that showed a lack of respect not only for her but for her family. What had his brother been thinking? But Gabriel knew the answer to that. As usual, Levi hadn't been thinking at all. Just doing whatever he wanted, never mind the consequences to anyone else. Gabe was only two minutes younger than his twin, but many days he felt years older.

His gaze strayed to Moriah again, and another surge of emotions swelled within him. It wasn't just her outer beauty that drew him. Moriah Byler possessed a humble, gentle spirit and an unmatched generosity that plucked at the strings of Gabe's heart. How many times over the years had he witnessed her offer to help an overwhelmed mother with her children, or go out of her way to care for an elderly member of their church? He couldn't bear to see her hurt in any way. All he wanted was her happiness, and if she found that with his brother, then he would have to learn to accept it.

Levi uttered more words, promising to care for her, to be a loving spouse. The same thing all Amish husbands pledge to do. Gabriel shifted in his chair and tugged at the neck of his shirt again. When would the ceremony *end*?

Finally, after three and a half hours had passed, Abel Esh, the gray-haired bishop, gave the couple his blessing. His beard, nearly down to the center of his chest, bobbed up and down as he spoke. Gabe glanced at Levi and Moriah's hands, their fingers intertwined.

As soon as the wedding ended, he shot out of the house into the cold winter air. He breathed in deeply, the crispness prickling his lungs. A pretty good snow had fallen a few days ago, the second in the month of November, but most of it had melted, leaving small piles of white slush and bigger pools of muddy water behind. The bright glare from the overhead sun added to his agony, its light betraying him as it seemed to bestow approval on Levi and Moriah's union.

He stuffed his icy hands deep into the pockets of his black trousers. He'd left his overcoat in Tobias's room, upstairs in the Byler's huge farmhouse, but Gabe wasn't ready to go back inside. Wearing only his thin dress shirt and a black vest, he figured he deserved to shiver in the cold for his sinful thoughts about his brother's wife.

Inside, the women and young boys were readying the front room for the wedding supper. He usually loved the food: the stuffing, creamed celery, fried and baked chicken, rolls, and probably twenty different types of casseroles and pies. Everyone in the community brought a dish to share among the almost two hundred guests in attendance. Even his father, who had become an excellent cook since their mother had passed away four years ago, had brought German potato salad, the twins' favorite. But Gabe doubted he could eat a bite.

A few more men braved the chill and came outside, but they had the good sense to wear their coats. Tobias and a few of his friends held baseball gloves and started a game of ball in the sprawling front yard. Rachel Detweiler appeared, dressed in her Sunday best—a dark, plum-colored dress with a black cape for an overcoat, complete with a stiff, white prayer *kapp*. She was a little thing, but not afraid of the boys, or of the muddy ground serving as their ball field. Slipping her hand in her own well-worn mitt, she intercepted a ball intended for Tobias, then whipped it back to Christian Weaver, who caught it cleanly, taking a step back due to the force of the throw.

"Go inside, Rachel," Tobias yelled at her, clearly annoyed that she had horned in on their game. "You should be in there helping the women get dinner ready."

"Go soak your head, Byler." Rachel looked up at him, one hand on her slender hip while the other slapped her mitt against the side of her thigh. "They've got plenty of help. If I wanna play ball, I'm gonna play ball. I don't care what you say."

Tobias looked at the other guys as if searching for backup, then shrugged his shoulders in defeat. Score one for Rachel Detweiler.

Gabe's lips twitched in an almost smile. Rachel was close to marrying age. It would take a strong fellow to deal with such a spitfire. He briefly questioned if there was a man in Middlefield who would be up to the challenge.

"They're serving the food." John Miller, Gabe's father, sidled up to his son. He put his huge hand on Gabe's shoulder. "You should go inside and eat."

Staring down at the smooth stones of the sidewalk, Gabe replied, "You go ahead. I'll wait until the next shift."

"Your brother is expecting you. Wouldn't be right not to be one of the first people to congratulate him."

Gabe turned and looked into his father's brown eyes, eyes that were similar to his and Levi's, except there were deep crinkles at the corners, new crevices he hadn't noticed before. Although a widower of four years, his father kept his marriage beard, which had reached to the front button of his shirt, with only a few strands of brown nestled within the gray. He had vowed never to remarry; his love for Velda remained as strong as it had been before she had passed away from cancer. Eternal, as he referred to it. They had been together over forty years, having the twins late in life. Their "miracle children," Gabe's mother had often called them. Their family had been an anomaly, a small one in the midst of many large ones.

Taking in the disapproval glinting in his father's eyes, Gabe relented. "I'll be in shortly."

"See that you are, *sohn.*" White puffs emitted from John's mouth as he said the words. He squeezed Gabe's shoulder once more, then turned away, his shoulders stooped from years of hard labor at the blacksmith's anvil.

Steeling himself, Gabe followed his father's footsteps into the house. He could handle this. He was skilled at masking his emotions about Moriah. He'd been doing it for so long. No one knew of his secret love for her.

Only God knew what was festering inside him. He aimed to keep it that way.

Moriah's face ached from smiling so much, but she wouldn't complain. After almost a half an hour accepting congratulations and receiving hugs and good wishes, she felt happiness beyond her expectations.

"Moriah!" A short, stocky young woman walked up to her. She

enveloped Moriah in a tight hug. When the woman released her, she smiled. "You don't remember me, do you?"

Tilting her head to the side, Moriah searched her memory, frowning. She couldn't recall ever seeing her before. "*Nee*, I'm sorry, I do not."

The young woman laughed, her cheeks plump and ruddy, her hazel eyes filled with merriment. "I'm not surprised, since we haven't been together since we were very young. I'm Katharine. Katharine Yoder."

Moriah's eyes widened. "*Mei* cousin!" She hugged her again. "I can't believe you're here! *Mami* said you wouldn't make it."

"And my *mudder* said she wouldn't miss her niece's wedding for the world."

"How was your trip from Paradise?"

"Long, but *gut*. We arrived yesterday. I haven't been out of Lancaster County since I was a small child, and I'm surprised at how different things are here compared to back home. You don't have as many tourists hanging about, and your buggies are a different color and shape." She reached up and touched her *kapp*. "Even your *kapps* are a slightly different style then what we wear." Katharine laid her hand on Moriah's arm and laughed. "But it is all still lovely. You are a beautiful bride, Moriah."

Moriah blushed at the compliment. While beauty was vanity, she did appreciate her cousin's kind words. They had been pen pals for almost fifteen years, since Katharine and her family had moved to Lancaster when the girls were both five years old. It warmed her heart to see her after all this time. "*Danki*, Katharine. Still, though there are some differences, we are all Amish, *ya*?"

"*Ya*. And family too." She took Moriah's hand and gave it a squeeze. "I'm so happy for you."

Katharine slipped away to visit with other family members, and Moriah spotted Levi a few steps away. Her new husband was in his element greeting the wedding guests. Filled to the brim with charm, he loved talking with people, and they seemed to gravitate toward him.

"*Danki,*" he said to his uncle Eli, who had just given them his blessing. Levi clapped the man on the back. "Me and Moriah appreciate you coming."

"Wouldn't have missed it. We always knew you two'd get hitched someday." He shook his head. "Makes a man feel old, it sure does, all these young folks getting married."

"*Ach,* age is just a number," Levi said. "You're fit as a fiddle, that's all that counts."

Eli grinned. "S'pose so." He looked at Moriah. "You take care of this boy, you hear? Needs a good woman to keep him in his place, dontcha know."

With a grin, Moriah said, "*Ya.* That I know."

Levi placed his palm at the small of her back. "I think I'm in good hands, Eli."

The warmth from his hand seeped through the fabric of her dress, causing a frisson of delight to course through her. She loved this man so much, more than she ever thought possible. Although her faith believed in eschewing pride for humility, she was proud to be his wife. She was Mrs. Levi Miller, from now until forever.

Suddenly the sound of a man clearing his throat reached her ears. She turned away from her husband to see his twin, Gabriel, standing before them. Eli must have discreetly disappeared, for there was no sign of him nearby.

"Congratulations, *bruder.*" Gabe extended his hand to Levi, who grasped it immediately and shook it with enthusiasm.

"Thanks, Gabe." Levi gently pushed Moriah forward. "Why don't you welcome your *schwei* into the family, your new sister-in-law?"

Moriah faced Gabe, the mirror image of her husband. His black hat was pulled low on his head, covering much of his sandy brown hair. Like Levi, he had broad shoulders and a barrel-like chest that tapered to a narrow waist. His cheeks were smooth, indicative of a single man. When their gaze met, she thought she saw something flicker in his brown eyes, eyes that were so similar to Levi's. Regret? She wasn't sure.

Yet while Levi always had a playful spark in his eyes, Gabriel's reflected his somber demeanor. He kept his feelings wrapped up tight, which made the brief dash of emotion in his expression even more puzzling. But as quickly as it had appeared, it left, and his stoic mask returned, firmly in place.

"*Daed* and I are looking forward to you and Levi visiting us soon."

"It won't be long before we will," she said. "Saturday for sure. We'll be staying with my parents until then."

Gabe nodded, then glanced away. "Saturday it is."

"Is that the best you can do?" Levi shook his head, grinning. "Give her a hug, Gabe. She's family now."

Gabriel hesitated, but finally he extended his arms to her and gave her a slight embrace. "*Willkum*," he said, then quickly released her, as if her touch burned him. He turned on his heel and made his way to a table with an empty seat next to his father.

Moriah tried to hide a frown. Why was he so reluctant to be near her? "Something wrong with Gabriel?" she asked.

Levi smirked, then gave her a knowing look. "No, nothing's wrong with him. Gabe's just being Gabe."

"I suppose." She cast Gabriel another glance, but he was involved in a conversation with a young woman who had sat down next to him. As far as Moriah knew, Gabriel hadn't actively courted anyone, and she always wondered about that, since there were many available, and interested, young women in their community. Maybe that one had piqued his interest.

"You know how my brother is," Levi continued. "Hard to figure out what's going on in that head of his. Heck, I'm his twin and half the time I don't know what he's thinking." He leaned in close, his breath warm in her ear. "I can promise you this—he's just fine with you joining the family. Everyone is, can't you tell?"

Levi was right. The last person to object to Moriah would be Gabriel. He had plenty of time to get used to the idea of his brother's marriage, since he'd been the first person they told they were getting married. He'd found out by accident, walking in on them when they were in the Miller's barn minutes after Levi had proposed. If Gabriel thought their union a bad idea, he'd had more than enough time to speak up.

But why was she concerned about what Gabe thought in the first place? She didn't need his permission or approval to marry his brother. Still, she wished their relationship could have been the way it was when they were younger. While Gabriel was more reserved and pensive than Levi, he could be just as charming and witty as his brother when he wanted to.

Levi glanced around the room. "Looks like everyone's happy," he said in a satisfied tone.

She looked up at him, forgetting about Gabriel. "Are you happy, Levi?" A tiny knot of apprehension formed inside her belly. All she wanted was his happiness.

He gave her a wink. "Of course I am. I'm married to you, aren't I?"

Moriah let out a relaxing breath. A tiny flutter swirled around in her belly as she gave him a loving smile. She was the luckiest woman in the world.

Turning her attention back to her guests, she saw them digging into their meals. Her stomach growled as the smell of the wedding dinner filtered through the air. When *Mami* brought out another huge basket of yeasty rolls, steaming hot from the oven, she couldn't resist any longer. "I'm starving," she whispered to Levi.

"You and me both. Let's eat."

With Levi taking the lead, Moriah followed him to one of the head tables, where her younger sister Elisabeth brought them two heaping plates and two large glasses of lemonade. Elisabeth leaned forward and whispered in Moriah's ear.

"Tomorrow morning, I want details." She wiggled her eyebrows.

Heat crept up Moriah's face. "Details?" she said, feigning ignorance. She loved her romance-crazed sister, but she could be nosy—and inappropriate—at times.

"You know what I mean." Moving back, Elisabeth winked at her sister, then handed a glass of lemonade to the next guest at the table.

"What did Elisabeth say?" Levi asked.

"Nothing." She hoped her husband didn't notice her blushing. Her sister might want "details," but she wouldn't get them. Moriah wasn't about to discuss her wedding night with Elisabeth. Five years separated them, but despite the age gap, they had shared nearly everything with each other. However, her wedding night with Levi was private, and it would stay that way.

The calm she'd experienced moments before evaporated, replaced by a new worry that tapped on her nerves. Would she disappoint him? She couldn't bear the thought of that.

Beside her, Levi talked with guests, grinning and laughing, unaware of the sudden turmoil churning inside her. Moriah stared at her food, her appetite gone.

Suddenly she felt Levi reach for her hand under the table and give it a squeeze, as if he had sensed the chaos in her mind. She tilted her head toward him and smiled. He grinned in return.

A semblance of peace washed over her, and for that she was grateful. With the smallest of gestures, Levi had calmed her down. She was thankful to the Almighty for Levi's love. He would be a fine husband and father. She knew of a couple of women in the community whose husbands treated them badly, and she pitied them. But with Levi, she wouldn't have that worry. He was kind, trustworthy, and loyal. They would be there for each other, through the good times and the bad.

Chapter 2

Tobias Byler could pinpoint the precise moment he had noticed Rachel Detweiler had become a woman. Last year, at a Sunday night singing in late May. She had just turned nineteen. Before that night he had thought of her as the biggest thorn in his side, a bratty, boyish-looking girl who acted way too big for her britches. Fiercely competitive, she often nagged him into sporting contests—usually fishing, volleyball, or softball. Lately she'd also become an expert corntoss player, tossing the corn bag easily into the hole of the wooden platform. He hated that she won their matches on a regular basis, and she never missed an opportunity to rub it in his face.

But that night six months ago, when he saw her at the singing, his attitude had changed. She was still a pest, but now he thought her a beautiful one. The plain, light-green dress she had worn that night, one that left everything to the imagination, accented her womanly figure. Until then he had never noticed how smooth her cheeks were, or how her bright blue eyes were framed by long, silky, light-brown lashes. He'd also never noticed how sweet her smile was, but that was probably due to her genuinely smiling at everyone but him. Usually he received a smirk or a haughty frown. Yet that spring night at the Yoder's, he would have done anything to have her grin at him the same way she had smiled at Christian Weaver.

Of course she didn't, and Christian had taken her home in his buggy after the singing. The two of them had never become an item, though. That had surprised everyone, including Tobias. Probably Christian too, even though he'd never said anything about it. Since then Rachel had allowed nearly every young man in the community to take her home after social events, save for him. Ordinarily this would have given her a loose reputation, except all the fellows knew Rachel wasn't interested in them like that. She was their pal, friendly to everyone, with one exception: him.

Of course, just because he thought Rachel was pretty didn't mean he liked her. How could he like a girl who kept showing him up in front of his friends? He had no choice but to put up with it. His father had always taught him to be a gentleman, to respect women and to treat them well. Not all the men in the community did that, but Tobias honored his father's wise edict. He hoped to emulate his parents' wonderful marriage.

But not—*definitely* not—with Rachel Detweiler. For some reason being friends with Rachel, much less having any other kind of relationship, was like searching for a rainbow in the middle of a thunderstorm. While wearing a blindfold. In other words, *impossible.*

Right now he was annoyed with her for joining their game. She had taken off her cloak, clearly warmed from the combination of the strong sunlight and the exertion of playing during his sister's wedding dinner. He and his friends had discarded their black overcoats as well, and Christian had already rolled up his sleeves. At least they were on opposite teams.

He picked up his old wooden bat, one his father had made

many years ago. Despite the nicks and chips accumulated from years of use, it still had a nice sweet spot. The handle had been worn down so that it matched his grip perfectly. He'd hit many a home run with this simple stick of wood, and he intended to take another trip around the makeshift bases today.

Stepping up to the flat rock that served as home plate, he stared her down. Rachel was rolling the grimy ball around in her right hand, not caring that her palm had turned black from the sticky mud or that her dress was smudged with it. He'd never admit it out loud, but she was a good pitcher too, which made him hot under the collar. No way would he let her strike him out. Not again.

"You don't scare me," she said, giving him a cool glare. "You couldn't hit the broad side of a barn."

Considering they'd moved their game from the Byler's front yard to the field behind the house, where the barn was in plain view, he now had the prime opportunity to make her eat her words. But before he could get set up in the batter's box, a fastball whizzed past him.

"Strike!"

Tobias glared at his younger brother Stephen, questioning the wisdom of having a thirteen-year-old referee their game. However, since Stephen was a stickler for rules, he had been everyone's unanimous choice for umpire.

"I wasn't ready," Tobias groused.

"You're in the box, you're ready." Always serious, Stephen pulled his black hat low over his brow and bent at the waist behind the home plate rock. "Play ball."

Tobias adjusted his grip on the bat. This time he wouldn't miss. He swung at the next pitch.

"Stee-rike two!"

Rachel smirked.

Ach, he hated when she did that. But he was just warming up. Now he would hit the broad side of *his* barn, and he couldn't wait to rub it in *her* face for once. When the third pitch flew by, he connected with a crack of the bat.

But instead of hitting the whitewashed wood structure a hundred yards away, the ball plowed right into Rachel's shin. Tobias watched in horror as she crumpled into a heap on the grassy ground, clutching her leg, her forehead touching the top of her knee.

"What'd you do that for?" Stephen hollered.

Tobias ignored him and threw down the bat. He sprinted toward Rachel, reaching her before anyone else. He knelt down beside her. "Are you all *recht*?"

She looked up at him with watery eyes, her teeth biting down on her plump bottom lip. He noticed her cheeks were rosy from the cold and exertion, and now probably from the intense pain. Without giving him answer, she folded herself into a tight ball and put her head down.

Tobias felt as if he'd taken a boot in the gut. He looked up at his friends—Christian, David Yoder, Isaac Stutzer, and his two younger brothers, Lukas and Stephen. Their expressions were filled with concern and . . . blame. More blame than concern, truth be told.

"I didn't do it on purpose," Tobias exclaimed.

"No one said you did." Christian hunkered down and put his arm around Rachel's small shoulders in a friendly, but somewhat intimate, gesture. "Rachel, can you stand?"

When she lifted her head, Tobias felt like he had been knocked in the stomach again. Tears streamed down her cheeks, but she didn't utter a sound, only nodded in response to Christian's question. She was trying to be tough; everyone could tell that. With Christian's help, she rose to her feet, gingerly putting pressure on her injured leg.

Tobias went to her other side and offered to prop her up. "Let me help you in the house."

"You've done enough." Her voice sounded hoarse. And angry. He caught the black expression on her face. Surely she didn't think he meant to hit her? He'd never stoop so low.

Christian intervened, pulling her closer to him. "Tobias, go tell your *mudder* we need a cold cloth. Lukas, let's get her to the kitchen. Mrs. Detweiler can take a look at her leg there."

Scrambling back to the house, Tobias burst through the back door, nearly running over a woman who was picking up a big pot from the top of the stove. "Where's *Mami*?"

"Land sakes, boy, watch what you're doing." Ida Yoder tightened her grip on the cast-iron pot. "She's busy in the front room, taking care of the guests. What do you need?"

"A cold cloth," he mumbled.

"Then get it yourself." Ida huffed and carried the stuffing out of the kitchen. "There's a cooler of ice in the barn."

Tobias ran back outside, passing by Christian, David, and Rachel, who were slowly making their way to the house. He dashed into the barn and found the cooler. He pulled his handkerchief out of the pocket of his good trousers, thankful it was clean. Laying it over his hand, he filled it with cold cubes before folding it into a pouch. He sped back to the kitchen, arriving just as Christian eased Rachel down on one of the chairs.

"*Mami*'s busy," Tobias explained, holding the freezing handkerchief in his hand, but he barely felt it as he focused his attention on Rachel. "All of the women are."

Rachel leaned back in the chair, her eyes screwed shut. "Just give me the ice," she groaned through gritted teeth.

Silently Tobias handed her the cloth. She bent over and lifted up her mud-spotted dress, resting the hem above her knee. His mouth went dry as he scanned her shapely leg, a sight he rarely witnessed. All Amish women wore their dresses to at least shin length, if not longer. He found himself staring at the view, until he spotted her injury. Despite her dark stockings, he could see the hard bump swelling on her shin. No wonder she was in such pain. He sucked in his breath through his teeth. "Rachel . . . I'm sorry."

"Don't talk to me!" Strands of her wispy blonde hair had escaped from her prayer *kapp*, lying against her cheek near her eyes. Before he could stop himself, he touched one of the feather-soft locks. Quickly she jerked her head up, gaping at him as if he'd lost his mind. He glanced around and saw his friends staring at him with the same shocked expression.

Snatching his hand back, Tobias cleared his throat. "Think I'll see if I can find your *mudder*." His voice cracked on the last word, and he ran out of the kitchen as if his pants were on fire.

Stupid, stupid. What had he been thinking, touching her like that? In front of his friends? Wouldn't be long before word got out that Tobias Byler not only slammed a baseball into Rachel Detweiler, but he's sweet on her too.

Threading his way through the mass of people in the front room, he caught sight of his sister, Moriah, and her husband, Levi. They'd finished their meal and were now visiting with friends. Although she'd seemed nervous before the ceremony, now she wore a smile. At least someone was happy today. He'd never been so embarrassed in his life.

Blades of searing heat shot through Rachel's shin, making her stomach churn. She gritted her teeth, refusing to let anyone, especially Tobias and the other boys, see her in pain. The ice did little to relieve the burning sensation. Tobias had said he would look for her *mudder,* but she wondered if he would keep his word. By the way he'd scuttled out of the room, she suspected his promise was just an excuse to leave the kitchen . . . and her.

Whatever. She was glad he was gone.

Christian knelt in front of her, concern etched on his lightly freckled, boyish face. Kind, considerate Christian. Tall, with dark brown hair and a five o'clock shadow that never seemed to go away. He'd always been like a big brother to her, convincing the other boys to let her play with them, never bothered when she beat him in a race or threw a better fastball.

Unlike Tobias, who took everything she did as a personal slight.

Christian fixed his gaze on her. "I should see what's taking Tobias so long. You gonna be all right?"

Rachel nodded, even though her shin continued to throb. The other guys had already abandoned her now that the excitement was over, saying something about apple pie as they'd left the kitchen. But Christian had stayed. "I'm fine. Don't worry about me," she said. "I'll survive."

He chucked her under the chin with a light tap of his fist. "I never do. You're the toughest person I know—male or female." Rising to his full height of six feet, he gave her a sweet smile, then left.

Moving her leg, Rachel gulped at the pulsating pain radiating from the lump. She gingerly touched the skin and felt warmth seep through her black tights. Tobias had hit her hard. If she'd been paying better attention, she would have jumped over it, and he probably would have had at least a triple, considering his speed. But she'd been so focused on striking him out, she hadn't thought about him actually hitting the ball.

She'd never admit it to anyone, but she considered him the most talented athlete in the settlement. And although she'd spent a good portion of their childhood defeating him in most of their games, he'd matured physically in the last year, and she doubted she could keep up with him much longer.

But Tobias Byler acted like he was oblivious to everything, so maybe he wouldn't notice that he could beat her. After all, either he didn't notice or he ignored the attention of several of the girls in the community.

She was sure his blasé attitude was insincere. There was no way he couldn't be aware of the female attention he received at the singings and frolics this past year. She'd heard the girls giggling over him time and time again, swooning about his mischievous blue eyes and crooked smile.

Sure, she might admit he was nice looking. But how could he not be, blessed with that mass of dark-golden hair that couldn't be restrained even under a hat. His forearms were finely muscled from hours and hours spent in his father's woodworking shop, sanding and carving rough cut wood into elegant pieces of furniture . . . Her cheeks suddenly heated, and a funny tickle started in her stomach. Probably a reaction from the injury. A part of her believed Tobias hit her on purpose; she knew he disliked her that much. True, she brought it on herself most of the time, but he was so infuriating, with his cocky attitude that he seemed to save mainly for her. Someone had to put him in his place. This time, however, she should have kept her mouth shut.

A lock of her hair dangled in her face again, and she remembered Tobias brushing it back. Why had he done that? That was the type of gesture a man made to a woman he was smitten with, or even a woman he loved. Didn't make sense, because he practically hated her. But he smoothed her hair nevertheless. He was a boy—no, a man, she had to at least admit that—filled with contradictions. If she lived to be a hundred years old, she'd never understand him.

Christian returned with her mother in tow. He had already explained to her what had happened during the game. After taking one glance at her leg, Sarah Detweiler told her daughter to go home.

"I'm fine, *Mudder*, really. I can stay."

"*Nee,* you need to put your leg up. That will help the swelling go down. Christian, would you mind taking her?"

"Not at all," he replied.

"But—"

"Don't argue with me." Sarah gave her a stern look, one Rachel had seen a million times before. "Aaron's home, he can keep an eye on you."

"More like I'll keep an eye on him."

"What was that?"

"Nothing." Rachel didn't want to get into an argument with her mother, especially in front of Christian, and particularly not about her brother, who was in the throes of his *rumspringa,* running around and giving the family fits. "I'll go."

"I'll get my coat and bring the buggy around," he said.

Sarah nodded her approval. "*Danki,* Christian."

When he left, Rachel looked at her mother, not missing the exasperated glint in her eyes. She steeled herself for her next comment, which was sure to come.

"Rachel, your dress." Sarah sighed as she scanned her daughter's attire. "We'll never get the stains out of it."

"I'm sorry, *Mudder.*"

"There was no reason for you to be outside with the boys, Rachel. Not when there is so much work to be done in here."

Glancing away for a moment, Rachel said, "I asked several women if they had anything for me to do. They said no. So I went outside."

Her mother leaned over slightly, her lips drifting into a frown. "We've had this discussion before. You are no longer a child, Rachel. You need to think about your future, about your responsibilities as a woman and soon, Lord willing, as a wife. No man is interested in a tomboy."

Rachel fought the urge to roll her eyes. Her mother had been saying such things since Rachel had turned thirteen, and they disagreed about it frequently. But she kept her annoyance at bay, trying to show her mother respect. *"Ya, Mudder."*

Apparently satisfied she'd gotten her point across, Sarah switched topics, softening her voice a tad. "Such a nice young man, that Christian."

"He's very nice."

"Didn't he bring you home from a singing one time?"

Surprised her mother remembered that, Rachel replied, "He did."

"I've always thought you two would make a good match." Sarah raised a light-brown brow. "But I only saw him that one time. Why hasn't he come around more often?"

Rachel leaned back against the chair and shrugged. "I don't really like him that way."

"But why don't you? He would make a good husband. He is kind and smart. Most of all, he is already a member of the church."

Rachel started to speak, but thought better of it. Her mother would never understand. She liked Christian, but when it came to romantic notions about him, she felt nothing. Weren't you supposed to at least feel *something* for the man who courted you?

But maybe she was looking at relationships from the wrong angle. Truly, there was nothing wrong with Christian. Nice looking, a complete gentleman, and as her mother had already pointed out, a member of the church, as she was. When she viewed him objectively, she saw a good Amish man, strong in his faith and devoted to his family.

Sarah took the damp, cold handkerchief—Tobias's handkerchief, Rachel couldn't help but notice—out of her daughter's hands. She crossed the kitchen and shook out the partially melted ice cubes into the large metal sink. "All right, then. If you don't like Christian, then I'm sure there are several other young men who could spark your interest. What about Tobias?"

Rachel scrunched her nose. "*Nee. Nee, nee, nee.* You see what he did to me."

"That was an accident," Sarah said, glancing over her shoulder.

"Maybe."

"I'm sure he feels terrible about it." Sarah turned around and folded the handkerchief into a small, neat square, then laid it next to the sink.

"That's the problem, *Mudder*. I don't think Tobias feels anything. About anything. He just floats through life, without a care in the world, thinking all he needs is his charm and good looks."

"Oh, so you think he's charming?" her mother said teasingly.

"I didn't say that." She swiveled in her chair so she could face her mother directly. "I never said he was charming."

"But you have to admit he's good-looking."

"I'm not admitting anything!" Now it was Rachel's turn to be exasperated. She turned back around, the pain in her leg growing more intense. She heard the soft ruffle of her mother's skirt as she neared.

Sarah put her hand on Rachel's shoulder. "There's no reason to get upset about this. I keep forgetting you don't like to be teased. Much like your *bruder*, Aaron."

"I am nothing like Aaron."

"*Ach,* I think you are more alike than either of you are willing to admit." She walked around Rachel's chair until she stood in front of her. She touched her cheek. "Just know that your *daed* and I love you. You are our only *dochder,* and we want what's best for you."

"Which is to get married."

Her mother smiled, her grayish eyes twinkling. "*Ya,* Rachel. You are of age now to at least be thinking about your future, which should include a husband."

Rachel expelled a heavy breath. She had no argument, because her mother was right. Deep down, she wanted to get married and have a family. Not necessarily right away, but eventually. At the moment she was happy and successful enough in her job as a waitress at Mary Yoder's Amish Kitchen. There really wasn't any urgency to find a suitable mate, even though her mother obviously felt otherwise.

The kitchen door slammed shut. Both women turned to see Christian walk into the room. "Ready?" he asked, looking at Rachel.

She hadn't expected him back so soon. He must have hitched up his buggy in record time.

"I can carry you, if you want," he added, looking directly at her.

Rachel couldn't believe he'd asked her that, especially in front of her mother, who would eagerly blow any hint of prospective romance for her daughter into epic proportions. But then she caught the teasing spark in his eyes, and she relaxed. "*Nee,* I can manage to walk to the buggy, thank you very much."

Sarah helped Rachel to her feet. "Your *daed* will be home soon to check on you. I will stay late and help Emma with the cleanup, but tell Aaron I'll bring him a plate home for supper." She gave Christian one of her trademark sweet smiles. "I know I'm leaving you in *gut* hands."

Rachel's cheeks burned. Could she be more obvious?

Fortunately Christian hadn't caught her meaning, or if he had, he graciously chose not to say anything. As her mother opened the door to the front room of the house, Rachel heard voices intermingling, then muffling when the door closed again.

Rachel fought the urge to breathe out a sigh of relief. She loved her mother, but that didn't mean she wasn't occasionally embarrassed by her. Taking a step forward, she winced as pain shot up her leg.

"Here, let me help you." Christian came up beside her and wrapped his arm around her waist.

She leaned against him only slightly, not wanting to appear as pitiful as she felt. He helped her into the buggy, placed a heavy quilt on her lap to keep her warm, then jumped in beside her. Within moments they were heading for her house a few miles down the road.

Several cars whizzed by as their buggy slowly made its way down the asphalt street. It shook as each vehicle zipped alongside them. Christian's horse, with its blinders on, remained unfazed, used to dealing with traffic. Rachel wrapped her black cloak more tightly around her, warding off the chilly, late afternoon air. A few clouds had appeared in the sky, with one large fluffy one blocking the sun, taking away its soothing warmth.

"You're awful quiet," Christian said suddenly, breaking the silence that had been between them since they'd left the Bylers. "Something bothering you?"

"*Nee*, not really." Not anything she wanted to talk about anyway. "My leg hurts, that's all. I do appreciate you taking me home."

"Don't mind at all." He pulled up on the reins a bit, slowing down his horse. "Gives me time to ask you something."

Turning her head, she looked at him, her curiosity piqued. "What?"

"I wondered if you'd mind me courting you."

Rachel's jaw dropped. "Did *Mudder* say something to you?" she blurted out, then wished she could take it back. Christian had been nowhere near the kitchen when she and her mother had their conversation.

He glanced at her, confused. "No, she didn't say a word to me. Should she have?"

"*Nee*," she said, slinking down in the seat.

Christian cast her a sideways glance. "*Gut*. Because I really don't want to talk about your *mudder* now. I want to talk about us. Or the possibility of there being an *us*."

One thing she could say about Christian is that he was to the point. He deserved her directness in return. "I'm surprised, Christian. This seems rather sudden."

"I guess it does in a way. But I thought I made it pretty clear last May that I liked you."

"I like you too." It wasn't a lie, she really did like him. She just wasn't sure she *liked* him.

"That's good to hear." He grinned at her, taking his eyes off the road for only a few seconds.

"As a friend," she quickly added, worried she'd inadvertently given him the wrong message.

His smile diminished somewhat. But he remained undeterred. "I understand that. But I think our friendship could grow into something else. Especially if we spent more time together." He gazed her again, his eyes latching onto hers. "Alone."

Suddenly the painful lump in her leg had become the least of her problems. Christian was serious, and from the determined look on his face, it didn't appear he'd give up easily. Uncertainty filled her. "Christian . . . I don't know . . ."

"Why won't you give us a chance, Rachel? We've known each other a long time. Our families are good friends. You're not seeing anyone else, and neither am I."

They were at the top of a gently sloping hill. The trees lining both sides of the road had shed their dead leaves, the naked, spindly branches pointing skyward. They passed by a white Amish house with the black buggy parked beneath a pristine carport, flanked by two fancy brick Yankee homes. Rachel spied her house in the near distance. Christian looked toward it and slowed his horse up even more. "Is it because you like Tobias?" he asked.

"What?" Rachel let out a strained laugh. "How could you even think such a thing? Tobias Byler is the last man I'd be interested in."

"Just checking. I thought maybe you two had something

private going on, especially after he touched your hair back there in the kitchen."

"I have no idea why he did that," she said, her face heating from the memory. She looked straight ahead, hoping Christian was doing the same so he wouldn't see the flush blooming on her cheeks. "Probably because he's *seltsam*."

Christian chuckled. "Okay, you proved your point, especially if you think he's weird. Tobias is definitely out of the picture." Then he sobered quickly. "Look, all I'm asking is that you give us a chance. If it doesn't work out, then no harm done. We both move on, and we'll stay friends."

She averted her gaze and looked at the countryside. The jagged tops of cut, dried cornstalks jutted out from a nearby field, presenting a raw and desolate landscape. Maybe she wasn't being fair. Maybe there had never been any sparks between her and Christian because she hadn't been open to the possibility. Maybe he and her mother had been right all along. Still, she wasn't completely sure.

Despite his efforts to prolong their ride, they arrived at her driveway. He turned onto a narrow dirt road and drove straight back to her house. He halted his horse, jumped out of his seat, and met her on the other side. Holding out his hand, he helped her out of the buggy, offering to assist her inside.

"I think I can manage," she said, limping toward her front door. "It doesn't hurt as much anymore."

"*Gut.* Glad to hear it." He paused for a moment, then reached down and lightly cupped her shoulders with his hands. "Promise me you'll think about what I said, Rachel."

She could feel the warmth from his palms through her cloak. Lifting her face, she gazed up at him. His black, wide-brimmed hat sat low on his head, nearly covering his eyes and shading the rest of his face. But she could still see his beseeching expression, and hear the pleading in his voice.

"I promise," she heard herself say softly.

His face split into a wide grin. "*Gut. Sehr gut.* You've made me one happy man."

Unable to resist his joy, she smiled back. Perhaps there was a chance for them after all.

Chapter 3

The movement beside her woke Moriah out of her light sleep. Her eyes opened and tried to adjust to the darkness as she sensed her husband getting up from their bed.

"Levi?" She heard the scratchiness of her voice as she sat up.

"Shh."

She couldn't see him in the engulfing blackness of the room. In the four months since their wedding she was still getting used to living in a different house, especially sharing a room with Levi. Leaning on her side, she picked up a small battery-operated flashlight and flicked it on. A chill cloaked the room, a byproduct of the typically cold February weather. Scanning the room, she spotted Levi by the closet, taking out one of his blue shirts. "What time is it?" she asked

"Time for you to go back to sleep." He slipped on the shirt, then pulled his suspenders over his shoulders.

"Where are you going?"

"Same place I've been going for the past month, Moriah."

"Gates Mills? I thought you were finished with that job."

Levi shook his head as he reached for his boots. He didn't

bother to sit down, instead choosing to hop on one leg, then the other, as he put them on.

She thought he'd said he would be finished working at that horse ranch this week. Or maybe that was just wishful thinking on her part. She threw off her covers, gooseflesh rising as the coldness of the room seeped into her skin. "I'll start some coffee."

"*Nee.*" He held up his hand, but he didn't come near her. Instead he reached for his black hat, which hung on a peg next to the closet. "I'll get some on the road."

Already out of bed, she wrapped one arm around her body, shivering in her white cotton nightgown. The light from the flashlight illuminated the distance between them. Although it was only a few feet, lately it seemed like miles separated them. And at times it did, as the affluent community of Gates Mills was farther than the twelve-mile limit a horse and buggy could manage. But physical distance wasn't their only problem. An emotional chasm had grown between them, and she had no idea why.

"When will you be back?"

He shrugged. "Not exactly sure." Finally, he looked directly at her. "Don't hold supper for me."

Unable to stand being apart from him anymore, she closed the space between them. "Tomorrow is our four-month anniversary."

"Already?" He put his hat on his head, but averted his gaze. "Time flies, don't it?" He went past her to walk through the doorway of their room.

"Levi?" she called out.

He stopped, then slowly turned around. "*Ya?*"

"I'm making a special supper for you tomorrow night. To celebrate. All your favorites. Liver and onions, green bean casserole, sweet cornbread, and cinnamon pumpkin pie. I even got your *daed's* German potato salad recipe."

"Sounds *gut.* Moriah, I got to go. My ride's probably already here. I'll see you later on tonight."

"Okay. I love—" But he was gone before she could finish the sentence.

She turned the flashlight toward the small clock near on the bed table. 5:45. Levi had given her the porcelain clock on their wedding night. Pure white, with a picture of a cherub painted in washes of pale blue and light pink on the base. It was fancy and looked expensive, but he had said he wanted to give her something special, something she could look at every day and remember him by. The clock wasn't really her taste, as she preferred simple, unadorned things, but she cherished the gift because it was from him, and he had seemed so pleased to give it to her.

Grabbing a quilt off the end of the bed, she wrapped it around her shoulders and looked out the window. She and Levi had moved into his family's house after they had married, and from the view from their bedroom—Levi's old room—she saw two figures moving in the shadows. One was Levi; the other had to be Gabe. The men talked for a few moments, then Levi walked off to the end of the driveway, where a white van arrived to taxi him to Gates Mills. He climbed in, and she watched until the van's red taillights disappeared in the darkness.

For over a month now, they had followed this pattern. Usually he left before she awakened and returned after she had fallen asleep. She had been so tired lately, and even when she tried to wait up for him, she usually didn't succeed. The only day he didn't leave was on Sunday, but even then it was as if he were gone. He picked at his food, seemed distracted during their conversations, and went to bed before her on Sunday nights, saying he was exhausted from working so hard during the week.

Tugging the quilt closer to her body, she wondered if this was normal, if the blissful bloom of the first weeks of marriage usually withered so quickly. She could barely remember the last time he kissed her, held her, shared the joys of marriage with her. Open displays of affection between a man and a woman weren't the norm among their people, but she hadn't thought that extended to the privacy of their home. Even her parents had shown their love for each other with tender words or a brief clasping of hands.

She must be doing something wrong. She had overheard some of the older women say that a husband's happiness often depended on his wife's competency. Maybe he didn't like her cooking, although he had never complained about it before. Or her housekeeping skills were lacking, even though not a speck of dust could be found in the house. Or perhaps she had disappointed him in more intimate ways.

Biting down on her lip, she chased away the thoughts. The wretched job in Gates Mills was the problem, not her . . . she hoped.

Turning from the window, she was tempted to crawl underneath the warm covers. Sleep beckoned her, but she had too much to do. Gabriel and his *daed* would open their blacksmith shop soon, and she needed to prepare coffee and breakfast for them. Gabriel and John had voluntarily relocated to the *dawdi haus,* a small three-room cottage situated a few feet behind the shop. Typically, a *dawdi haus* was built to house aging Amish grandparents, but the houses and shop had been in John Miller's family for years. He had inherited them when his father had passed, and he had gifted the main house to Levi and Moriah as a wedding present. Ever since, he and Gabriel had spent most of their time either in the small cottage or in the shop. They had never once asked her to fix their meals. But she enjoyed doing it, and wouldn't think of leaving them to cook for themselves. They were her family, and it was her responsibility, and joy, to take care of them.

Dressing quickly, she made her way downstairs to the first level of the house, leaving the flashlight behind. She knew the way in the dark, and when she reached the kitchen, she turned on the tall gas lamp in the corner and started on her morning chores, distracting herself from her troubling thoughts about Levi and their marriage.

"You're going to Gates Mills *again*?" Gabe watched Levi grab two leather bags of horseshoes and tools and hoist them over his shoulder. Despite the early hour, Gabe had been in the shop for half an hour already. After Gabe retrieved his tools, he followed Levi outside, his irritation with his twin rising.

Levi headed to the end of the driveway, where he'd arranged for a taxi service to pick him up. Although their Old Order community forbade their members from driving an automobile, the *Ordnung*—the unwritten rules their Amish community followed—allowed them to pay a driver to take them longer distances. Some communities had different rules for their members concerning travel by car and other "modern" conveniences, and while his church allowed its members to ask Yankees to take them long distances, members weren't permitted to own cars themselves.

The bags were heavy, but Levi easily hauled them as if they were filled with feathers instead of metal. "They have a lot of horses," Levi said, not bothering to turn around and look at Gabe.

Gabe continued to dog Levi's heels. His brother had been gone every day save Sundays for the past month, working on that fancy horse farm in Gates Mills, a ritzy suburb of Cleveland. Levi had started shoeing their horses when the farm's owner, Mr. Johnson, had come to Middlefield to check out their blacksmith and farrier business. Their shop was so simple it didn't have an official name, but the Millers' reputations as excellent smiths and shoers had extended beyond their settlement. Now Levi spent more time away than in the shop.

Gabe pushed his hat off his forehead. "I need you here, Levi. The Stutzers placed a big order that they need by the end of next week. *Daed* and I can't do it by ourselves."

"I gave the Johnsons my word, Gabe." Levi finally looked at him. "Besides, they pay more than the Stutzers ever could. Mr. Johnson's also asked me to break one of his fillies. Said he'd triple my going rate."

Gabe couldn't believe what he was hearing. "You would take money over helping out a neighbor?"

"I've got a wife to provide for, remember?"

Gabe winced. Salt rubbed into a raw wound. He didn't need his brother to remind him about his marriage to Moriah. All he had to do was look at the short growth of beard on Levi's chin, the Amish man's wedding ring, to remember who his twin had married. He'd distracted himself with work and tried to avoid Moriah, but he couldn't get her out of his head and heart.

Absently Gabe rubbed his own smooth cheek and forced himself not to think about Moriah. He looked at Levi, unable to understand the man's eagerness to work for outlanders, especially ones who lived over an hour away. The blacksmith shop made enough to provide for all of them. They didn't need any extra income. What they needed to do was help out a fellow member of the church.

"My ride's here." Levi's boots crunched in the icy snow as he stepped toward the street.

"What about the Stutzers?"

"I'll try to be home early. I can pitch in then." A large white van pulled up beside him. Without another word, Levi climbed into the vehicle and shoved the sliding door shut.

Resentment churned inside Gabe as he watched the van crest the hill. His brother had been acting strangely the past couple weeks. He briefly wondered if there was trouble at home. If there was, it was none of his business. And if there wasn't, he didn't want to know about their perfect marriage either.

"Forgive me, Lord," he whispered, his breath hanging in puffs in the frigid air. "Forgive me for my sin." He had repeated that prayer so many times that he wondered if God heard it anymore. He forced himself to focus on the problem at hand—how to fill the Stutzer's order without Levi's help. Tomorrow would be too late. And lately *Daed* had been unsteady on his feet, something that unsettled him even more than Levi's peculiar behavior. The other day he'd almost fallen near the blazing forge, which would have seriously injured him. His father had shaken off Gabe's concern, saying he must have tripped over something. But Gabe knew better. He hadn't missed the sudden appearance in their kitchen of several types of herbal tea used to cure illness and increase strength.

Shivering, Gabe headed back to the warmth of the shop and lit the forge. There was no way to get around it—he would have to hire some help. The names of several employment candidates popped into his mind, and then he thought of Aaron Detweiler. The boy had been in a peck of trouble over the past few months, having left the family fold for his *rumspringa* as soon as he turned sixteen, only to get involved with drugs. He'd returned to the Detweiler's four months ago, after spending a few months in the Geauga County jail. Aaron wasn't the first Amish teen to find living outside the community perilous, and he wouldn't be the last. But at least he was trying to turn things around. As far as Gabe knew, he wasn't working anywhere steady other than his family's farm.

Gabe's own *rumspringa* had been uneventful, as he had chosen to join the church at eighteen and had no desire to experience the Yankee world. Levi, however, had snuck out a few times at night to hang out with non-Amish teens, unbeknownst to their father. Gabe doubted even Moriah knew about that secret part of Levi's life. But he had joined the church as well, and put those worldly dabblings behind him.

It was decided then. As soon as *Daed* came to the shop, Gabe would visit the Detweilers and offer Aaron a job. If and when Levi decided to become dependable again, there would be enough work for all four of them. Everyone needed a chance to redeem themselves. Gabe thought it a blessing he could offer Aaron that chance.

The scent of fresh-brewed coffee, combined with the peppery aroma of breakfast sausage and scrambled eggs, filled the air. Moriah covered the eggs with helpings of savory Swiss cheese she had picked up from the Middlefield Cheese House, then divided them over four slices of bread. She added a patty of sausage on top and finished the breakfast sandwiches with four more pieces of buttered bread. She wrapped them in foil, filled a thermos with steaming coffee, and packed it all in a large wicker basket. In her mind she was already planning their lunch meal—a platter of hearty slices of meatloaf, brown gravy, mashed potatoes with plenty of butter and milk, and apple crisp for dessert.

While she delighted in preparing and serving Gabriel and John their meals, her feelings were often pricked by Gabe's reception. John, of course, was always grateful, and always praised her cooking talents. But Gabriel often said little more than thank you. Although Levi had seemed distant as of late, Gabriel acted indifferent toward her, even more so since her marriage. She had hoped their relationship would improve, but it hadn't. But she determined that his attitude wouldn't keep her from taking care of them. As two single men, they needed some pampering every once in a while.

She donned her coat, then walked the short distance to the blacksmith shop. Like the main house and the *dawdi haus,* it was painted crisp white, with a black roof and plain wooden door. Outside, she could hear the echo of metal clanging against metal. She hung the food-laden wicker basket on the crook of her arm and opened the door with her free hand.

Heat immediately blasted her body, engulfing her in warmth, a welcome contrast to the coldness of the outdoors. The tin ring of a bell sounded as she shut the door, and both Gabriel and John looked up. John gave her a smile, while Gabriel acknowledged her with a small nod.

"I hope that's what I think it is," John said, as he put aside a fat metal file and walked toward her. He took a few steps, then touched the side of a table, as though trying to gain his balance.

She hadn't noticed John being so unsteady before, but then again, she didn't spend much time in the shop. Moriah set the basket of food on a nearby table. While John peeked inside, Gabriel stayed at the anvil, pounding away at a red, glowing piece of metal. John rarely worked the anvil anymore, preferring to let his brawny sons do the hard labor. She didn't blame him—he'd spent many years putting in long and exhausting hours as a blacksmith. He'd earned the well-deserved rest.

She caught sight of Gabriel again. His shirt sleeves were rolled up to his elbow. The muscles flexed beneath his skin as he slammed the hammer down. Quickly she glanced away, feeling a twinge of guilt for staring at her brother-in-law. "What did you bring us today, *dochder*?" John asked, rubbing his callused hands together.

Glad for the diversion, Moriah named off the items as she withdrew them from the basket and laid them on the table. "Sausage and egg sandwiches and a thermos of coffee."

"*Gut, sehr gut*. Everything smells delicious, Moriah. *Danki*."

Her lips formed into a smile, genuinely happy that her father-in-law was pleased with her offering.

"Gabriel, come and eat," John said as he picked up a sandwich. He peeled back the foil and inhaled, closing his eyes and grinning. "Manna from heaven."

"In a minute." The sizzling sound of hot metal meeting cold water filled the air, and for a moment Gabriel was completely obscured by a cloud of steam. He withdrew the cooled piece of iron, balanced it on the anvil, and walked toward her and John. His gaze remained cast downward, as it usually was whenever he and Moriah shared the same company.

"You have to try one of these. They're still hot." John handed Gabriel a sandwich. Gabriel accepted the sandwich, then unwrapped it and took a bite. He nodded his approval, but his face remained unreadable.

Moriah took out two coffee mugs from the basket. She unscrewed the lid off the thermos and poured John and Gabriel each a cup of coffee. She handed Gabriel his first.

His gaze flicked to her as he took the cup from her hand, but he took two steps back and looked at the floor again. Downing the sandwich, he balled up the foil and took a swig of the coffee before putting the mug back on the table. "Got to get back to work."

"Gabriel, you can take a break." John took a big bite of sausage, cheese, and egg. "We'll get the work done, *sohn*."

As Moriah listened to John, her stomach suddenly felt like it had been turned upside down. Perspiration beaded her forehead as she inhaled the mixed scents of black coffee, sausage, and coal burning. The aromas made her gag. She reached out to grab the table as the room started to swirl.

"Moriah, you all right?"

John's voice sounded far away. Where had the table disappeared to? Suddenly she couldn't see anything.

She sensed something behind her just as she tilted backward. Something solid. Closing her eyes, she fought for consciousness.

The instant Gabe saw Moriah sway, he rushed to her. He'd just managed to move behind her when she fell against him and started sliding to the floor. Grabbing her shoulders, he drew her closer to his chest, calling out her name.

"Moriah?"

Her head lolled for a moment and she mumbled something incoherent.

John reached for a nearby chair and dragged it to Gabe. "Let her sit down, Gabriel."

Gabe eased her into the chair as his arm cradled her shoulders. Her complexion had paled, and her normally peach-toned lips were nearly white. Bending his legs at the knees, he crouched down beside her, one arm still across her shoulders.

"I'll get a cold rag," John said, and he shuffled over to the sink on the other side of the shop.

Gabe heard the trickling of water in the sink as he scanned Moriah's features. Her eyes were closed, but she was still conscious. "Moriah? Can you hear me?"

She nodded, her eyes opening. Some of the color seeped back to her face now that she was seated. "What happened?" she asked in a breathy, surprised voice.

"You passed out . . . I think." He searched her face again. "Are you all right?"

"I don't know." She licked her lips, which were still stark white.

His gaze went involuntarily to her mouth. Under other circumstances, he might have enjoyed being so close to her, only to emotionally flog himself later, but now all he could think about was her welfare. "Do you need something to drink?"

"She needs this." John handed her a wet rag. The faded red cloth was filled with stains. "Wipe her face with it," he instructed. "Don't worry, *sohn*. That rag might look filthy, but it's clean."

Carefully Gabe dabbed the damp cloth against her smooth forehead, then slid the rag over the plumpest part of her cheeks. She closed her eyes again, leaning even further against him.

"Did you eat something this morning?" John asked.

Opening her eyes, she shook her head. "I wasn't very hungry."

Gabe glanced up at his father, whose expression had suddenly become inscrutable. John took one of the sandwiches and handed it to her. "Here, take a bite of this. I'll go get you some water."

She shook her head. "I don't—"

"No arguments, Moriah. Eat it." John turned and trekked back to the sink, where they kept a small supply of clean glasses and coffee cups.

Moriah brought the sandwich to her mouth and took a small bite. She chewed for a moment, then swallowed. Clearly she was forcing the food down.

Concern filled Gabe. She didn't look well at all. "Moriah, are you sick?"

"No . . ." Her eyes suddenly widened. The paleness of her cheeks gave way to a rosy red as she refused to look at him.

And at that moment Gabe *knew*. She was carrying his brother's child.

A jumble of emotions passed through Moriah. Embarrassment that she'd almost fainted in the shop. Appreciation for the way John had taken charge and made her eat something. With a bit of food in her stomach, she felt less queasy. She hadn't eaten anything that morning because the thought of consuming even one bite of food made her stomach turn. But now she knew that to ignore her body's hunger signals would be even worse.

She also felt something else, something completely unexpected. As Gabe still stayed beside her, crouching on the ground, looking at her with genuine concern, she felt safe. Protected. Cared for, and in a way she'd never felt before, not even with Levi. How could she feel that way in her brother-in-law's presence, but not her husband's?

Perhaps it was the hormones from the baby. If today's near fainting spell didn't prove she was pregnant, she didn't know what would, other than a pregnancy test of course. But she didn't need to take a test to know there was a new life growing inside her. She had suspected it for a while, since she'd missed her last monthly cycle. She brought the partially eaten sandwich up to her mouth to hide the smile twitching on her lips.

"I think you're coming out of it." John handed her a cup of water, then propped his hip against the table. The overhead lights in the shop, powered by the white propane tank in the backyard, illuminated the salt and pepper colors in his hair and beard. "You shouldn't skip breakfast, young lady. Didn't your *mudder* always tell you that?" The twinkle in his brown eyes indicated he was only half scolding her.

"*Ya*. Don't worry, I won't miss a meal again."

He nodded, apparently satisfied with her answer.

She glanced at Gabe, who was still crouched by the chair. An odd expression spread across his face, and this time he was looking at her. Although he seemed to look right through her, as if he had something else on his mind. Something that bothered him, from what she could tell. "I'm okay now," she said, sensing that he needed the reassurance.

"What? Oh." He jumped to his feet. "I'm glad." He stepped away from her to stand behind John, reverting back to his habit of not looking directly at her.

Sighing inwardly, she wondered if she would ever understand

her brother-in-law. She took another small bite of the sandwich, then felt refreshed enough to stand up.

"Are you sure you're all right?" John asked, stepping toward her. Gabe had already returned back to the forge.

She felt normal, as if she hadn't been overcome with dizziness only moments ago. "I'm fine," she said sincerely. "I'd planned to visit my family today, and I feel well enough to do so."

"Are you sure?" John didn't look convinced.

The reverberating sound of Gabe's hammer against the anvil filtered through her ears. "I'm sure. Thanks for taking care of me. I appreciate it." She smiled. "If I start to feel strange again, I'll turn around and come home."

"You'd better." The twinkle was gone from his eyes, and she knew he was serious.

"I will." She turned to say good-bye to Gabe, to thank him for keeping her from hitting the floor. But he was engrossed in his work and didn't even look up when she moved toward the door.

Had she imagined his earlier concern? If his current indifference was any indication, she had.

She left the shop, confused by Gabe's bewildering treatment of her. Maybe he was unhappy that she had displaced him from his house. Both she and Levi had insisted he stay in the main house with them, but he had been all too eager to move into the *dawdi haus* with John. Maybe his curt behavior didn't have anything to do with his living arrangements. Maybe he just wanted to get away from her.

Tamping down the hurt, she returned to her kitchen and cleaned up, forcing Gabe from her thoughts. Instead she focused on the baby. *Mine and Levi's.* She couldn't wait to tell him about the pregnancy. A baby would bring them closer together, she was sure of it. As she finished up her chores, she praised God for the blessing growing inside her.

A short while later she arrived at her mother's house, still not feeling any ill effects from her earlier fainting spell. The sun had risen fully, but was obscured by a flat, grayish sky that cast a cloudy pall over everything. On the other side of the black asphalt driveway stood her father's woodshop, where he and her brothers made the handcrafted furniture the tourists always seemed to crave. Normally she could hear them working, but the shop doors were closed tight against the winter cold.

"*Mami*?" she called out when she entered her parents' home through the front door. An odd sensation came over her as she scanned the living room. Now that she and Levi had settled into their own place, she found it strange coming back here, even though she had spent so many hours in this sparsely furnished but cozy and welcoming room, sitting on the comfortable brown sofa near the coal fireplace, reading a book or talking with her siblings. She had spent her entire life in this house, but now it was no longer home, despite everything being so familiar to her.

"In here, Moriah." Her mother's voice came from the kitchen at the back of the house.

Moriah walked through the living and dining rooms, breathing in the scent of freshly baked bread. Baking day. The scent, instead of making her nauseous, beckoned her. She followed the delicious aroma into the kitchen.

"You must have read my mind, daughter." Emma brushed the back of a flour-covered hand over her damp forehead. Although it might be thirty degrees outside, the radiating heat from the stove made the kitchen toasty. "I just started a fresh batch of sticky buns. I could use your help."

"What would you like me to do?"

"You can start by rolling out that dough."

Moriah went to the sink and washed up before sitting down at the table. She then dipped her hands into the canister of flour and grabbed the glob of dough and a wood rolling pin. Immediately she set to work.

Her mother removed two finished pans of buns from the oven and began spreading them with cream cheese frosting. "I considered keeping Elisabeth and Ruth home today from school to help, but thought better of it. Besides, Ruthie would howl if I even hinted at not allowing her to go to school."

Imagining her twelve-year-old sister, Ruth, throwing a tantrum wasn't too difficult. But fifteen-year-old Elisabeth, who was in the eighth grade at the Amish-run school, wouldn't have minded missing a day or two. Or more, for that matter. She hated school and couldn't wait for her last year to end.

Moriah felt a bit relieved that she wasn't here. Elisabeth would try to pump her for more personal information about her relationship with Levi, which she'd done the day after their wedding night. Moriah had ignored her probing questions until Elisabeth had finally given up. Her sister then launched into a detailed report about her latest crush, whom she swore she was madly in love with. Moriah highly doubted that, as Elisabeth's targets of affection were usually discarded on a weekly basis.

"How are things at home?" Emma asked, smearing a knife full of frosting onto the second batch of hot rolls. "Levi doing well?"

"He's fine, *Mami.*" To reassure her doting mother, she repeated,

"Everything is fine." The words *I'm pregnant* danced on the tip of her tongue, but she kept the knowledge to herself. No need to worry her mother. Also, she wasn't ready to tell anyone about the baby. Not until she told Levi first.

"I hear his shop is very successful. They've gotten quite a few Yankee customers."

"*Ya.* Levi's working with one now, in Gates Mills."

Emma turned and looked at her daughter. "Really? I didn't know John let his boys make house calls to outlanders."

"He hasn't before. But Levi insisted, and Mr. Johnson seems like a nice man." Moriah had met him the day he'd come to check out the Millers' shop.

Emma's brows furrowed. "How often is he gone?"

Moriah paused before answering. She didn't want to cause her any worry—or hear a lecture about Levi spending too much time in the "devil's playground." Besides, he would be finished with that job soon.

She was pondering a suitable answer when Tobias suddenly burst into the kitchen from the back door. He paused and gave the air a long, satisfied sniff, then bellowed with enthusiasm, "Sticky buns. Talk about good timing." His hand shot out for a freshly iced bun, but Emma snatched them away.

"These are for your *daed* and your brothers. You can have yours when you come back."

"Back from where?" His blond eyebrow arched from beneath his hat.

"The Detweilers'. Sarah left one of her pie plates here, and I keep forgetting to give it back to her."

Tobias looked pained. "Why can't Lukas or Stephen take it?"

"Because you came in first. That makes you the lucky one."

Emma smiled and tapped the brim of his hat with her finger. Her lighthearted nature warmed the Byler home, creating a comfortable atmosphere of laughter and playful teasing. She handed him a glass pie plate. "Here you go. Oh, and take this batch of sticky buns with you and give it to Sarah."

"Now you're just torturing me," Tobias said with exaggerated drama. "I can't eat these, *and* I have to smell them all the way to the Detweilers'?"

"I'm sure you'll manage."

He turned and looked at Moriah, acknowledging her for the first time. "Hey, sis, why don't you take these to the—"

"Oh no you don't." Emma shooed him out the door. "I won't have you pawning your responsibilities off on your sister. Now go!"

Moriah laughed at the helpless expression on her brother's face as he disappeared outside. She knew he wouldn't refuse *Mami* any request, but he had a good time ruffling her feathers before capitulating.

"That boy," Emma said, shaking her head as she plopped down at the table. "He'll be the death of me, I'm sure of it. Why can't he just say 'yes, ma'am' like my other two sons and get on with it?"

"Because then you'd think there was something wrong with him." Moriah grinned as she turned the dough and continued rolling. She was glad she'd decided to visit her family today. It lifted her spirits, making her concern over her relationship with Levi seem far away.

Emma sighed. "You're right. I just wish he'd find a nice girl to court. But he's too busy playing games and having fun."

"Now that's not quite true, *Mami*. You know he works hard in the shop and around here."

"*Ya*, that he does. But he certainly has plenty of free time. More than your father had at that age." She brushed a few specks of flour off the table. "I thought maybe he liked that sweet Rachel Detweiler, but she's been seen with Christian Weaver quite a bit."

"Rachel and Tobias can't stand each other, *Mami*."

"There's a fine line between passion and hate, Moriah." Emma sighed and leaned her elbow on the table, putting her chin in her hand. "Doesn't matter what Tobias thinks about Rachel, she's pretty close with Christian now. Sarah suspects they'll be wed this fall."

"She does?"

"*Ya*. She's planting plenty of extra celery in the garden this spring. You know, Tobias needs to pay attention to what Christian's doing. He needs to put childish things behind him and start thinking about his future. Like you did when you married Levi. Although that young man dragged his feet for so long we didn't think he would ever get around to asking you."

Moriah hid her frown. Her mother's words stung a little, digging deeper into Moriah's insecurity.

Emma must have noticed, because she quickly added, "Doesn't matter anyway. You two are married now. And happy, *ya*?"

"*Ya*. We're happy, *Mami*."

With a grin Emma said, "*Gut, gut*. Then my prayers have been answered, praise God."

Her pricked emotions assuaged, Moriah couldn't resist the chance to rib her mother. "Maybe you should pray for patience with Tobias."

"Believe me, I do. Every single day of my life."

Chapter 4

Tobias couldn't believe his bad timing. The last thing he wanted to do was go to the Detweilers'. He hadn't seen much of Rachel since he zinged her leg with the baseball last November, and that suited him just fine. She'd been keeping company with Christian, even sitting next to him during the singings. Neither of them had been at the last frolic, and Tobias remembered someone mentioning that they had spent the day in Ashtabula, shopping with Christian's family.

Tobias gripped the reins tighter, barely hearing the clopping of the horse's hooves against the slushy roads. Guess things were pretty serious between Christian and Rachel. Not that he cared. She could marry whomever she wanted, and he liked Christian. Although he wondered how a calm, soft-spoken guy like Christian could handle Rachel's crazy moods. Especially when she was angry, those gorgeous eyes of hers sparking, that pert mouth emitting a diatribe that would burn even the most seasoned man's ears. A spitfire, that's what she was. She could be so passionate—

He jerked on the reins. Where the heck did that come from? *Passion* and *Rachel* in the same thought? Heat crept up on his neck, and his coat was suddenly too warm, even though it was thirty-something degrees out.

Maybe his *mami* was right. He should find some nice girl to court, someone to marry and have a family with. Several of his buddies had already chosen their wives, and Christian seemed well on his way to doing so. Perhaps if he had his own girl to focus on, he would quit thinking about Rachel Detweiler all the time.

But then again, women tended to complicate things. His life was fine the way it was—good job, fun friends, nice home, a great family. He was young, only nineteen. Plenty of time for him to get married—if he even wanted to.

A few moments later he pulled up to her house and turned in the driveway. He brought the buggy to a stop, then hitched up his horse. If he was lucky, Rachel would be at Mary Yoder's restaurant, serving her customers some of the authentic Amish cooking that drew tourists and locals looking for home-style meals or tempting baked goods. But nothing could beat his mother's sticky buns. He would just leave them with Mrs. Detweiler, then rush home to finish the load of work waiting for him. He hated working late. Why his mother hadn't sent Moriah to run this errand was beyond him. Not like his sister had anything else to do.

On the Detweilers' front porch, he knocked on the white oak door, his knuckles hurting from the cold. While he waited, he breathed out white puffs into the chilly air. He had just formed his mouth into a perfect *O* to see if he could make a circle with his breath when the door opened.

Rachel planted her hands on her hips. "What are you doing?"

His lips froze in the *O* shape as he stared at her. Wow, she looked pretty in her midcalf-length dress and white *kapp*. Light purple was a good color for her. It brought out the blue in her eyes, eyes that were suddenly looking at him as if he had totally lost all his marbles. For the second time in ten minutes, he felt a rush of heat surge over his face. "Sticky buns," he said, thrusting the plate at her.

The plate wobbled in his hand, nearly tipping over until she reached out and grabbed it. When she did, their fingers touched for the briefest of moments. Tobias wanted to slap some sense into himself. No wonder she thought he had lost it—he was starting to think the same thing.

"Thanks," she said, still giving him a wary eye. "I'll give these to—"

"Who's at the door?" Sarah Detweiler appeared behind her daughter. "Oh, Tobias, hello. What brings you by?"

"Sticky buns," he repeated, then fought the urge to roll his eyes. Apparently those were the only two words in his vocabulary this morning.

"From Emma?" Sarah took the buns from Rachel. "They smell marvelous. How about you come inside and we can share them together? I just put a pot of coffee on to perk."

Rachel's eyes grew wide, and Tobias could tell that the last thing she wanted to do was share sticky buns with him. That helped him make up his mind. "I'd be obliged, ma'am," he said, walking past Rachel and removing his hat. He hung it on a peg near the door, then slipped off his snow-covered boots. He turned and gave Rachel a big, smug smile.

She responded with a glare.

"Goodness, Rachel!" Sarah said. "Shut the door; you're letting in all the cold air."

Rachel dutifully closed the door. She started to head to the kitchen when Sarah stopped her. "Why don't you and Tobias get settled in the living room? I'll bring out the buns and coffee. How do you take yours, Tobias?"

"Black," he said, grinning even wider as he saw Rachel's frown. "If you please."

"Rachel?"

"None for me," she mumbled, then scooted past Tobias into the front room, which served as the Detweilers' visiting area. She plopped down on the most comfortable looking chair and crossed her arms, her mouth in full pout mode. He followed her into the room and could almost feel the daggers shooting from her eyes. Her resentment cast a pall over the neat, plainly furnished room.

Tobias caught the warning glance Sarah gave her daughter before heading to the kitchen at the back of the house. He lowered himself in the chair directly across from her, his eyes never leaving hers.

"Don't you have work to do?" she asked, tilting her head and looking at him dead on, as if she could wish him away if she glared at him hard enough.

"Don't you? Thought you'd be at the restaurant."

"I'm off today. You still haven't answered my question."

"I just can't resist my mother's sticky buns." He smirked.

"Then you should go home and eat them there." She met his gaze, unflinching.

"But I wouldn't want to disappoint your mother."

"I'll explain why you left."

"Then you'll look like a fool, because I'm not leaving." He put his hands behind his head and leaned back in the chair, reveling in the fury he saw building inside her. Good Lord, she was fun to rile up. The spark that leapt to her eyes affected him, like touching a lit match to a stick of dynamite.

Rachel suddenly jumped from her seat. "You are the most *infuriating* person I have ever met."

"Wow. That's a big word," he said drolly. "You been reading the dictionary in your spare time?"

"Ooh," she said, going to him. She poked him in the chest. "You are *seltsam,* Tobias Byler!"

He grasped her hand midpoke, not even caring that she had called him weird. Instead of letting go of it, he held on. His own hands were rough, scarred, and gouged from working with wood since he was a child. Her hands, in contrast, were small and soft, with slender fingers that he had a sudden urge to intertwine with his own. Their gazes instantly met, and for the life of him he couldn't move away from her, even if he wanted to. Which he didn't.

"Nothing better on a cold winter morning than coffee and sticky buns," Sarah's voice sounded in the hallway, as if she were warning them of her approach.

They both jumped apart, Rachel snatching her hand out of his grip and flinging herself into the chair. Tobias looked at Sarah as she entered the room and placed the tray on the coffee table. While she settled herself on the sofa, he gave Rachel a quick glance, and was surprised to see the blush blooming on her cheeks, making her look even prettier than before.

Sarah looked up and directed her attention to Rachel, a frown forming on her lips. "Are you feeling all right, daughter? You look flushed."

Her mother's comment seemed to only intensify the reddening of Rachel's face. "I'm fine."

Suddenly, his pleasure at putting her on edge disappeared, replaced by a tiny bit of shame, and a large dose of confusion. Since when did he have the urge to hold her hand, especially since everyone knew she and Christian were courting?

The parlor, which had been so welcoming and comfortable minutes before, now seemed stuffy and claustrophobic. He scrambled up from his chair, assailed by an uncontrollable urge to get out of there. When he started to speak, the words came out in a foggy croak, so he cleared his throat and tried again. "I gotta go, *Frau* Detweiler."

Surprise crossed Sarah's features, her blue eyes so similar to Rachel's. "So soon? You haven't even had your coffee yet. Surely you can stay for just a little while."

"I know, but I just remembered I promised *Daed* I would do something for him." He grappled for a more thorough explanation, but his mind went blank. "Something important" was all he could come up with. He nodded toward the tray. "I'm sorry to put you to so much trouble. *Danki.* I appreciate the hospitality." Spinning on his sock-clad heel, he dashed to the front door, yanked on his boots, and grabbed his hat, then flew down the steps to his buggy. He slapped the reins on the horse's flanks.

As the horse and buggy sprinted home, he felt a tingle in his hand. The hand that had held Rachel's. He glanced down at it, remembering how much he liked the feel of Rachel's skin against his.

Dummkopf. He should have never accepted *Frau* Detweiler's invitation. Now she probably thought he'd lost his mind. With a hard shake of his head, he tried to clear the scene from his mind. If Rachel's mother thought he was crazy, she wasn't the only one.

"What on earth has gotten into that boy?"

Rachel shrugged, but she didn't look at her mother.

"Did you two have a fight? Rachel, look at me." Sarah moved closer to her daughter. "Did he say something to you?"

"*Nee, Mudder,*" she replied, hoping her mother didn't notice that Rachel's face was perilously close to exploding with embarrassment. As if that wasn't bad enough, she was dealing with some other emotion she couldn't define. A tickling, yet tingling sensation that started as soon as Tobias had touched her hand. "He's just *seltsam.*"

Sarah frowned, the parentheses-shaped lines around her mouth deepening. "That's not a nice thing to say, Rachel Anne. It doesn't matter how you feel about someone, when they are a guest in your home, you are to treat them with kindness and respect. Part of the duties of a good wife is to make her home a welcoming place. Not just for family, but for the community. Tobias is a part of this community, whether you like it or not."

Properly chastised, Rachel leaned back in the chair. "Sorry."

With a nod, Sarah picked up the untouched tray from the coffee table. "Besides, it doesn't hurt to keep your prospects open."

Rachel popped up from her chair. "What do you mean?"

"In case things don't work out with Christian."

"Things are fine with Christian." At least she thought they were. True, their relationship was building slowly . . . very slowly. Probably at a slower pace than she had expected. But that wasn't necessarily a bad thing. She and Christian both needed to be sure about their feelings for each other before they became serious. They were suitably matched—they had a deep connection to their families and faith, they enjoyed reading, and . . . well, she knew there were more things they had in common, she just couldn't think about them right now. One thing she did know for sure, Christian was better for her than Tobias could ever be.

"Don't be surprised if he changes his mind," Sarah said.

"Tobias?"

"*Christian*," Sarah said as she walked out the door. "Men can be fickle, you know."

Rachel fell back in her chair. She didn't know about men and their inconsistencies. In fact, she knew very little about men at all. True, she had brothers, but they were all several years older than her, except for Aaron. While her friends in school had spent their younger teen years crushing on one boy or another—with Tobias as the object of their affections at some point—she had focused on schoolwork and grades. Her diligence paid off, she had made straight As all through her school career. While she was proud of that accomplishment, her singular devotion to her studies—and her relentless competitive streak—had come at the expense of some of her friendships. Then she took that same ambition and applied it to her job at Mary Yoder's Kitchen, not paying much attention to the social opportunities she might be missing.

For the first time she regretted not being a little less ambitious and a little more pacifying. Then she might have gained an insight or two on how men ticked. Or maybe not. Maybe this had nothing to do with her, and everything to do with Christian.

Was he having second thoughts about their relationship? The good Lord knew she had more than a few.

Rising from her chair, she straightened up a small pile of Family Life magazines on the end table and began fluffing the already full sofa pillows. She should have a talk with Christian. A serious talk, not the superficial conversations they normally had. She should find out what his intentions truly were. When she agreed to date him, she had done so with an open mind and—she hoped—an open heart. But every time they were together, it seemed they treated each other more as friends than romantic interests. Her mother had probably picked up on that as well.

"Rachel?"

Rachel turned around to see her mother poke her head in the doorway of the parlor. "*Ya*?"

"When you're finished in here, I need you to clean the upstairs bedrooms."

"Aaron's too?"

"*Ya*. You do such a wonderful job, even better than I do." Sarah smiled. "Your husband will be very lucky indeed to have such a good housekeeper."

Rachel managed a half smile and wondered if her mother had lost her mind. *Mami* was clearly obsessed with Rachel's future marriage—when or if it ever happened.

But her mother's compliment about her cleaning skills warmed her; Rachel abhorred untidiness and had always kept her room in order. Still, she didn't relish straightening up Aaron's room. She wondered if he was even out of bed, despite it being midmorning. Since his return from jail, her parents had been dealing with him as if he were made of thin glass. They said it was because he was still in drug recovery, but Rachel was keenly aware of the difference between the way they treated her and her older brothers, though her brothers now were married and out of the house.

The bulk of the chores often fell to her, even more so after Aaron had fallen in with a bad crowd during his *rumspringa*. He had been belligerent, lazy, and argumentative, especially with their parents, something she had never done. While she had experimented with a few forbidden things during her own *rumspringa,* such as borrowing one of those little music players and trying on one of her Yankee friend's makeup, she didn't have the rebellious streak her brother possessed. Since his return, he had stayed holed up in his room for the most part, and she hadn't talked to him much. If anyone asked her to describe her brother, she doubted she could do it, other than give just a physical description. She didn't know him anymore.

Yet she still had to clean his room.

As she passed by the front door on the way to the stairs, she heard someone knocking. Glad for the reprieve, however slight, she turned around and answered it, surprised to see Gabriel Miller standing at the front door.

"Good morning, Rachel."

"Good morning, Gabe. What can I do for you?"

"Is Aaron around?"

"Why don't you come in?" she offered, remembering her mother's words about hospitality. "I haven't seen him this morning, but I'll check upstairs."

"*Danki.*"

"Would you like to sit down in the parlor? I could bring you a cup of coffee. We have some sticky buns too."

"No, I'm fine. But thank you. I'll just wait here."

Rachel dashed up the stairs and stopped in front of her brother's room. The door was shut, so she knocked. Even though she didn't strike the door very hard, it opened in response. She expected to see him asleep in bed, but his bed was already made, their grandmother's black-and-white quilt neatly pulled over it. She stepped inside and saw him sitting in a chair beside the only window, staring out into the barren, snow-covered field behind the house. Unsure of her brother's mood, she looked around the room. Nothing amiss. A small chest of drawers sat next to the tiny closet. A round, braided rug, made by their mother from pieces of leftover, faded rags, covered the middle of the wood-planked floor.

"Gabe Miller's here to see you," she said in a soft voice.

Slowly he turned around and faced her, his expression blank, as it had been since he'd returned from jail. Without verbally responding, he pushed back his chair and walked passed her to exit the room. Not even a single thank-you for her trudging up the stairs to fetch him.

A passage from Romans entered her mind as she battled the resentment rising within her. "Do not let the sun go down on your anger." Easy for Paul to say.

As she thought more on the passage, her ire cooled. She really did need to work on managing her anger. It seemed she'd been more and more volatile lately and didn't fully understand why.

Well, might as well clean Aaron's room while I'm here. Examining the small space, she searched for what needed to be cleaned and straightened. After five minutes she realized, surprisingly, that there was nothing for her to do. He had done it all.

"I need someone four days a week." Gabe and Aaron stood on the Detweilers' front porch, Aaron in a simple broadcloth shirt, pants, and socks. Gabe figured the boy must be freezing, but if he was, he didn't say anything. Instead he silently listened to Gabe's offer, nodding in understanding every once in a while.

"Mostly you'll be cleaning up around the shop, oiling the

tools, and helping me out at the forge when necessary." Gabe thought about adding the duty of keeping his father away from the forge, but he wouldn't humiliate his *daed* like that. He would keep an eye on him himself. "The pay is pretty good, but not as much as you'd get at one of the factories around here. I know for sure that Dillen's pays more. I gotta be honest about that."

"Not worried about the pay."

Gabe stroked his chin as he sized up the seventeen-year-old. He had a thin frame, but that was to be expected from his recent drug use and time spent in jail. Blond fuzz covered his scalp. When he first came home, he looked something like what the Yankees called a skinhead, but at least he wasn't completely bald anymore. The kid's face was, however, completely unreadable. Blank was the best description he could come up with.

"You've heard my offer," Gabe said. "And my terms. What say you? Will you take the job?"

Aaron nodded slowly. "*Ya.*"

Gabe grinned. "Be there at seven sharp tomorrow morning. Levi and I usually start at six, but we won't need you until seven."

"I can start this afternoon, if you want."

Gabe considered his offer for a moment. "All right. Do you need a ride?"

"*Nee.* I'll walk."

"Then let's say in a couple hours. I can show you around the place, tell you how we run things." He held out his hand and Aaron clasped it in a gentleman's agreement. He scanned the young man's lack of winter attire. "You better get inside before you freeze," he said.

"I'm fine," Aaron replied with a shrug. He turned and went inside.

Satisfied, Gabe descended the steps, unhitched his horse, and headed home. He'd closed down the shop for an early lunch while he went to talk to Aaron. His father hadn't minded or questioned him; he just went back to the house and said he would have some tea and read for a while. The old man looked tired, and Gabe wasn't in any hurry to have him back in the shop again.

As he made his way back to his house, he passed by the Byler's and recognized Levi and Moriah's buggy in the driveway. Her beautiful face immediately came to mind, and he remembered her near fainting spell earlier that morning. The past four months had been difficult, knowing that she lived only a few feet away from him in the main house.

And now she carried Levi's child. Another blow, even though he had known it would eventually happen. He slapped the reins against the horse's flanks. The sooner he accepted that Moriah was lost to him, the easier life would be. Every night he prayed the same prayer to the Almighty—to free him from this prison of sin and covetousness. His prayers were still unanswered.

God rewards the faithful in His time, not man's. Gabe knew this, and clung to it. God would answer his prayer eventually and release him of this burden, of that he was sure. In the meantime, He was molding Gabe into a new vessel, one worthy and strong enough to serve Him. As a worker of iron, he was well acquainted with the heat and pressure and power necessary to change raw material into something useful.

He just wished the process wasn't so painful.

Chapter 5

Butterflies danced a jig inside Moriah's belly as she prepared supper, although she wasn't exactly sure if it was caused by nerves or nausea. First thing this morning, she'd had to run to the bathroom. Levi had already left for Gates Mills, saving her from having to explain to him why she was throwing up. He would find out why tonight, during their anniversary dinner. She had spent the previous day cleaning the house from top to bottom, hoping Levi would notice her efforts. Unfortunately, he hadn't, or at least he hadn't said he'd noticed.

She placed her hand over her stomach and stirred the simmering liver, spooning the brown gravy over the meat and onions. Liver had never been one of her favorites, and she wasn't sure she would be able to eat a bite. But Levi loved it, and she wanted this meal to be special.

Remembering her promise to John about not skipping meals, she decided she'd eat at least a small portion with Levi tonight. The aroma of yeast rolls and a fresh-baked apple pie filled the kitchen. She knew he liked pumpkin pie better, but she'd forgotten she had used all of the canned pumpkin at Christmastime. Even though February was drawing to a close, the food cellar still held plenty of apples from the fall harvest. She had even sliced a few hearty wedges of cheddar cheese to accompany the pie. She hoped Levi would be pleased.

She placed the rolls in a basket and wrapped a tea towel over them to keep them warm. When the liver and onions finished simmering, she turned off the burner and placed a lid on top of the pot. Glancing at the battery-run clock on the wall, she saw she'd finished just in time. Levi would be home any minute. When he had been late last night, he had promised to be home in time for supper tonight. Anticipation filled her as she went to the sitting room and sat on the sofa by the large picture window, waiting for the familiar white van to arrive. She imagined what his reaction to her news would be. An image of his handsome face lit up with joy came to mind. Surely he would be as happy as she was about the baby. Of that she had no doubt.

"*Moriah . . . Moriah.*"

The sound of her husband's voice penetrated her mind. Moriah opened her eyes, surprised to find herself in a darkened room. A strong hand touched her shoulder, shaking her gently. Then soft, glowing light flooded her eyes.

She squinted, trying to figure out where she was, then realized she had fallen asleep on the sofa in the sitting room. Moving to an upright position, she focused on the man turning away from the gas-powered lamp he had just lit. Through sleepy eyes, she smiled as she looked at his back. He hadn't even had a chance to take off his coat and hat. He must have had to work late, but she was glad he was finally home. Now she could tell him about their precious baby.

But when he turned around, her anticipation dimmed. Although many people had difficulty telling the twin brothers apart, she never did. "Gabriel?"

His expression solemn, he came and sat down next to her on the couch. A strange thing for him to do, since normally he kept his distance from her.

"Moriah, are you awake?" he asked, his voice quiet, but with a slight edge to it. "Fully awake?"

She rubbed her eyes to rid them of sleep, then looked at him. "*Ya,* Gabriel. I'm up." Only then did she see the distress in his brown eyes. "What is it? What's wrong?"

He turned from her and looked at the wall for a moment before slowly rubbing the back of his neck. Then he took off his hat and set it on the end table next to the sofa.

The longer he took to answer, the faster the panic built inside her. Finally, she couldn't take it anymore. "Gabriel, what is going on?"

Without a word he reached into his pocket and withdrew a folded piece of paper. He handed it to her. "Levi sent this," he said tightly.

Her gaze dropped to the note. She stared at it, not wanting to accept it from him. Her throat tightened at the thought of reading it, sensing it contained something she didn't want to know. She raised her head to see Gabriel's expression, but his eyes darted from hers, as if he couldn't bear to look at her directly. His reaction only fueled the anxiety rising inside her. He pushed the note toward her again. This time she took the paper and unfolded it. She first noticed a business heading stamped at the top: *Johnston's Farms.* Had something happened to Levi at the horse farm?

Moriah,

This is a hard letter for me to write. You have to know up front that I never meant to hurt you. In my own way, I did love you.

Tears sprang to her eyes, blurring the small, uniform lines in front of her. Not hurt her? Did love her? What kind of words were those? She blinked, and round circles of moisture dotted the page. She forced herself to read on.

I am leaving you and the Amish. I haven't felt right about being Amish for a long time, but I thought I didn't have any choice. Everyone in my family joined the church, and it would have broken my mother's heart if I hadn't joined. But Mami is gone, and I want to be free.

I don't want to follow rules all the time. I don't want to be stuck in four-hour church services or banging on a forge until I die. I've found my place with the Yankees. There's no drudgery, no self-denial. Only total freedom to be who I am.

I hope you can understand why I had to do this, Moriah. And I hope someday you will forgive me. I think we'll both be better off.

Levi Miller

Moriah let the letter slip through her fingers and drop to the floor. Slowly she rose from the couch and wrapped her arms around her body. She'd let the fire go out in the stove. She had to get more wood and light the stove. Maybe then she would feel warm again.

Gabe wasn't sure what he expected when Moriah read his brother's note, but the silent way she left the room wasn't it. Alarmed, he jumped up from the sofa and followed her. As he entered the kitchen, the faint scent of rolls mingled with liver and onions hung in the air. One glance at the kitchen table and his heart broke even more.

She'd obviously taken pains to make the setting perfect. She had covered the table with a white linen cloth, the one his mother had reserved for special occasions. A small gas lamp bathed the room in soft light. A basket of rolls, the red tea towel covering the bread in an attempt to keep it warm, sat next to a sunken apple pie that looked like it had been out for hours.

His gaze jerked from the table when he saw Moriah walking out the back door, without a coat or wrap on. Although spring was only a month away, the damp night chilled the bones. "Moriah," he called, following her out the door. "Where are you going?"

"Stove's out," she said, her voice monotone and barely audible. "I shouldn't have fallen asleep."

He came up behind her as she bent to pick up several split pieces of wood. "Go inside, Moriah," he said. "I'll get the wood."

In the darkness of the night he couldn't see her expression, but he could see the shadow of her movement as she nodded her head. She went back inside, her steps slow, as if she were in shock. Gabe realized she probably was.

He snatched up enough wood to make a decent-sized fire, then dashed back inside where Moriah stood in the middle of the kitchen, staring at the withered pie on the table. "I should have made pumpkin," she mumbled. "He likes pumpkin better than apple."

Concern filled him as he shoved the wood in the opening of the stove. He moved beside her and led her to a chair. "Sit down, and don't move. I'll get the fire started." He started back to the stove but added for good measure, "Don't move."

He lit the stove. Soon the kitchen would be warm. Hopefully

that would help; she appeared so cold. He could see her body trembling, her fingertips a bluish hue. Remembering the quilt he saw lying over the back of the couch in the front room, he went to fetch it. Within moments he came back and put it around her shoulders, then sat down next to her.

He was glad to see she had gathered the quilt closer to her body. At least she wasn't completely catatonic. "Do you want some coffee? Tea maybe?"

"Coffee," she said, then looked up at him, her eyes not so empty now.

As he moved around the kitchen, easily locating what he needed—she hadn't rearranged anything since moving into the house—he thought about his brother. That Levi would leave the church, leave his *wife* . . . Gabe could barely comprehend it. That he would do such a thing by an impersonal letter added even more fuel to the angry fire stoking inside him.

Levi had sent Gabe a letter as well, through the driver that had taken him to Gates Mills for the past couple months. In the short note, he had said he was leaving the church and the community—to do *what,* Gabe didn't know—and told him not to try to contact him. Right now Gabe didn't care if he never saw his brother again. The coward had left it up to him to deliver the news not only to Moriah but also to their father.

As the coffee perked on the stove, he dropped his head in his hands. How could he tell *Daed* what Levi had done? Did his brother not realize their father's increasingly fragile state? Was he so selfish that he didn't care if their father died from the heartbreak of knowing his son had chosen the world over God?

"Gabriel?"

He looked up at the sound of Moriah's voice. Her features

seemed less pale, less haunted. But the pain was still evident in her eyes, in the downward turn of her mouth. He hated seeing her suffer this way.

She stood up from her chair and walked over to him. Placing her hand on his arm, she said, "Let it go, Gabriel. Let your anger for Levi go."

How did she know what he was thinking? He followed her gaze to his hands, which were clenched so tightly the knuckles where white. When she looked at his face, he relaxed his hands.

The coffee pot finished percolating. Gabe started to reach past Moriah's shoulder for a cup from the cabinet when she stopped him. "I'll get it."

"*Nee,* Moriah. Let me do it."

She shook her head. "I can't just sit here. Do you want some?"

He nodded, not wanting to argue with her, then went to sit down as she took two white ceramic mugs from the cabinet and poured coffee into them. She spooned a little sugar into Gabe's, then poured cream into hers before sitting back down at the table and handing him his cup. Surrounding the mug with her hands, she stared into the caramel-colored liquid.

"How do you do it?" he asked after a few moments of silence.

She glanced up. "Do what?"

"Stay so calm." A few moments ago she'd seemed ready to fall apart. Now she was a pillar of strength. How she managed to regain her equanimity he had no idea.

"I'm not calm," she said. The tremble in her lower lip as she spoke revealed the truth behind her words. "I don't know what I feel right now, but it's definitely not calm." She looked back at her coffee, but didn't make a move to drink it. "Does your *daed* know?"

He shook his head. "I didn't want to wake him."

"What time is it?"

"Twelve thirty."

With a sigh, she said, "I must have been asleep for hours. I was waiting for Levi . . ." Her hands tightened around the mug. "Why is he doing this?" Her voice sounded thin.

"I don't know." Gabe stood up from his chair and started pacing the room, his coffee untouched as well. "It doesn't make any sense."

"Did he say anything to you about leaving?"

"*Nee.* Not a word."

"Did he . . ." She paused, her gaze averted. "Did he say he was . . . unhappy?"

Gabe immediately caught her meaning and sat back down. "*Nee,* not ever. Moriah, I'm sure that whatever crazy thing is going on inside my brother's head, it has nothing to do with you." But as he said it, he saw a tear roll down her cheek.

"He doesn't love me. Not anymore." She wiped her face with the back of her hand, still not looking at him. "I wonder if he ever did."

"Moriah," Gabe said, lowering his voice. How he wished he could take away the pain, the humiliation she so clearly felt. "This isn't your fault."

Her head snapped her head up. "But what if it is? What if he left because I wasn't a good wife? What if I pushed him to do this?"

He couldn't imagine her being anything but the perfect wife. "I don't believe that."

"Just look at this supper," she said, her voice rising an octave. "The rolls are burned."

"Moriah, they're fine—"

"And I know he likes pumpkin pie more than apple, but I didn't have any pumpkin. I should have bought some; I should have prepared better. A good wife would have put her husband's needs first, right?"

Her words were coming out faster now, and the worry that had filled him when she first read Levi's letter returned. "Pie is not a need, Moriah. He would have been fine eating apple, trust me."

She stood from her chair, letting the quilt fall to the floor. She kept talking as if he hadn't said anything. "I must have done something wrong, something horrible for him to leave me. I wasn't good enough. I wasn't pretty enough, or desirable enough, or . . ."

Gabe couldn't take listening to her tear herself down. He leapt from his chair and went to her, putting his hands on her shoulders. "Stop it, Moriah. Stop saying things that aren't true!"

Her eyes filled with moisture, and she reached up and grabbed his shirt. "I should have made pumpkin, Gabriel. I should have made pumpkin . . ." She fell against his chest and sobbed.

Instinctively his arms went around her. He could easily rest his chin on her head, and he wanted to do just that, to press her against his chest and never let her go. He squeezed his eyes shut.

He knew he should step away, but he stroked her back, even pressed his cheek against her *kapp*, breathing in the sweet smell of her. While Levi would cast her away, Gabe would treasure her forever.

But she wasn't his to treasure. With a huge effort, he lifted his head, stilled his hand, and stepped away from her. His shirt was damp with her tears and pain. When she looked up at him, her eyes brimming with tears, it took every ounce of his resolve not to draw her against him once more.

"I was going to tell him something tonight," she whispered,

her cheeks and lips shiny with moisture. "I was going to give him the best news in the world."

Gabe sucked in a breath. He didn't have to hear the words; he already knew what she was about to say.

"We're having a baby." Somehow she managed a watery smile. "I'm pregnant with Levi's child." She laid her palm flat against her stomach. "This baby was going to fix everything between us, Gabriel. Draw us closer together, make us a real family." Once again she leaned against him, pressing her cheek against his shirt. "Now what am I going to do?"

Gabe continued to hold her, convincing himself he was only offering her comfort, even though with every fiber of his being he longed to offer her more. Most of all he wanted to take on her pain as his own. But he couldn't. He could only give her solace, and weak solace at that. "I don't know, Moriah," he said, reveling in her nearness while wallowing in his own guilt. "I don't know."

"Gabriel . . . Gabe, *sohn,* wake up."

Gabe's eyes flew open at the sound of his father's voice and the touch of the old man's hand on his shoulder. He straightened to an upright position as the kitchen came into focus. A dull ache spread across his shoulder blades. Glancing around, he realized he'd fallen asleep at the table. Arching his back, he looked up into his father's concerned eyes. "What time is it?" he asked, his voice still heavy with sleep.

"Past seven thirty. When you didn't show up at the shop, I got worried. Aaron had to come get me to unlock the door."

Gabe rubbed the back of his neck. "I'm sorry, *Daed.*" He

surveyed the kitchen once again. The fire had burned out in the stove, and a chill hung in the air. He spied two nearly full cups of cold coffee on the table. Then the prior evening's events replayed in his mind.

Soon after Moriah had told him about the baby, he had managed to convince her to go upstairs and sleep. Despite the fatigue that had seeped into her features, she had resisted. Finally, she agreed to rest for the baby's sake. He had planned to stay up, to be there if she needed him. Sometime during the night he must have fallen asleep on the table.

The impact of her pregnancy continued to swirl around in his brain. A baby. Moriah was pregnant, and her husband gone. His heart squeezed in his chest at the thought of the pain she must be going through. There was no option of divorce in their faith. Levi would be her husband until death, whether he was here or not.

"Gabe? Are you gonna tell me what's going on here or am I gonna have to drag it out of you?"

His father's voice yanked him out of his musings. Gabe looked at the old man, dread spinning in his gut. He didn't want to tell him about Levi, but he had no choice. He couldn't prolong it; his father would find out soon enough anyway. Unless . . .

Unless Levi came back.

Once his brother knew about the baby, he'd have to return. He'd put away self-centeredness for the sake of his wife and child. They would work out their problems and be the family God intended them to be. Then his father wouldn't have to know anything about his son's betrayal.

Gabe popped up from his chair, his decision made. "I need you to do me a favor, *Daed*."

A bewildered expression crossed the older man's face. "Sure, *sohn.* Anything. But I still want to know what's going on."

"You will, soon enough." He went outside and grabbed a few chunks of wood, then started the fire in the stove. The wood crackled as the fire burned through the bark. He dumped the stale contents of the coffeepot in the sink, then started a fresh brew. Moriah would probably want a cup once she awakened.

"Gabriel?" John questioned, sitting down at the table. "Are you going to tell me what you need me to do or not?"

"Sorry. Can you stay with Moriah? She's upstairs, asleep. She's not feeling well."

John raised his bushy brows in surprise. "Where's Levi?"

Gabe hesitated for a moment before answering. "Gates Mills," he said.

John frowned. "He didn't come home last night?"

"He had some extra work to do." Gabe checked the stove again, even though the fire was at the perfect temperature. He hated lying to his father, and he couldn't look at him while falsehoods flew out of his mouth. But it was necessary, at least for the moment. "Levi will be back later tonight." *Lord willing.*

That simple explanation seemed to pacify John. "Good. I have half a mind to tell that boy to quit working for those Yankees. We need him here. It isn't as if we're desperate for money. The Lord has seen fit to provide us with everything we need."

"*Ya,* He has." Eager to end the conversation before his father asked more questions, Gabe searched the kitchen for his hat and coat, then remembered he left them up front. He took a deep breath to steady his nerves, inhaling the rich scent of coffee brewing. "I'll be gone for part of the day, *Daed.* Please stay here and keep an eye on Moriah. I'll close the shop, but Aaron can do a few things in there. If I'm not back by the time he's finished, go ahead and send him home."

"That's a fine boy you hired," John said. "I can tell he's going to be a *gut* worker. Hard to believe he spent time in jail."

Gabe nodded, only half-listening to what John was saying. "I'll see you this afternoon."

After grabbing his coat and hat, he rushed to the shop. Aaron was already at work sweeping the floor, even though it didn't need it. He had swept it thoroughly the day before.

"Aaron," Gabe called.

Aaron looked up, then set the broom aside before shoving his hands in his pockets and lumbering over to Gabe. "What can I do for you?"

His standard question. Since starting work two days ago, Aaron Detweiler hadn't said much and mostly kept to himself, but he always asked Gabe and John what he could do for them. Gabe had confidence that he was leaving the shop in good hands. "I've got some errands to do, and I'll be gone most of the day. *Daed*'s inside the main house, but I don't want him working out here today. I'm closing up the shop, but I hope you'll do a few things for me." Aaron nodded and listened carefully to Gabe's instructions. "When you're done, just let *Daed* know before you go home."

Aaron nodded again but remained silent.

"*Danki.*" Gabe hurried out the door and hustled to the end of the driveway. He sprinted along the road to the telephone box situated in between his property and the Fishers', his neighbors. The church's *Ordnung* allowed the Millers to use cell phones for their business, but they hadn't made the switch yet. Four families, including his, shared this telephone for business or emergency purposes only. Today constituted an emergency. He called Guy Thompson, a fellow he knew who ran a taxi service for many of the Amish. As the hollow-sounding ring repeated in Gabe's ears, he prayed Guy was home.

"Thompson," a man with a low, gruff voice answered on the fourth ring.

Gabe offered a quick, silent prayer of thanks. "Guy, this is Gabriel Miller."

"Hey, Gabe. How are you?"

"Doing all right," Gabe said, but that was far from the truth. Inside the dense wool of his gloves, his palms broke out into a sweat while his stomach churned. Confronting his brother was the last thing he wanted to do, and he knew he needed God's help to keep his temper when he saw him. He fought to keep his tone steady. He didn't need Guy asking any questions. "I need a ride. Are you available today?"

"Sure am. Where you wanna go?"

"Gates Mills," Gabe said, letting out a frosty breath. "I need to see my brother."

Moriah's eyes ached as she struggled to open them. Somehow she had managed to fall asleep, but she didn't know when or how. She had only agreed to go upstairs to placate Gabe, who had insisted she get some rest. Thank the Lord he had been there last night. What would she have done without him? Uncharacteristically, he had been kind to her, giving her comfort, trying to reassure her that everything would be all right, even though she could see in his eyes how deeply Levi's betrayal had affected him. When he told her she had to sleep for her baby's sake, she finally, albeit reluctantly, agreed.

But when she'd begun to climb the stairs, the tears came again. Over and over she had asked herself how Levi could do this—to her, to their families, to himself, to their community. Didn't he realize what it meant for him to leave their faith? He had agreed to live by the tenets of their church for the rest of his life when he had been baptized. How could he break that vow? And why would he break their marriage vow?

She couldn't shake the thought that somehow his leaving had to be her fault. What she had done to fail him. What she could have done differently.

She'd cried until she had fallen asleep.

Now, with bright winter sunshine streaming through her window, she forced herself to wake up. Breathing in the air of a new day, her sorrow multiplied as she looked around her bedroom. The room she had shared with Levi for the past four months. Every bit of her surroundings reminded her of him. She spied the open closet door, taking in the dark outline of his black Sunday suit. He had looked so handsome in his stark-white shirt and black vest. Her gaze fell on his spare pair of work boots, one boot lying sideways as if it had been cast asunder.

She sat up and threw off the covers. The emptiness of this room, the dreams that would be unfulfilled, they all assaulted her.

She glanced down and saw that she wore the same dress she'd had on yesterday. Shoving away her thoughts, she rose from the bed and trudged to the closet, swallowing the lump in her throat. As she reached toward her dresses, she tried to ignore Levi's shirts, particularly the one she'd sewn and given to him on their one-month anniversary. She had commemorated each monthly anniversary with something special. Last night was to be the most special of all.

Blinking back tears, she grabbed the first dress she touched and carried it to her bed, tossing it on top of her scattered bedclothes. Within minutes she had stripped off her wrinkled dress and was in her underclothes, her exposed skin pebbling in the cold air. She hadn't bothered to start the small propane heater in the bedroom last night, and she felt the chill seep into her. But instead of dressing, she shut the closet door and stared at her reflection in the mirror hanging on the back.

Her hand went to her flat stomach. Soon the new life inside her would grow, stretching out her belly more than she would think possible. She remembered when her youngest sister, Ruthie, had been born. Her mother had been so swollen Moriah thought she would pop. She wondered if her baby would do the same thing to her.

Her teeth started to chatter, but she didn't care. The cold numbed her, both outside and in. She could stand here forever, not feeling a thing. No pain. No regrets. No heartache.

Nothing.

"Moriah?"

The faraway sound of her father-in-law's gravelly voice travelled up the stairs.

"Honey, are you awake?"

Her body began to shake violently as the cold set into her bones. She noted that John's voice was steady, and she realized Gabe hadn't told him about Levi. She briefly wondered why, but figured he had his own reasons. She wouldn't say anything either, not wanting to be the one to break the bad news to him. She also didn't want to raise his suspicions, so she quickly dressed, then pinned up her hair with shaky hands before fastening her *kapp*. Slipping on her shoes, she went downstairs, hoping her father-in-law wouldn't notice the redness in her eyes.

John stood at the bottom of the staircase, one gnarled hand

resting on the simple banister. "*Gude mariye,*" he said, his kind gaze giving her a once over. "Gabe said you were feeling poorly last night. Are you doing any better this morning?"

"I'm f-fine," she said, unable to keep her teeth from chattering.

His good-natured expression changed to one of concern. He reached out and touched her forehead with the rough pads of his fingers. "Goodness, you're freezing." John put his arm around her shoulders and shook his head. "Chilled to the bone. Didn't you have the heat on last night?"

"I forgot," she said as he led her to the kitchen. "Guess I was too tired last night."

"You must have been. Well, we'll warm you right up."

They walked into the kitchen, and her cold body welcomed the heat emanating from the stove. The aroma of fresh coffee comforted her as she sat down at the table.

John walked over to the stove and picked up the percolator. "Gabriel made some coffee before he left. Thought you might want some. Would you like a cup?"

Bless Gabriel. Moriah wrapped her arms around her body. How stupid of her to stand upstairs and freeze. That's all she needed to do—catch a cold and get sick. She had more than herself to think about now.

"Or would you rather have some tea?" John turned and looked at her. "My own special brew. Will fix whatever ails you." He smiled.

Not knowing what John's "special brew" consisted of, or if it would be safe for her baby, she shook her head. "Coffee will be fine."

John poured her a cup of coffee. "Sugar? Cream?"

"Black," she said, even though she hated the taste of black

coffee. But she didn't want to put him to any trouble. Knowing Gabriel, he had probably asked his father to stay with her. Yet another reason to be grateful for her brother-in-law. She needed the distraction of John's company.

Her father-in-law placed the mug in front of her, then set his own mug in front of him before he sat down.

"Where's Gabriel?" Moriah said, breathing in the scent of the strong beverage. Her stomach performed an unexpected summersault. Maybe she should have had the tea instead.

"I don't know. Said he had to go somewhere, and he'd be gone most of the day. He left Aaron in charge of the shop."

Moriah nodded, bringing the drink up to her lips. She surmised Gabriel had gone to see Levi, to convince him to come back to the community. A glimmer of hope flickered inside her. Levi's return would be the best thing for everyone, but where would they go from there? Levi didn't love her. He didn't want her. How could she deal with that?

She would have to accept it with patience and humility.

Her father-in-law leaned forward, his smile slipping somewhat. "Moriah, are you sure you're all right? You've turned awful pale all of a sudden."

Her belly bubbled and gurgled, and nausea rose up in her throat. Perspiration beaded on her upper lip. The coffee suddenly smelled putrid and rank. She shoved away from the table, her hand covering her mouth.

"Moriah?"

Flying to the bathroom, she slammed the door behind her, kneeled over the toilet, and threw up.

"You should really try some of my tea," John said from the other side of the door. "Does wonders to settle the stomach."

Chapter 6

"Oh my, these dogs are howling." Gladys Johansson plopped her ample behind on the low concrete-topped brick wall directly across from Mary Yoder's restaurant. The plump waitress slipped off one of her tennis shoes and rubbed her chubby foot. Wisps of her dyed-red hair swayed in the cold breeze, revealing her silvery roots. "Yep, I'm gonna have me a good soak in the foot tub tonight. Just me, my bubbles, and some trashy reality television. The perfect way to spend an evening."

Rachel grinned as she sat next to her Yankee coworker. Mary Yoder's Amish Kitchen was owned by Yankees but employed both the Amish and outlanders. It was only two in the afternoon, but Gladys obviously planned to begin her evening as soon as possible.

Their morning shift had just ended, and Rachel was waiting for Christian to pick her up. He had made the offer after the singing last Sunday evening and she had accepted. Two days had passed since then, and she was kind of looking forward to seeing him.

Gladys shoved her foot back in her shoe, wiggling her heel back and forth until it was completely encased in white leather, then bent over and tied the laces. After one last stretch, she stood, then slung her black purse over her shoulder and turned to Rachel. "Sure you don't want me to give you a ride home, honey? It'll only take a few minutes. I'll just bring my car around and off we'll go."

Rachel tugged her navy blue *reck* closer to her body, the wool blend soft and warm. Despite the cloudless sky, the sun offered little heat. February in Ohio could be brutal. "No thanks, Gladys. Christian is coming to pick me up."

"The fellow who's had breakfast here a few times? The one who always sits at one of your tables?"

"No, that's Tobias. And he only sits at my table so I can *serve* him. He lives to aggravate me."

Gladys tilted her head. "Hmm. I thought he sat there because he was sweet on you."

"Hardly. We can't stand each other."

"Oops. My mistake." Gladys smiled and headed toward the restaurant's huge parking lot. It wasn't unusual for Mary Yoder's to serve tour bus travelers, so there was plenty of room for parking. "You lovebirds have a wonderful time."

Rachel waved good-bye to her coworker, then tucked an errant strand of hair into her *kapp* as she waited for Christian to pick her up. A few minutes later his buggy pulled into the parking lot. He steered his horse alongside her, then waited for her to climb in on the passenger's side. When she was settled, he handed her a lap blanket. "This will help you warm up."

She smiled as they pulled away. He really was the perfect gentleman. As he made a right turn onto North State Street, she glanced at his unassuming profile. Inside the buggy, only inches separated them. Since they were courting, she thought they should be sitting closer to each other. She scooted to the left until the skirt of her gray dress touched his black pants, expecting him to notice her bold move.

But Christian kept his gaze straight ahead as he guided his horse along the road. The black winter covering of the buggy buffered them from the harshest parts of the wind and cold. Traffic whizzed by, some cars giving them a wide berth and others coming perilously close. It made sense that he would have to keep his concentration on the road, but she had hoped for at least some kind of reaction. Even a small glance would have been encouraging.

She tried a different tack to gain his attention. A man's heart could definitely be reached through his stomach; that's one thing she'd known since she was a child. Her dad and brothers were never stingy with the compliments when it came to eating the foods they loved, which in the Detweiler home were plentiful. She took the small white sack she had brought from the restaurant and opened it up. Immediately the buggy filled with the nutty, sweet scent of homemade pecan pie.

"Smells good," Christian said without turning to look at her.

"I brought you a piece of the pecan pie I made at the restaurant. It's fresh from the oven." She gave him what she thought might be a pretty, charming, appealing, and desirable smile. The kind that didn't hide any secrets. Hopefully he would notice it soon, since it hurt to contort her mouth in such a foreign way.

He gave the pie a cursory glance before staring straight at the road again. "I'm allergic."

Her smile slid from her face. "You're what?"

"Allergic to nuts. I thought you knew that. All kinds of nuts—hickory, walnuts, and especially pecans. Make me swell up so much I can't breathe."

Rachel stared down at the piece of still-warm pie encased

in a foggy, clear plastic box. She'd had no idea he was allergic to nuts.

"Nice thought, though." He gave her a quick smile.

She smiled halfheartedly back and returned the pie to the bag. Even though he couldn't enjoy the treat, he seemed to have appreciated the gesture.

Suddenly he scooted over to his left, creating another space between them. "Don't mean to crowd you," he said.

Rachel's shoulders slumped. This wasn't working out at all like she had planned.

They rode the rest of the way to her house in silence. *Boring* silence. She had no idea courting could be this dull. Christian was a nice guy, but not much of a conversationalist.

When he pulled up to her driveway, he got out of the buggy and met her on the passenger side. When she stepped on the ground, he asked, "Can I take you to the frolic this Sunday night?"

"*Ya.*" Although she thought she should be more excited about it. Why weren't her emotions cooperating?

He grinned. "I'll see you then." Turning around, he started to climb back in the buggy, but stopped and faced her again. Before she knew it, he leaned forward and kissed her on the cheek, then turned and left.

Rachel watched him go, even more confused than before. Her fingers pressed against her face where his lips had touched. Her first kiss. Granted, it was a peck on the cheek, but that was more than any boy had done before. His unexpected show of affection surprised her, but that was her only reaction. Frowning, she kicked a pebble on the driveway and walked toward her front door.

Shouldn't she have felt something else when he kissed her?

Instead, she felt nothing, other than bewilderment over what she should do about Christian, if anything. She couldn't shake the feeling that something wasn't right between them. Her lack of response to his kiss only reinforced it. Maybe things would change once they spent more time together. Even though she had known Christian all her life, he mostly kept to himself, and rarely revealed much to her. In many ways he was like her brother Aaron. A mystery wrapped up in an enigma. She didn't truly "know" him, not like she thought she should. She wondered if she ever would.

Gabe repeatedly clenched his fists until his knuckles ached as he stood in front of the truck-stop counter. Guy had picked him up over two hours ago, but he'd also picked up three other men and dropped them off in Ashtabula to work on a construction project. Now they were at a truck stop for gas and coffee, and Guy was flirting with the woman at the cash register. She was far too young for Guy, who was well into middle age and had the soft gut and silvery hair to prove it. Gabe tried to keep from tapping his foot as Guy paid for his gas and beverage, flashing his yellowish grin.

The girl was clearly bored with the attention. "Thanks. Have a good day." She handed him his receipt, the tiny silver ball underneath her bottom lip glinting under the fluorescent lighting. Then she pulled her cell phone out of her pocket and started texting.

"I sure will, sweetheart," Guy said, baring his teeth again, oblivious to her ignoring him. "I'll see you tomorrow."

She nodded, her gaze not moving from the small screen of her lime-colored phone. Her fingers, the nails coated in black polish, flew fast and furious on the tiny keyboard.

"Yep. That one's mine," Guy said, as they walked out of the store. He gave Gabe a contrite look. "Sorry, Gabe. Shouldn't be talking like that in front of you."

"Shouldn't be talking like that at all," Gabe mumbled.

"What?" Guy asked over the cacophonic sound of passing cars and semitrucks.

"Nothing," Gabe said, deciding he needed to keep his mouth shut. He didn't want to say or do anything to jeopardize his ride to Gates Mills. It would cost him a pretty penny to get there, as Guy would have to hang around to bring him back. But if he could convince Levi to come home, it would be worth it.

They climbed into Guy's minivan, and Guy turned the key. Country music blared from the speakers. Gabe tuned it out. He glanced at the illuminated clock on the dashboard. Nearly two o'clock. The day was wasting away. He clenched his fists again.

Guy snapped off the radio. "Something bothering you, Gabe?"

Gabe relaxed his hands and placed his palms on his thighs. "No. I'm fine."

With a shrug, Guy grabbed his Styrofoam coffee cup with one hand while his other hand lay limply over the steering wheel as he maneuvered his way onto Interstate 90. "You seem kind of keyed up, that's all."

"Nothing's wrong." He turned and looked out the window. The bare branches of trees lining the interstate spiked into the cloudless sky. Black slush coated the freeway while a thin layer of pale white snow glistened on the grassy land. His mind whirled as he thought about what he would say to his brother. What he could do to convince him to return home.

Then his mind shifted to Moriah, as it always did. What if Levi refused to come home? What would she do then?

The hour-long drive seemed to drag. Guy had turned the radio back on and spent the rest of the trip singing off-key. Gabe normally didn't mind Yankee music, even though he heard it only on rare occasions. Radios and any type of music players were forbidden by the *Ordnung*. Yet when he did hear it, he kind of enjoyed it. The songs were a welcome change from the monotone singing at church services.

But not today. The music sounded like buzzing bees in his ears. He ground his teeth as Guy exited the freeway and headed toward the Johnston's horse ranch. When the impressive metal gates rose into view, Gabe pointed. "Turn here."

"Yep." Guy spun the steering wheel and passed under an arch with the letter *J* curved around the top of the gates. Gabe grudgingly admired the extraordinary scroll work.

Guy drove up the long driveway toward a huge brick house with a circular driveway of red-stone pavers. A fountain made of sand-colored stone stood in the center, holding an urn-shaped centerpiece emblazoned with a huge lion's head.

Gabe had been here only once before and, as before, was struck by the size of the house and the property. Gates Mills was an exclusive community, and Johnston's Farms was just on the outskirts of the village. He knew the Johnstons had only one child, a daughter. Why would they need a house that big for only three people? The imposing dwelling looked large enough to house two large Amish families.

Guy let out a low whistle. "Nice. Very nice." He turned to Gabe. "Want me to drop you off here?"

"No. I need to go to the horse barn." He pointed to part of the brick driveway that led to the back of the property. They followed it until the neat pavers turned into a windy but well-kept dirt road. A four-wheeler with two riders whizzed by, seemingly heading for the same destination. As the minivan neared an extravagant, bright-red barn with a white roof, Gabe held up his hand and signaled Guy to stop. "Drop me here."

Guy applied the brakes. "When do you want me to pick you up?"

"Give me an hour."

"Sure enough."

"Thanks," Gabe said as he opened the door.

"Hey," Guy called as Gabe stepped to the ground. "Good luck with whatever this is you're doing. Seems really important."

"It is, Guy. It is." He shut the door and watched for a moment as Guy backed up and turned around, then headed for the main road. Gabe swiveled around, his shoe crushing and sliding against the slushy, dirty snow. He took in the two-story structure in front of him. Even Gabe could tell it was top of the line. He imagined the extraordinary horseflesh occupying the stalls inside. Behind the barn was a wide pasture, bordered by a thick white oak fence. Although the field was covered with snow, when spring came there would be enough grass for at least twenty horses to eat their fill.

The rumbling sound of the four-wheeler filled the air again. Gabe jerked his head around and saw the shiny red machine with its two riders coming toward him. The vehicle stopped a few feet behind him, and both riders got off, their faces hidden by their black helmets. Gabe fully turned just as they both took off their headgear.

His mouth dropped open as he looked at his twin brother, wearing a new black-leather jacket and blue jeans. He had shaved his beard and his hair was cut short over his ears, with a big hank of brown bangs hanging over his forehead. The other rider, a woman with long, free-flowing red hair and brightly painted red lips had her arms around Levi's waist, as if he were her personal property. Laughter filled the air as they looked at each other, oblivious to anyone else around them.

A wave of nausea threatened to cut Gabe at the knees as he watched the two of them cavorting around. He thought of Moriah, miserable and pregnant, not understanding what had happened to her husband and her marriage. Meanwhile Levi was having the time of his life with another woman.

Gabe couldn't stand to watch anymore. He stormed toward his brother, shoving aside the anger threatening to bubble to the surface.

Levi's and the woman's laughter abruptly stopped as they noticed Gabe approaching. Levi's eyes narrowed into angry slits. "What are you doing here? I told you not to come."

The woman standing beside him moved even closer, until her body was pressed up against his. She flipped her unbound hair over her shoulders. Even in the dull light of the gray sky Gabe could see how beautiful and shiny it was. As he breathed in, he could smell the heady scent of her perfume. "Who is this?" she asked, peering at him. Then her eyes widened. "You have a twin?"

"Yes." Levi spoke in a low, guarded tone.

She gaped at Gabe, then looked at Levi. "You never told me."

"The subject never came up."

Gabe cringed inside. "I need to talk to you. Alone." He spoke in Pennsylvania Dutch and gave the woman a pointed look. Clearly she had a major part to play in his brother leaving his wife.

"Excuse me?" The woman turned to Levi. "What did he say?"

Levi scowled. "He wants to speak to me. Alone."

She lifted the corner of her upper lip in an indignant smirk. "Does he know who he's talking to?"

Just as Gabe was opening his mouth to say that he knew exactly who he was talking to, Levi intervened. He pressed his cheek against her forehead and said, "Go on in the house, honey. I'll be there in a bit."

"But—"

"It's fine. Let me talk to him."

She looked at Gabe again, her green eyes assessing him coolly. "Okay." Even though they stood in the cold, she didn't suggest that Levi and Gabe go inside the barn, or even in the house, to have their conversation. Instead she turned, tilted up her head, and kissed Levi fully on the lips.

The sickening lump in Gabe's belly expanded as he witnessed his still-married brother kiss her back with enthusiasm. When they were done, the woman walked past Gabe, tossed him a look of conquest, then headed back into the expansive house, her helmet tucked underneath one arm.

Levi looked directly at Gabe. His face suddenly flushed, and he stepped back and looked away, wiping his mouth with the back of his hand as he did.

At least his brother had the decency to appear embarrassed. "Who is she?" Gabe asked, fighting to keep his tone even.

"A friend," Levi said after a long pause.

"You looked more than friendly to me."

Levi turned his gaze back on his brother. "I know why you're here, Gabriel, and it won't do any good. I'm not coming back."

Gabe stepped toward him, shoving his hands into the pockets of his coat to keep from clocking Levi across the face. "You have to."

"*Nee,* I don't. You can't make me. No one can. Not you, not the bishop or ministers. When you go back, you tell them not to bother visiting here, because nothing they say will make me change my mind." Levi walked over to the four-wheeler and set the helmet on the seat. Then he turned around, his expression determined. "This is my home now."

"This?" Gabe yanked his hands out of his pocket and thrust out his arms wide. "This is where you *work,* Levi. You are an employee here, nothing more."

"That, *bruder,* is where you are mistaken."

"Your home is in Middlefield. With your *wife.* Remember her?"

"Of course I do," Levi said hotly. "But I took care of it when I wrote her that letter."

"A letter? You think a letter will absolve you from everything? Your marriage vows, your church vows?" His breath hung in frosty clouds as he paused, still struggling to remain calm but finding it harder with each passing minute.

Levi stormed toward him, anger sparking in his eyes. "*That* is why I'm not going back."

"What? You don't want to hear the truth?"

"I don't want to hear *your* version of the truth. You don't get it, Gabe. You've been sheltered—we all have. All we do is follow rules. Don't wear this. Don't talk like that. No electricity. No music. No *life.*" He took a step back. "I can't do it anymore. I want to live. I want to be free to be myself, my real self. I can't do that and be Amish too."

"And what are you free to do, Levi? Get your hair cut? Wear Yankee clothes? Cheat on your wife?"

Levi turned his head. "It's not like that."

"That's what it looked like to me."

Whipping his head around, Levi said, "There you go again, judging me. My perfect brother. Never commits a sin." Levi's eyes narrowed. "Except in his heart."

Gabe froze. Surely his brother didn't suspect . . .

"You have no right to say anything to me, not when you've been lusting after Moriah for years. You thought I didn't know, but you weren't very good at hiding it." He crossed his arms. "I thought you'd be glad I was gone. Then you could have her for yourself. In fact, why don't you? This is what you've always wanted, isn't it? It just kills you that she chose me over you."

Years of resentment and bottled anger suddenly burst. With one hand, he grabbed Levi by the collar of his new, slick jacket and made a fist with the other, ready to plow it into his brother's face.

But Levi didn't cower. He didn't flinch. He stared Gabe straight in the eye and said, "Go ahead. Hit me. Show me what I've known all along—you're no better than I am."

Gabe paused, his fist raised in midair. If he hit his brother now—and Lord knew he wanted to more than anything in the world—he would prove Levi right. Violence of any kind was not permitted by the *Ordnung*. How could he hit his brother, then turn around and tell him what to do afterward?

Slowly he lowered his fist and released Levi's jacket. His brother stepped back and adjusted his collar, his gaze not leaving Gabe's. Finally, Gabe looked away, the anger and energy flowing out of him.

"You're not denying you love her," Levi said.

Gabe let out a long breath. Why bother admitting what his brother already knew? "Moriah's pregnant," he said flatly. "She told me yesterday."

Levi suddenly paled. "I . . . I had no idea."

"No one did. She was going to tell you last night. Instead, she got your letter."

Running a hand through his newly short hair, Levi began to pace. "What am I gonna do?" Over and over he mumbled as he stalked back and forth, arguing with himself in low tones.

In Gabe's mind, there was only one answer, and he didn't understand his brother's struggle. "It's an easy decision, Levi. Come home. If not for your own sake, then for your child's."

"You don't understand." Levi stopped and gave Gabe a haunted look. "Taylor's pregnant too."

"Taylor? Who's Taylor?"

"The woman you just met. Taylor Johnston."

Gabe's heart fell to his knees. "You didn't."

"I couldn't help it. She's special—"

"So is your wife," Gabe gritted out.

He stared at the snowy ground. "Look, I love Taylor."

"Seems to me you love what she can give you." Gabe gestured to Levi's clothes. "Did she buy those for you? Did she tell you to cut your hair, shave your beard?"

"So what if she did? She didn't make me do anything I wasn't ready to do." Levi looked directly at him. "I love her, Gabe. More than I ever loved Moriah."

Shaking his head, Gabe asked, "How is that possible? You've known her for a couple months. You've known Moriah for years."

"But I never loved her. Not like this. I should have never married Moriah. I should have known it wouldn't work when . . ." He stared off into the distance.

"When what?"

Levi leveled his gaze at his brother. "You remember when I went to Indiana last spring?"

"*Ya.*"

"I never told anyone this, but I . . . met someone else."

"A Yankee?"

"*Nee,* she was Amish. I had planned to stop courting Moriah, but when this girl found out about her, she didn't want anything more to do with me."

"Sounds like a smart *maedel.*"

Levi leaned against the seat of the four-wheeler. "She is."

"I suppose Moriah didn't know anything about this other *maedel.*"

He gazed down at the ground. "*Nee.* She didn't. But it didn't matter, because I came back home and proposed. I thought if I married her, when I was fully committed, I would never look at another woman again. I really wanted things to work out with her."

"Levi, I don't understand why they can't."

"Don't you see? It isn't Moriah; it's me. Ever since we got married I've been feeling smothered."

"But you said you loved her—"

"That was before I knew what love really was!" He jammed his hands into his pockets and looked down on the ground. "Moriah was convenient, Gabe. She was always there, always available. She's a nice girl, a *wunderbaar* woman, but she's suffocating me. The only time I can breathe is when I'm here with Taylor." He looked up.

"Taylor has given me everything I've dreamed of, things I didn't even know I wanted. All this?" He gestured to the barn, the house, the land. "It will be mine someday. That's more than I'll ever have working my fingers to the bone in the shop."

"Do you really love all this excess, Levi? Is this all about money?"

Levi shook his head. "*Nee.* It's not about the money. Like I said, I love Taylor."

"But Moriah is pregnant! How can you abandon her like this?" Gabe walked up to him. "Levi . . . I don't understand. How can you leave your child behind?"

Suddenly Levi's shoulders slumped. His tortured eyes met Gabe's. "I have to, Gabe. I can't go back. Not ever. My life is here now. And that's how I want it to be." He nodded, as if trying to convince himself that his words were true. "Her family and the rest of the community will take care of her and the baby."

Shock coursed through Gabe. He barely recognized his brother any more. "You'd let someone else raise your baby?"

Levi swallowed, hesitating before he responded. "In this case, *ya. Ya,* I would."

"You have a responsibility to Moriah first, Levi. If you're willing to give up one of your children, then let Taylor find someone else."

"Her father would tear me apart."

"We could protect you. If you confess your sin, the whole community will stand behind you."

Levi let out a bitter laugh. "There you go again, branding me with your righteousness. I won't confess anything, because I have nothing to confess. Even if her father had nothing to do with it, I'd still want Taylor. It's best for everyone."

"Except Moriah. You know the *Ordnung* doesn't permit divorce, under any circumstances. She'll never be able to remarry."

"You think she'd be better off trapped in a loveless marriage?"

"I want her happy. She'd be happy to have her husband back."

"I doubt it."

Gabe was getting nowhere with his hardheaded twin. His brother was rationalizing his choices, twisting everything to satisfy his own selfishness.

Stepping toward Gabe, Levi said, "You could take care of her. I know you love her, Gabriel. You can have her now, if you want to."

Gabe couldn't believe what he was hearing. "Levi, she is married to you! She will always be married to you. I'm not an adulterer."

"Except in your heart."

His nostrils flared. "You have no right to accuse me of anything."

Levi paused. "You're right. But you would be a better friend to her than I would be a husband. We both know that."

"What about *Daed*? Have you thought about him? How he will feel once he knows you've left us?"

His brother looked out over the snowy landscape. "He'll understand," he said in a low voice.

"You know he won't."

"He'll have to. And he'll move on, just like he did after our *mami* died."

"Levi, what if—"

"Are you even listening to me?" Levi sprang up from the seat of the four-wheeler, getting directly into Gabe's face. "I'm not. Coming. Back. Not ever. The sooner you and everyone else understand that, the faster we can all move on." He snatched his helmet off the four-wheeler, his expression dark and angry. "We've got nothing more to talk about, Gabe." Stalking past his brother, he headed for the house, never once looking back.

A wave of frustration flowed over Gabe as he stared at Levi's back, threatening to pull him under. Nothing he said made any impact on his brother. Then his anger diminished, replaced by deep sadness as he realized that Levi fully intended to leave the Amish, and nothing would change his mind. Levi hadn't even asked about the state of their *daed*'s health. He'd already written off his family, fully embracing a woman and a life he barely knew.

Chapter 7

Moriah tapped her fingers against the kitchen table, the sound a steady, monotonous tattoo that broke the silence of the empty house. John had left a short while ago after she'd convinced him she'd be all right until Levi came home. She had gone along with the ruse, unable to tell him about her husband's letter. He had seemed so weary by the end of the day, she knew he needed to lie down and rest in his own room, in his own comfortable bed.

She stilled her fingers, antsy but annoyed with the noise. Rising from her chair, she peered out of the kitchen window into the dark, cold night. The sun had disappeared beyond the horizon an hour ago. Gabriel should have been home by now.

Her stomach twisted itself into another knot. Not only because of the nausea of the pregnancy, but because her mind was completely occupied with Levi. Had Gabriel been able to persuade him to return? Maybe Levi had been drinking when he wrote the letter, so he wasn't in his right state of mind. But she dismissed that outright—his words had been clear, his writing steady. Besides, she had never known her husband to touch alcohol. Letting out a sigh, she crossed her arms over her chest to ward off the sudden chill that had infiltrated her body.

Where was Gabriel? More importantly, would he have Levi with him?

All she wanted was for her husband to be here, to tell her the letter was a mistake, to reassure her that everything would be all right between them from now on.

But something deep inside chipped at her, causing fresh wounds, telling her that her hopes were fruitless. Nothing would be the same again.

A sharp knock sounded behind her. Whirling around, Moriah ran to the door and flung it open. She took one look at the man standing in the doorway and for a fraction of a second, her heart soared. Levi had returned!

But it wasn't Levi gazing at her. It was Gabriel, his eyes filled with sorrow and regret. Her hopes had played tricks with her eyes, and her heart.

She stepped back until her waist banged the countertop. Reaching behind her, she gripped the cold Formica, forcing herself not to sway. She'd fallen apart in front of Gabriel the night before; she refused to do it again.

"I'm sorry, Moriah." His voice was thick, as if his vocal cords had tightened up. "I tried talking to him. I really did."

The droop of his shoulders spoke more than his words ever could. She realized he had taken the burden of his brother's betrayal on himself and had tried to make everything right. But he couldn't, and it was tearing him apart. She could see that, plain as day. Forgetting about herself for the moment, she gestured for him to come inside.

"Cold night tonight," she said lamely, shutting the door behind them. "Come warm yourself."

He took off his hat, walked into the kitchen, and dropped into the nearest chair. Moriah followed him. Looking into his ragged face, she said, "It's all right, Gabriel. Thank you for trying."

Gabriel ran his hand through his hair as he tossed his hat on the table. With a sigh he looked at her. "He's not coming back, Moriah."

"I know." She sat across the table from him, a numbing cold infiltrating her body, as if she'd been submerged in a tub of ice. "What did he say?"

Gabriel stared down at his fingers. He curled them inward to his palms, making two fists. "He doesn't want to be Amish anymore. Too many rules."

From his vague explanation to the way he avoided looking directly at her, she suspected he wasn't telling her the whole truth. "That's it?"

"*Ya.* That's it."

His words sliced through her. "Did you tell him about the baby?"

A long moment passed before he answered, compassion in his eyes. "*Ya.*"

She swallowed. "I see." She had to look away from him, unable to face the pity she saw in his gaze.

"I can't believe he did this to you," Gabriel muttered. "I could . . . I swear, Moriah, I could—"

With a gasp, she glanced up to see his full mouth stretched in a straight line. His hands were still clenched so tightly she thought his knuckles would snap. "What did you do?" she whispered, afraid to hear the answer.

His hands relaxed. "*Nix.* I did nothing."

She breathed out a sigh of relief. "Praise God."

"How can you say that? He deserves the worst for what he's doing to you."

"Gabriel," she said softly, reaching for his hand. "Just because he turned his back on our beliefs doesn't mean you should."

His eyes met hers, anger still sparking in them. "How can you not—"

"Hate him?" She looked away. A part of her did, but she had to overcome it. She had to be strong for their baby's sake. Tending the bitter weed of hate would only cause it to grow and overtake every aspect of her life. That wouldn't be fair to the child blossoming inside her. "God will see me through this. He will see us all through it . . . even Levi." Her eyes moistened, and she looked at him through misty vision.

He disengaged his hand from hers, and for a split moment, she missed its comforting warmth.

"I have to tell *Daed*," he said. "I don't know what this will do to him."

"Wait until morning," Moriah said. "He was very tired."

"I'm worried." Gabriel sat up and rubbed the back of his neck. "He's not as strong as he used to be, but he still wants to work in the shop. I'm afraid he'll hurt himself. But how can I tell him to quit?" He let out a bitter, flat chuckle. "It's not like I can just fire my father."

They were silent for a long time, lost in their own thoughts, dealing with their own emotions.

Then Moriah finally said, "I'll move back home tomorrow."

Gabriel's gaze shot to her. "You don't have to do that. You can stay here. *Daed* and I don't mind."

"*Nee,* I cannot. This isn't my home anymore."

"Moriah, it will always be your home. You can stay here as long as you like."

She shook her head. "Gabriel, I have to leave. You know that. You and your father can move back into the house. I'll be fine with my family. Once I tell them what happened, they'll understand." She closed her eyes, humiliation rising through her at the thought of telling her parents that her husband had left her, and for no other reason than he didn't want to be Amish anymore.

Pushing away from the table, she said, "I'll pack my things in the morning. Would you mind taking me back home?"

He stood and stepped toward her. "Moriah, I mean it. You don't have to leave."

Her bottom lip began to quiver. Why couldn't she be strong? Pressing her teeth down for a split second to quell the movement, she then said, "I want to go home. I need my family right now. So does my child."

He opened his mouth as if to protest once more, but then clamped it shut. "I understand. I'll take you home whenever you're ready."

"*Danki.* And thanks for trying to convince Levi to come back. I know it had to be a hard thing to do."

"Harder than I thought." He looked at her for a moment. "I don't think you should be alone tonight. Mind if I bunk in downstairs? I can sleep on the couch."

A tiny thread of relief wound its way through her. He must have read her mind, as she dreaded being alone in the big house. Too many memories, too much loneliness. "I don't mind. In fact, I'd appreciate it."

Tobias nursed the last dregs of his coffee in the nearly abandoned dining room of Mary Yoder's. There were only three other customers left in the restaurant—a tiny, elderly couple eating two crumbly pieces of apple pie and a rotund man, who looked only a few years older than Tobias, busily slurping the last watery droplets of his iced tea.

He didn't know what he was doing here. Mary Yoder's served good Amish food, but his mother's was ten times better. Besides, he'd already had dinner and dessert at home a couple hours ago before hitching up his horse and ending up at the restaurant. For some reason he'd felt restless tonight, and spending the evening at home alone didn't appeal. Everyone had plans for tonight—his parents were visiting an elderly neighbor, Elisabeth and Ruth were spending time with some of their girlfriends, and Stephen and Lukas were making some extra money helping their cousin clean out a barn in West Farmington.

He'd thought about doing some extra work in the woodshop, but he'd spent the entire day in there. All work and no play made Tobias dull indeed. At least he thought so. Although he did have a good time working today, except for cutting his fingertip on one of the saw blades. But he'd cut his fingers and hands so many times over the years. One more slice on his skin didn't make a difference.

Tapping his foot on the carpeted floor, he sucked down the last drink of coffee and signaled one of the bus girls for the check. She was about the age of his sister Elisabeth, who couldn't wait to finish school and start working outside the home. No doubt so she'd have ample opportunity to flirt with guys. He'd noticed how boy-crazy she'd gotten in the past couple months. He suspected his mother would have her hands full once Elisabeth turned sixteen.

The bus girl nodded at Tobias and went to get his server. When Rachel appeared, he hid a smile. As she had when he arrived, she looked less than pleased to see him. With determined steps she walked to the table, crossed her arms as she usually did when she was around him, and looked down the length of her cute little nose. "What do you want now?"

He leaned back in the chair, his restless spirit inexplicably easing. He pointed to his coffee cup. "I'm done."

"About time." She pulled out a computer-printed ticket from inside her apron, as if she'd been waiting all day to give it to him. "Here." She put it down on the table. "You can pay up front." She took the cup from the table and walked away.

He looked at the amount on the ticket, then stood. Digging out his leather wallet from his trousers, he felt two pennies in his pocket. He knew leaving such a cheap tip would get a rise out of Rachel, and he couldn't resist the opportunity. Retrieving the coins, he dropped them on the table, then walked out of the dining area and into the gift shop.

He passed Amish crafts of all kinds and noticed a couple of wooden train sets his brother Lukas had made a few months ago, hoping to sell them for an extra bit of pocket money. There were also candles, books, and stuffed animals available for purchase. He approached the empty bakery counter where the cash registers were located. The manager, a Yankee woman, took his ticket and rang up the total. "$1.25," she said.

He gave her two dollars, then took out another five from his wallet. "Could you give this to my server, please? Just don't tell her it came from me. If you could add it to the rest of her tips, I'd appreciate it."

The manager tilted her head and gave him a strange look, but nodded. "I'll be happy to do that. Are you sure you don't want to just put this on your table, though?"

"Positive." He stuffed his wallet back in his pocket and adjusted his hat. "Thanks for the coffee. You all have a good evening."

"You do the same."

Tobias grinned as he left the restaurant. *Ya,* Rachel would be steamed when she saw the measly tip he left her. He almost wished he could witness the volcanic explosion of temper when she picked up the two cents. As he entered the parking lot and headed for his buggy, he thought about the spark that would light up her blue eyes, the lovely rosy glow that would spread across her creamy cheeks, the—

"Tobias Byler!"

He halted in his tracks at the zinging sound of Rachel's voice behind him. Turning around, he watched with amusement as she stomped forward, fury pulsating from her like an old wood stove belching heat.

Boy, he'd gotten her good.

"What is *this*?" she said, holding out the pennies in her hand. "Do you think this is funny? I work hard for my tips. Very hard." She threw the coins at him.

He held up his hands in a weak defense as the pennies ricocheted harmlessly off his pants leg. "You gave me *one* cup of coffee," he said blandly. "That's it. Big deal."

"You . . . *you* . . ." Her body started to tremble as she sputtered.

Was she that angry? Suddenly realizing that it was below thirty degrees and all she had on was her short-sleeved dress and apron, he whipped off his coat. "Here, put this on. You're freezing."

She stared at the jacket as if it had thorns poking out of it. "No, thanks."

"Then go inside and warm up."

"Not until I get my real tip. The tip you owe me."

"Rachel, don't be stupid," he said, still holding his *reck* out to her. Her teeth were chattering. Why did she have to be so stubborn? "Get inside where it's warm."

She held out one shaking hand. "M-my m-money."

"I'll give it to you—if you put on my coat."

Her eyes grew wide at his insistent request. In fact he was a bit surprised by it himself. But he couldn't stand to see her shivering out here, and he knew she wouldn't leave until she got her money. At least she would be a little warmer while he fished out his wallet.

Without a word she took the jacket and wrapped it loosely around her shoulders. The dark blue, woolen fabric practically engulfed her.

"Rachel! What are you doing outside?"

"Oh no," she whispered.

Tobias looked up to see Rachel's boss holding open the front door of the restaurant. Quickly Rachel spun around and ran back inside, taking his coat with her.

A blast of cold night air hit him as the glass door shut behind Rachel. Great. Now *he* was shivering out here in the cold.

For Pete's sake, this was crazy. He couldn't drive all the way home without his coat. Although the winter curtain on his buggy would keep some of the frigid air at bay, it would be a miserable ride. He plodded back to the restaurant, opening the front door for the elderly couple as they exited.

"Aren't those Amish just the nicest people?" the petite woman said.

"*Hmmph,*" the man grunted as he leaned on his cane. Together they hobbled over to their car.

The cloying scent of about a million varieties of candles hit Tobias's nose as he walked back into the restaurant. Women really loved those things—his mother lit them all the time. He scanned the gift shop area and saw there was no one behind the counter or in the front of the building. What should he do? Go back and ask for the manager? Or just walk through the empty restaurant and call out for Rachel? After weighing his options, he decided to search for himself.

The third time he said her name, the manager appeared through the door separating the kitchen from the dining room. "We're closed, sir. Was there something else you needed?"

He felt heat creep up his neck. Somehow every time he tried to one-up Rachel he always ended up looking like a fool. "I came to get my coat, ma'am."

"Did you leave it in the dining room?" The blonde-haired woman walked farther into the large room and began looking at the tables and chairs.

"No, I didn't. Rachel has it."

She frowned. "Were you the one she was talking to outside?"

He nodded.

"I'll go get her." The manager started toward the kitchen, then stopped and turned around, annoyance coloring her expression. "I don't know what kind of game you teenagers are playing, but this is a place of business and Rachel is an employee. I want you to remember that in the future. I'm sure you would like your friend to keep her job."

"Yes, ma'am. I'm sorry."

A few moments later Rachel appeared from the kitchen, carrying his *reck*. "Here," she said, thrusting it at him. When he took it from her she headed back to the kitchen, but he stopped her.

"Hang on," he said, pulling out his wallet again, feeling bad that she could have been fired over his little, and obviously not very funny, joke. He took out a five-dollar bill and handed it to her. This was becoming the most expensive cup of coffee he'd ever had.

She looked at the money with disdain. "Now you're being insulting. No one gives a five-dollar tip for a cup of coffee."

Yeesh, I cannot win with this woman. Either I give her too little or too much. "Would you just take it? Before your boss comes out here and you lose your job and I get another lecture."

"Fine." She took the bill out of his hand. "You know there are lots of other places that serve coffee."

"*Ya*, there are," he responded as she placed her hand on the metal doors that led to the kitchen. Then for some unknown reason he blurted out, "How are you getting home?"

"My cousin Melvin is picking me up," she said, then started toward the kitchen again.

"Not Christian?"

She spun around and faced him. "If you must know, he and his parents left for Holmes County today. They're spending a long weekend with his mom's sister down in Charm. His uncle broke his arm, and he needs some help with the chores."

"Rachel?"

The manager came out of the kitchen and approached her. She held a small yellow Post-it note in her hand. "Your cousin just called." Handing Rachel the note, she turned around and left.

Tobias watched Rachel's expression as she read the note. From the look on her face, he could tell it was bad news. "Melvin can't pick me up. He's got an emergency. A couple of his cows have gotten loose."

"That's not *gut*. I wouldn't want to be searching for a cow in the dark."

"Me neither." She tapped the note against her chin, her light brows furrowed. "I'm sure someone here can drive me home."

"I could take you."

She gave him a dubious look.

He really needed to figure out a way to tape his mouth shut. Why he was offering to subject himself to her company in the small quarters of his buggy? She was already furious with him for stiffing her. The smart thing to do would be to let her fend for herself. Except he didn't like the idea that she might not be able to find a ride home.

To his further surprise she seemed to be considering his offer. She wrinkled her cute nose. "Are you sure?"

He nodded. "No problem." At least he hoped there wouldn't be. With Rachel Detweiler, he never knew for sure.

She expelled a deep breath. "All right," she said slowly, with an expression that suggested she'd just agreed to walk off the plank of a very tall ship. "Not like I have much of a choice anyway."

"Gee, thanks." He had half a mind to tell her to forget about it if she was going to act that way.

She ignored his response. "It'll take me about half an hour to finish up. You can wait up front." With that, she disappeared into the kitchen.

Her gratitude was underwhelming. And irritating. "Why, thank you for offering, Tobias," he muttered in a high falsetto, mimicking her voice. "I appreciate you coming to my rescue. Thank goodness you were here tonight. I don't know what I would have done without you."

He turned around to make his way to the front of the store, only to run smack-dab into the manager. Somehow she'd snuck up on him.

The woman was about half his height, but intimidating nevertheless. She peered at him with disapproval over her red, wire-rimmed glasses. Tobias didn't have to be a genius to figure out that she'd overheard him mocking Rachel.

"I'll just wait up front," he said, lowering his hat over his eyebrows and quickly walking past her.

"Good idea," she called out after him.

Tobias hoped Rachel would hurry. After tonight, he'd probably never show his face in Mary Yoder's again.

As she took off her work apron and put on her *reck*, Rachel thought about Tobias's offer. Although she would never admit it out loud, and never to Tobias, she was grateful to him for taking her home. But he'd really annoyed her with that two-cent tip. She took her job seriously, working hard to serve her customers, a fact that hadn't gone unnoticed by her boss—and usually showed in her tips. For Tobias to come in, only order a coffee, then leave her a two-cent tip . . . well, obviously it infuriated her, and she'd made a pretty big idiot of herself in front of him, something he'd probably expected. Somehow she had to figure out a way to keep him from getting under her skin.

But if he wanted to make her miserable, then why did he offer her his coat when they were outside? Not only did he offer it, he'd insisted she wear it. Then he asked if he could take her home. She thought he'd rather see her walk along the side of the road in the darkness, shivering, as he pulled his buggy past her, all cozy inside. Instead he wanted to make sure she was warm and that she got home safely.

She'd never figure that man out.

She found her boss and apologized again for running out of the restaurant.

"You're going home with him?" she asked quietly from the back of the gift shop. They could see Tobias near the front of the store by a book rack, reading the back cover of one of the several Amish novels available for purchase.

"He's *taking* me home. My other ride couldn't make it. Don't worry, I've known him forever. He's harmless. Irritating, but harmless. I'll see you tomorrow. Have a good evening."

"You too."

Rachel came up behind him as he put the book back on the rack. "Do people really read that stuff?" He gestured to the books with his thumb.

"*Ya.* We sell a lot of those. Along with the cookbooks."

"The cookbooks I can see. Everybody has to eat. But novels?" He shrugged. "Never was much for reading myself."

"I remember," she said, thinking back to their days in school. Tobias passed his classes, but barely. More often than not he was busy goofing around with all the other boys, driving the poor school teacher to exasperation. The young woman, *Fraulein* Lucy, had only been a few years older than the oldest student, and had her hands full with a couple of the boys, Tobias included. Rachel thought she had probably dropped to her knees and thanked the Lord for several hours the day they had all graduated.

"Are you ready?" he asked, walking toward the exit.

"Yes." She followed him as he opened the solid glass door. But instead of passing through it ahead of her, he paused and opened it wider. "After you," he said.

She smirked at him as she strolled through, but secretly she was impressed. The gesture was something Christian would have done, but was unexpected from Tobias. Neither had she expected him to hold the buggy door open for her, which he also did. Tonight he was full of surprises.

Soon they were on their way home. Although the night was cold, it was beautiful out. The inky black sky resembled rich velvet studded with sparkling diamonds. The stars weren't exactly clear through the window in the curtain covering the front of the buggy, but she could still see their twinkle. Suddenly a shiver ran through her and her body shook involuntarily.

"Cold?" he asked.

"*Nee,*" she said, but she was lying. She crossed her ankles and pressed her legs together as she bent forward slightly, hugging her arms. Her coat didn't seem warm enough tonight.

"Here," he said, reaching behind her and withdrawing a thick quilt. Then he handed her the reins. "Hold this."

She arched a brow as he tucked the quilt around her waist, letting the heavy blanket fall over her legs and trail to the floor. Instantly she felt warmer. He took the reins from her and steered the buggy to the right, turning on Nauvoo Road, right behind the Middlefield Cheese Factory.

"Why are you being so nice to me?" she asked, bewildered by his unexpected behavior.

"*Mei mami* raised me right." He turned and grinned.

She could barely see his smile, except for the gleam of his

white teeth. They weren't perfectly straight, like Christian's. The two top front ones overlapped slightly, and his bottom teeth were a little crooked. Yet she hardly noticed as he continued to grin at her.

How could she, when her heart was thumping a million miles an hour.

She jerked her gaze from his and stared straight ahead, trying to figure out why she was having a hard time catching her breath. This was Tobias, for heaven's sake. The thorn in her side, the pain in her behind . . . The most handsome man she'd ever seen.

"Besides," he added, breaking into her disturbing, but not all that unpleasant, thoughts. "I can never resist a damsel in distress."

With that remark, any schmoopy thoughts she currently had for him disintegrated like ashes in the wind. "I am *not* a damsel in distress. I just needed a ride."

"And a blanket to wrap around you," he added. "And a pretty *wunderbaar* guy to take you home."

"You are so full of yourself, you know that?"

"Not at all. Now you . . . that's a different story."

She looked at him. "Excuse me?"

"You know what I'm talking about."

"No, I don't." She flung the quilt off her lap. "Stop this buggy. I'll walk."

"Don't be dumb," he said, the teasing hint in his voice disappearing.

"I mean it. If you don't stop, I'll jump out."

"For the love of—" He yanked up on the reins. "This is what I'm talking about, Rachel. You're the most difficult woman I've ever—"

Bright, fast-moving lights suddenly appeared out of the

darkness. They headed toward the buggy. Rachel lifted her hand to shield her eyes from the blinding light.

"Rachel!" Tobias yelled as the lights came upon them.

The roar of an engine sounded in her ears as the car clipped the side of the buggy, causing it to flip over. Her scream pierced the air.

The buggy turned over, breaking loose from the horse's hitch. Her body was thrown against the top of the buggy as it hit the ground. Her eyes slammed shut. Something cupped the back of her head. Then everything came to a stop.

A heavy body lay partly on top of her. Heavy and warm and solid. She opened her eyes. In the darkness of the upside-down buggy she could barely make Tobias out. But she felt him. His hand remained at the back of her head, his other arm stayed pinned protectively behind her back. Most of his body rested against the length of hers.

Their breathing intermingled in the small space, coming in short, gasping spurts. This was the first buggy accident she'd been in, and thank God they hadn't been killed. But Rachel wasn't completely positive she had to catch her breath solely from the accident.

"Are you okay?" he said softly, his mouth close to her ear.

A shiver traveled through her, but she wasn't the least bit cold at all, not while she was cradled in Tobias Byler's strong embrace, feeling his warmth against her. "I-I think so."

"You're trembling."

Her mouth suddenly dry, she swallowed. "I know. I-I can't seem t-to stop."

Her eyes now adjusted to the darkness, she could see him move his head. Their eyes met, the lightness of his blue irises visible to her. She could read something in those gorgeous eyes. Something that made her shiver even more.

Her *kapp* had dislodged during the accident, and a lock of her hair was askew. She drew in a sharp breath when he slowly pushed it back from her face, his fingers lingering on her cheek, his embrace tightening.

Without thinking she kissed him.

It was barely a brush on the lips and lasted less than half a second, but it was a kiss nevertheless.

"Hey! Anyone in there?"

A beam of light shone on the buggy. Rachel saw the shock on his face, knowing it mirrored her own.

"Are you two all right?" A man knelt down beside the overturned buggy. "What happened?"

Tobias climbed out of the buggy's opening, then turned and looked at Rachel with a strange expression, as if he didn't recognize her. He extended his hand to help her out, and when she came to a standing position, he cleared his throat and said, "Got hit by a car."

"What about you, hon? You okay?"

Rachel squinted at the kind man holding the flashlight. She tried to straighten her *kapp*, which was practically dangling from the side of her head, but she was fumbling so much she just made it worse. "I think so," she finally answered, shoving in a pin and hoping the *kapp* would stay put. But she was anything but fine.

"My horse," Tobias exclaimed, spinning around. His gaze darted around in a panic. He faced the helpful stranger again. "Have you seen my horse?"

"Down the road a bit," the man answered. "Seems to be all right though. Scared, I imagine. Looks like you took quite a spill."

Rachel turned and looked at the buggy, taking in the wheels. One of them was twisted, probably ruined. The full impact of what happened suddenly hit her. She'd known several people from her community and neighboring ones who had been killed in car-and-buggy accidents. That she and Tobias were still alive, much less with not a scratch on them, was a miracle.

"We should call the police," the stranger said. "They'll want you to file a report."

"There's no need to do that," Tobias said. "I'll get my horse, and I'll come back in the morning for the buggy."

"But, son, this was a hit and run. The person that did this needs to be caught and prosecuted."

"That's not our way," he replied.

He tugged on his black knit skull cap, seemingly perplexed by Tobias's response. "Well, all right. If you're sure."

"I'm sure."

"How about if I give you two a ride home?"

Rachel met Tobias's gaze. They were at least two miles from her house, and over three miles from his. It would be a cold walk, but she didn't relish the idea of letting a complete stranger drive her home.

"We'll be fine," Tobias said, saving her from having to answer. "Thank you for your kindness. It's appreciated."

A confused look crossed the man's face. "I feel bad leaving you two out here in the cold. I can drive down the road to a phone and call someone for you. I accidentally left my cell phone at home."

"We'll be okay. We must go now. I need to find my horse." In dismissal, Tobias tilted his head at Rachel and started walking.

Rachel looked at the kind gentleman. "Thank you for

stopping. We both appreciate it. Tobias . . . he's just worried about his horse."

"I can understand that. I'm glad you're both okay."

"Me too. And thanks again."

When the man walked back to his car, she turned to follow Tobias, who was already heading down the road.

Tobias suddenly started up short. "Wait a minute," he said to Rachel, then dashed back to the buggy.

Rachel watched the red taillights from the car disappear into the darkness. She crossed her arms in a vain attempt to keep warm.

Tobias ran up to her, carrying the quilt. Without a word he wrapped it around her shoulders, then started walking again. Although the moon wasn't completely full, it cast enough silvery light for them to find their way.

A flurry of emotions swirled inside her as she tried to process what had just happened between them. She'd kissed Tobias Byler. Not only that, but she had felt *something* when she did it. A warm, fuzzy feeling. A good feeling. No, not just good. *Wunderbaar.*

She'd never felt that way about Christian. Guilt overpowered her. She shouldn't be feeling about Tobias this way. Or thinking about him this way. Or wishing they hadn't been discovered so soon. Her thoughts and loyalties should only lie with Christian.

But they didn't.

She was the lowest of the low.

Burdened by her guilt and falling farther behind as Tobias hurried his steps, she heard the whinny of his horse up ahead. The animal stood a few feet from the road, beside an open field. Tobias ran and caught him by the bridle. She heard him talk in soft, hushed tones to the horse, calming the animal until he came to a complete stop.

The buggy hitch was still attached to the harness. Tobias quickly detached it and left it in the field. Another piece of equipment he would have to get in the morning.

Rachel had finally caught up to him when he turned and faced her. There were a few houses on the road, interspersed among wide open fields. The glow of a single streetlamp mixed with the moonlight, but she couldn't see his expression. She wasn't sure she wanted to.

Why, oh why, had she kissed him?

"We can ride home," he said matter-of-factly, as if nothing had happened between them.

"There's no saddle."

"I've ridden him bareback before. Don't worry, he's a good horse. Smart too. He'll lead us back to your place." He held out his hand to her.

She looked at it, hesitating. Her shoulders had started to hurt, undoubtedly from the spill in the buggy, and her toes were numb with cold. To refuse his offer would be stupid. Slipping her hand in his, she allowed him to help her on the horse. When she was situated, he slung his body up in one smooth motion, then positioned himself behind her.

She could feel the heat seeping from his chest to her back, even through the quilt. His nearness embarrassed her, but thrilled her at the same time.

"Hand me the reins," he said, his tone as assured and confident as it normally was.

She did as he asked, and they were on their way. Sometime during the ride he wrapped his arm around her waist. When she turned her head to look at him, he said, "Don't want you to fall off. We've had enough accidents tonight."

"I'm sorry about your buggy," Rachel said, though she knew he wasn't just talking about his buggy.

"Just glad we weren't hurt," he said.

It didn't take long for them to reach her house. Before he could get off his horse, she slid down the animal's back and handed him the quilt.

Looking up at Tobias, she knew she had to fix this. "I'm dating Christian," she said, a little too loudly, as if the volume of her tone could hammer that point home for both of them.

"I know," he said solemnly, laying the quilt in front of him over his horse's back.

"Just wanted to make that clear."

He nodded, looking down at her. "He's my friend. I don't want to hurt him."

"*Gut.* I'm glad we understand each other."

Tobias paused for a moment, as if he wanted to say something. Then he nickered to his horse and steered the animal around before making his way down the driveway.

Rachel watched him go, her heart heavy with guilt over the kiss. He must think her an idiot. Worse yet, a betrayer. Yet guilt and shame weren't the only emotions pulsing through her. Something had awakened inside her tonight after she kissed Tobias. She wasn't sure what it was, but she knew she would never be the same again.

Chapter 8

Moriah awakened before sunrise, double-checking her suitcase to make sure she had packed up all her belongings the night before. She looked at the clock Levi had given her on the nightstand, but she didn't care about the time. For a few moments she contemplated taking the clock with her. But what would be the point? It would only serve as a reminder of her failed marriage. Turning, she left the clock behind as she exited her and Levi's bedroom for the final time.

She entered the kitchen and set her suitcase against the wall next to the back door. As she glanced around the kitchen, taking in the old-fashioned wood stove, gray Formica countertops, and the unadorned window over the metal sink, she fought back tears. She had spent so many hours in here, preparing meals, studying recipes, trying to make sure every bit of food she made would satisfy her husband. Yet it was all for naught. This was no longer her kitchen. No longer her home.

The door opened and she turned around. Gabriel walked in, a few pieces of wood in his arms. He laid them down next to the stove and removed his hat. "I didn't expect you to be up."

"I couldn't sleep."

"Neither could I." He held her gaze for a moment, then put his black hat on one of the three pegs next to the door. "I'll make some coffee."

"*Nee.* I can do it."

Gabriel held up his hand. "Are you hungry? I make a mean plate of scrambled eggs."

The thought of food made her stomach flip over, but she nodded. He seemed so eager to prepare breakfast for her that she couldn't bear to turn him down, even though she knew he was doing it out of guilt over Levi. She remembered other times he had taken on his brother's burden. More than once when they were in school, the teacher would confuse the twins. Often it was Levi getting into trouble, but Gabriel didn't protest if he was the one being punished. Since Levi wasn't here to make things right, she had no doubt Gabriel would try to.

Gabriel squatted in front of the stove and threw a couple handfuls of crumpled up newspaper into the firebox. He added two small pieces of dried cordwood, then struck a match and lit the fire. "This will be going in no time."

Moriah nodded, then sat down at the table. She held her head in her hands. When she felt Gabriel's hand on her shoulder, she jerked up.

"Moriah?"

The worried expression on his face touched her. "I'm all right." She sat up straighter and tried to force a smile. She wasn't successful.

"Can I get you anything? Are you cold?" He knelt down beside her. "What can I do to help you, Moriah?"

She couldn't speak for a moment. While she appreciated

Gabriel's concern, she couldn't help but question it. He'd kept her at arm's length for so long. Now he was treating her with such compassion, such tenderness. She didn't know how to react.

John suddenly came in through the back door, his expression a mask of concern. "There you are," he said, looking at Gabriel as he shut the door behind him. "You weren't at the house when I woke up, and it didn't look like your bed had been slept in. Had me worried for a minute." His gaze went to Moriah, then back to Gabriel, who was now standing. His bushy brows furrowed. "Want to tell me what's going on here? Where's Levi?"

Gabriel expelled a long breath. "Sit down, *Daed*."

Shaking his head, John said, "Now I'm really worried. If you have something to say, just say it."

Moriah watched as Gabriel quickly told his father about Levi. John sank down in the chair and never said a word. Silent tears streamed down his wizened cheeks. Gabriel walked over and put his arm around his shoulders.

Sorrow filled her as she witnessed Gabriel trying to comfort his father. He knelt down, and John wept on his shoulder. For the hundredth time she wondered why Levi would do this. How could he hurt all of them so deeply? She wiped at the tears dangling on her eyelashes, not wanting Gabriel to see her crying also. He couldn't comfort them both, even though she knew he'd try.

John sat back in his chair and swiped at his face with the back of his hands. "I don't know why Levi did this, but we can't lean on our own understanding. God is in control." He looked at Gabriel, then at Moriah. "He will see us through this. I trust in that, and I hope you do too." He held out his hands. "We need to pray for Levi."

Moriah hesitated to take John's outstretched hand. Pray for Levi?

"Levi made his decision, *Daed.*"

She looked up to see that Gabriel hadn't moved either.

"*Ya,* but we don't know what has influenced that decision." John kept his hands out, palms facing up. "We can pray against whatever has come between him and his faith and family. We can also pray that he comes back."

Drawing the slightest bit of hope from her father-in-law's words, she slipped her hand into his roughened one. After a bit more hesitation, Gabriel finally did the same. Moriah closed her eyes and listened with a heavy heart as a father prayed, through fresh tears, for his wayward son.

The next morning, after spending her first night back at home, Moriah laid on her bed, staring at the ceiling but not really seeing anything. She rolled over and tucked her covers under her chin. She didn't want to get up. Elisabeth, who she shared a room with, was already dressed and downstairs. Fortunately her sister had the good sense not to ask any questions about what had happened with Levi. But eventually she'd want to know. Everyone would.

With a sigh she realized that it was Sunday. A church Sunday. Services were held every other week, and the whole community would be there. They'd know Levi was missing, and the questions would fly. Part of her wished she had stayed with Gabriel and John. At least then Gabriel would have run interference, sparing her the pain of having to explain to everyone that her husband had left her.

But that would make her just like Levi, wouldn't it? Refusing to take responsibility, fleeing from the consequences. She wouldn't do that. She wouldn't put more of a burden on Gabriel. He had put up with enough.

A soft knock sounded on her bedroom door. "Moriah?" The sweet sound of her youngest sister Ruthie's voice penetrated through the wood.

"*Ya?*"

"*Mami* wants to know if you're coming down for breakfast. She made your favorite. Buttermilk pancakes. She even made some strawberry syrup to go with them."

Moriah's stomach growled, but she had no appetite. She thought to tell Ruthie no, but knew she had to eat for the baby. "Will you tell her I'll be right down?"

"*Ya.*"

She listened to Ruthie's retreating footsteps, gathering her courage to go downstairs. When Gabriel had dropped her off late yesterday morning, only Ruthie and her mother had been home. Her brothers were still in the woodshop with their *daed,* and Elisabeth was visiting a friend. After exchanging a few words with her mother, Moriah had gone upstairs, and stayed up there until her mother and father had come to talk to her. She didn't want to face a barrage of questions from her siblings.

At that point she explained everything to them. Her mother had cried, but her father had remained silent and stone-faced. Moriah had never seen his countenance so stoic. Her father had always been an easygoing person, quick to laugh like her brother Tobias, but pensive when need be, like her brothers Lukas and Stephen. After a few moments he stood up and walked out of the room, never saying a word.

"Don't worry about your *daed,*" her mother had said, wiping her tears with her handkerchief. "He needs some time."

"*Mami,* I'm so sorry."

"Oh, Moriah, sweetheart." Her mother grabbed her hand and squeezed it tightly. "You don't have to apologize. This isn't your fault."

"Isn't it? He wouldn't have left me if I had been the wife he needed."

Emma Byler frowned. "No more talk like that, daughter. The blame is squarely on Levi's shoulders, not yours. You understand? Blaming yourself doesn't do any good."

"I know," she whispered. "I just can't help feeling so . . . awful."

"My sweet *kind.*" A tear escaped out of her mother's red-rimmed eyes. "I hate to see you going through this. I'm glad you came home. We'll help you through this. All of us will."

Now, lying in her bed, thinking about that conversation with her mother, she knew she had to lean on her family almost as much as she had to lean on God. Just because her life was a mess didn't mean she could avoid them, or anyone else. Church attendance had always been mandatory, and she would be expected to be at the service with her family. She'd always loved attending church services in the past. She loved spending that special time with the community, and the hymns and sermons fed her soul. But today, she wanted to stay in bed. She didn't want to go, but she knew she'd be expected.

Rising from her bed, she put on her Sunday dress, fastened her *kapp,* slipped on her shoes, and headed downstairs to the kitchen. The hum of her family engaged in quiet conversation reached her ears before she made it to the kitchen.

But when she entered the room, all activity stopped. Everyone except her mother and Elisabeth were already seated at the table.

Moriah turned her gaze on each one of her siblings. Tobias had an uncharacteristically sullen expression on his face, along with a dark bruise on his forehead. She briefly wondered how he'd been injured. Lukas, the only black-haired member of the family, looked at her with a mixture of pity and concern. He'd turned eighteen last month, but had an old soul. Thirteen-year-old Stephen kept his focus on the plate in front of him, even though it was empty. Ruthie gave her a look of encouragement that far surpassed her tender age of twelve. Elisabeth finally turned around, carrying a basket of fresh-baked biscuits. She went straight to Moriah and held them out to her. "Want a biscuit, *schwester*?"

With a smile, Moriah took one. "*Danki,* Lis."

"No problem. Welcome back. It'll be nice to have another set of hands around here. I'm tired of washing the dishes all the time."

"Hey," Ruthie said, scowling. "I wash them too, you know."

"When you don't have your nose planted inside a book. Which is never."

"All right, all right, girls," Moriah's father said, holding up his hand, palm facing outward. "Let's stop arguing and sit down for prayer."

"Yes, *Daed,*" Ruthie and Elisabeth said simultaneously. Moriah didn't miss the taunting looks that passed between them.

When everyone was seated, the family joined hands. "Dear heavenly Father," Joseph said. "We thank Thee for bringing us together and for the abundant meal You've given us. We also thank Thee for bringing Moriah to us today, Father. Let her know that she is deeply loved, not only by You, but by all of us. Amen."

Her eyes burning, Moriah opened them and looked at her family, who had immediately started tucking into their meal. For the first time since she'd read Levi's letter, she didn't feel utter despair. This was where she was meant to be. With her family. Her father hadn't needed to petition God to show her how much she was loved. She felt it all around her.

Gabe watched the barn entrance for Moriah. He wouldn't blame her if she had decided to stay home. By now it had spread through half the community that Levi Miller had left his wife and the church. The hard wooden bench felt less comfortable than ever, and he shifted in his seat as he looked at his father surrounded by several men, including the bishop and two ministers. He knew they were offering words of comfort, but he also knew that words were meaningless. Thousands of words, even delivered with good intentions, wouldn't heal the fissure that had formed in his father's heart.

Over the past twenty-four hours, Gabe had watched his father weaken physically. If he thought his father would even consider it, he would've taken him to the doctor, but he knew *Daed* would have none of it. A firm believer in alternative medicine, John Miller would put his faith in the healing power of God and in the other natural remedies he preferred, especially the teas he insisted on drinking.

Gabe watched as his *daed* sat on the edge of the bench in the front of the cavernous room, his shoulders in a permanent hunch, his long white beard touching the center of his chest as Amos Helmuth, one of the ministers, sat next to him, speaking to him in low tones.

The chill in the air began to fade as warm bodies filled the barn. The men took their seats on the left side of the barn, while the women found their places on the right side. The scent of fresh hay filtered through the air. Gabe took one last look at the barn entrance before sitting down in the back of the church. Not only did he not see Moriah, he didn't see the rest of the Byler family either. Had they decided to skip church? He wouldn't blame them if they had. Levi's decision had shamed both of their families.

Abel Esh, the bishop, stood at the front of the room and opened the *Ausbund,* the Amish hymn book. The hymn leader signaled for the congregation to begin singing. Every voice chimed together in an a capella chant, the haunting monotone echoing off the wooden slats of the barn.

They were nearly finished with the first hymn when out of the corner of his eye, Gabe saw Joseph Byler take a seat on the opposite end of his bench, flanked on both sides by his sons Tobias, Lukas, and Stephen. None of them looked at him, instead directing their attention to the ministers up front. On the other side of the room, Gabe caught sight of Moriah, seated between her mother and her sister Ruthie. He didn't see Elisabeth, but she often sat with her friends.

Suddenly Moriah turned, meeting his gaze, as if she knew he was looking straight at her.

His heart soared at the calm he saw in her eyes, a serenity he hadn't seen since before Levi had left. He had wanted her to stay in the large house, not only out of guilt for what his brother had done to her, but also because he wanted her near. She was so fragile, so vulnerable, and with good reason. His brother had been right about one thing—Gabe wanted to look after her. But she had insisted on moving back home, and he could see now that it was the right decision.

The hymns continued, one after the other, but Gabe did little singing. He surreptitiously kept his gaze on Moriah throughout the first hour of the three-hour service, unable to keep from looking at her, wishing she would acknowledge him, but also hoping she wouldn't. She seemed completely involved in the singing, and other than that one time at the beginning of the service, she kept her attention focused on the bishop.

After the singing ended, Abel stood and began his sermon. The words passed through Gabe's ears, his mind not registering anything but the plights of his brother, Moriah, and his *daed* weighing heavily on his soul. He vowed to keep close watch on his father, and considered hiring another part-time employee, at least until *Daed* had a chance to recover from Levi's departure. He couldn't risk anything happening to his *daed*. Not when he'd already lost his brother. He couldn't lose the only immediate family he had left.

When the service finally reached its conclusion, the congregation rose to sing another hymn. After the dismissal, he turned to look for Moriah, but she was already headed to the Eshes' house, probably intending to assist with lunch preparations. He wouldn't have blamed her if she hadn't stayed, but he wasn't surprised that she would offer to help. Throughout this ordeal, she had continually surprised him with her inner strength.

He suddenly heard the hushed tones of his father and Joseph Byler behind him. Turning, he saw his *daed* speaking to Joseph and the bishop. Gabe could see his father's eyes were glistening with tears. "*Danki* for listening to me, Joseph. I ask you to forgive my son. I beg you to forgive my Levi for what he has done to your daughter and your family."

Gabe quickly went to his father's side. "*Daed*," he said in a low voice.

Joseph stilled them both by putting his hand on John's shoulder. "Don't take your son's burden on yourself."

"But I have already. Can't you see? His burden is mine. It always will be."

Gabe looked at Joseph, who remained silent for a moment. Finally, he dropped his hand from John and spoke. "We'll pray for Levi to realize his folly and return. When he does, we will welcome him home."

"*Danki,* Joseph," John said quietly. He stared at the ground as Joseph turned and walked away.

The bishop drew Gabe to the side. "Your *daed* is in a bad way, Gabriel."

With a nod Gabe said, "He's taking this hard."

"Of course he is. None of us blame him for that. But perhaps it would be best if you took him home. The ministers and I will come by this afternoon and see how he's doing." Abel looked squarely at Gabe. "How both of you are doing."

Giving his father a quick glance, Gabe suddenly felt as tired as his *daed* looked. He didn't want to be here, fighting to keep his composure while worrying about John. "*Ya.* I will take him home."

Fortunately, John readily agreed to leave the Eshes'. "Not much in the mood for socializing," he said wearily.

"Me either." They walked to their buggy. Before John got in, he looked at Gabe. "Will we ever see him again, Gabriel? Will I ever see my son again?"

More than anything Gabe wanted to tell his father that Levi would return, that everything would be back the way it was. But he couldn't because nothing would be the same for any of them again. Yet he refused to take away his *daed*'s hope. The old man needed something to cling to, even if it was a lie. "I don't know," he finally managed. "I don't know."

Moriah watched John and Gabriel as they headed for their buggy. *Poor, poor John.* Her heart went out to her father-in-law. Yesterday as they'd prayed together, his strength and faith had given her hope. But today the man was obviously consumed with grief over what Levi had done. And there was Gabriel, right by his side, offering his support. He had not only been Moriah's rock that first night, but he continued to be his father's as well.

She turned around and started to go inside to help with lunch. But something stopped her, causing her to look at her father-in-law and brother-in-law again. While everyone was gathering for the afternoon meal, John and Gabriel were alone. And despite what Levi had done, she was still part of their family. Even though she was suffering with her own pain, she didn't want to leave them alone. She had to find a way to help somehow.

She went inside and found her mother with the other women in the kitchen. Making her way over to her mother, she whispered her intentions in Emma's ear. *Mami* looked surprised, but she nodded, then went to find the bishop's wife.

Moriah hurried back outside just in time to see Gabriel step up to get inside the buggy. She called out his name and rushed toward him.

He stopped and looked at her, his visage grim.

"Is he all right?" she asked.

"I have no idea." He lowered his voice, adding, "He's taking this very hard."

"I know."

"Gabriel?" John called to his son.

Both Gabriel and Moriah peeked inside the buggy. When John's gaze met hers, he smiled. "Such a sweet *maedel*," he said. "You didn't deserve this. I'm so sorry for what Levi has done."

"We should be going," Gabriel said as he climbed inside. He seemed to be in a hurry, but then he paused. "Will you be all right?"

Moriah nodded, but wondered if she'd ever be all right again.

Seemingly satisfied with her response, Gabriel touched the reins to the flanks of the horse and pulled out of the Eshes' drive.

Moriah watched as they left, her heart not only bleeding for herself but also for Gabriel and John.

Gabe and John rode home in silence. Once they reached the house, he helped his father into the bedroom he had shared with his wife for over forty years. The modest space still held reminders of their mother—a quilt she had made as a child draped over the back of the rocking chair she had used to rock Gabe and Levi to sleep. An old Bible passed down through her family lay on the nightstand next to the bed, on the side where she used to sleep.

A nearly unbearable sense of sadness engulfed him. He'd never missed his mother more than now. He had grieved deeply for her after she died, but Levi had been there to share that grief. Both of them had been close to her, Levi even more so.

She would have known what to do about *Daed*. Gabe had no idea how to handle his father's pain. Even after his wife had died,

John Miller had been strong. Now, with Gabe's arm supporting him, guiding him to his bed, he was a broken man.

"*Daed,* why don't you lie down for a little while? I'll bring you some lunch in a bit."

John sat down on the edge of the bed, but he shook his head. "I'm not hungry." He looked up at Gabe. "I was right in asking Joseph for forgiveness."

"That's what Levi needs to do."

"He can't. Not now."

"You mean he won't."

Squaring his shoulders as if he had a sudden burst of strength, John said, "I know what I mean, *sohn.* Levi is lost. He's strayed away from God. I don't know what led him down this path, but I do know that he has to seek out the Lord and ask His forgiveness. Only when he's given himself fully to God will he be able to come back." He bent over and took off his boots, then stretched out on the bed, closing his eyes. "You're right. I am tired."

"I'll leave you alone." Gabe turned to go. "Come downstairs when you're ready." He slowly shut the door behind him and made his way to the first floor of the house. As soon as his foot landed on the bottom stair, he heard a knock on the front door. He opened it and saw Moriah standing on the porch. His eyes widened with surprise. "What are you doing here?"

"We brought you lunch."

Gabe looked beyond her and saw *Frau* Byler coming up the porch steps, carrying a large picnic basket. Joseph was tending to their horse. He looked back at Moriah, who gave him a small smile that warmed his heart.

"We thought you and John might be hungry."

"Come on in." He opened the door wide and gestured for the

two women to step inside. He then went out to help Joseph with his horse and buggy. When the men returned, they were welcomed by a feast of sliced ham, bread, pickles, potato salad, rolls, banana bread, and two different kinds of cookies. Gabe was thankful for the bounty, and for the generosity of the Bylers.

"*Daed*'s upstairs," Gabe stated as he went to the sink and washed his hands. "He said he wasn't hungry, but I know he'd want to be down here to thank you for bringing such a *wunderbaar* meal."

"Don't worry about bothering him," Emma said as she filled their glasses with iced tea. "He should rest. We have plenty and this will all keep 'til later.

They took their chairs, and Gabe sat across from Moriah. After prayer they started to eat, but it became evident that no one had much of an appetite. Moriah just picked at her food, and her mother soon noticed.

"You have to eat, Moriah," she said, her voice soft and gentle. "Even when you aren't hungry, your baby is."

Nodding, Moriah ate a spoonful of potato salad. A long, awkward stretch of silence soon followed. Gabe's attention kept swaying to her. He wished there was something he could do to fix the situation. But he couldn't do anything. And he hated that helpless feeling most of all.

As they made their way home from church, Rachel and her mother rode in silence. Sarah stared straight ahead as she guided the horse and buggy down the road. Her black bonnet obscured her face, keeping Rachel from discerning her thoughts, although she suspected she already knew what Sarah was thinking about. She was thinking about it too.

The entire community had been abuzz this morning at church. Soon everyone knew that Levi Miller had left his wife and the Amish. Rachel could barely believe it. She didn't know Levi well, but she had thought he and Moriah had a good marriage. They were still newlyweds—how could there be trouble in the relationship already? Yet having marriage problems was one thing. Leaving the church was an entirely different story.

She'd known a few people who had "yanked over" by leaving their faith, mostly rebellious teens and young adults who had gotten a taste of the Yankee world and started to chafe underneath the *Ordnung*. Usually those who left hadn't been baptized and were allowed to come back to the community and socialize with their family and friends. She knew of only one woman who had moved away after she had joined the church. Rachel had heard she had fallen in love with a Yankee, but she didn't know if that was a rumor or not, because the woman had never returned. When she left, she was immediately put in the *bann*. Maybe the shunning had kept her away, not an outlander. Rachel could only guess at the true reasons.

Leaving the church had never been an option in Rachel's mind. She had always known she would become Amish when she was old enough to make the decision about baptism. The trappings of the world had never appealed to her, and she had never had the desire to break the *Ordnung*. Why would anyone want to, when their faith offered them so much?

Back at home, Rachel and her mother prepared a cold lunch. Aaron hadn't attended church that morning—he had still been in his room when they'd arrived home. Again, her father, Emmanuel, along with her mother didn't say anything when he came downstairs without a word. Rachel couldn't figure out why he was allowed to do whatever he wanted to do.

"I'm going to visit Emma," Sarah had announced when they finished with dinner. "She needs our support. Rachel, please wash the dishes. I'd like you to come with me."

Rachel had just popped the last bit of her ham and Swiss cheese sandwich in her mouth and she froze midchew. Alarm shot through her at the thought of going to the Bylers. She had managed to avoid Tobias at the service that morning, only seeing him briefly before church had started. Thank goodness they hadn't crossed paths. That would have been embarrassing. Either he hadn't seen her in the service or he was ignoring her, and she would bet a week's tips he'd disregarded her on purpose. The last thing she wanted to do was run into him again, especially after what had happened between them two nights ago.

"Can't I just stay here?" she had pleaded, hoping her mother would change her mind. "I have some reading I want to catch up on."

"Rachel, I'm surprised. You would put a book ahead of the Byler's troubles?"

"Bible reading," Rachel clarified, a twinge of guilt pricking at her as she said the lie. If her mother let her off the hook, then she felt duty-bound to crack open the family Bible. She found the High German translation hard to read, but she had some serious confessing to do about her newfound feelings for Tobias.

"As impressed as I am by your devotion, I think that can wait until later. Emma, Joseph, and Moriah left right after the service and I want to see if they're all right. I should think you would care about their welfare as well," Sarah said again, rising from her chair and adjusting her crisp, white apron.

"I do. But—"

"But what?" Sarah paused, lifting one brow.

Rachel couldn't explain her real reason for not wanting to go the Bylers, so she dropped the issue. "Never mind. Just give me a few minutes to finish the dishes."

"*Danki,* Rachel."

As Rachel took her *daed*'s plate, he said, "Don't forget Aaron's too."

Rachel pinched her lips together as she accepted her *daed*'s dish, then went to collect Aaron's. Part of his sandwich still remained on the white plate. "Are you finished?"

"*Ya.*" He got up, pushed his chair back where it belonged, then left the room without a word of thanks. Their father departed shortly after, saying he had some work to do in the barn.

That was two hours ago. Now it was late afternoon, and as they approached the Byler's, Rachel's insides started to churn. She hoped Tobias wasn't home. If she was lucky he'd be out visiting one of his cousins or something. But she doubted he would be out having fun, not after what happened to Moriah. She gripped the side of the buggy seat as her mother turned into the driveway.

"Please tether the horse," Sarah said as she parked the buggy. "I'll meet you inside."

Rachel did as she was asked, then procrastinated by stroking the horse's velvety soft nose. She wasn't in a hurry to go in the house and see Tobias again. The weather had warmed several degrees since the other day, and the sun was out in full force. At least she could be thankful for that. When she couldn't stall any longer, she turned to go inside, but paused for a moment when she spied the wrecked buggy parked behind *Herr* Byler's workshop. The vehicle was completely mangled, and she said a quick prayer of thanks that neither one of them had been hurt. She spun around on the heel of her black shoe, only to run smack-dab into Tobias's chest.

"Whoa," he said, as his arms went around her shoulders to steady her.

She just had to pick that moment to breathe, to inhale the scent of his clean Sunday shirt, which was now inches from her nose. For the briefest of moments she reveled in his nearness, until common sense took over and she stepped back.

"Sorry about that," she said, her hand touching her *kapp* as she tried to steady her nerves.

"It's all right."

The despondent tone of his voice caught her attention. She looked up to see his glum expression.

"What are you doing here?" he asked flatly.

"We came to see how your *daed* and *mami* were doing." And because she couldn't stop herself, she added, "Don't worry, I didn't come to see you."

He ran his hand through his hair, revealing a yellowish bruise on his forehead. A reminder of the accident. As if either one of them needed another one. "*Gut.* That makes me happy."

But he didn't sound anything close to being happy. "What do you mean by that?"

Shoving past her, he headed to his damaged buggy. "Never mind."

Turning around, she followed him. "That's not an answer. I want to know what you meant."

He knelt beside the buggy's broken axle. "You know, Rachel, the world doesn't revolve around you."

"I never said it did."

"You don't have to."

"Excuse me?"

Remaining in his crouched position, he looked up at her, any remnant of his trademark gloating and teasing gone from his crystalline blue eyes. "Go inside. I'm not in the mood for your drama."

She crossed her arms. "I am not dramatic."

He glanced at her folded arms, then went back to inspecting the axle.

Changing her stance, she moved toward him. "This is about the other night, isn't it? You're blaming me for what happened."

"Not your fault we got hit by a car." He jerked on the axle, checking its stability. It immediately came loose. He groaned.

"I'm not talking about the accident." Why was she even bringing this up? She'd told herself that she didn't want to see Tobias, but here she was, not only seeing him, but also trying to engage him in a conversation they really shouldn't be having in the first place. What was wrong with her? "I think you know what I mean."

He stopped his inspection and rested his forehead against the lower side of the buggy. The motion pushed his hat farther back on his head. "That's not your fault either," he said quietly.

"*Ya,* it is. I should have never kissed you. I must have knocked my head really hard to do something as crazy and stupid as that." She looked away. "Not like it was good or anything."

Slowly he rose from the ground and looked at her, eyes filled with fury. She'd never seen him so mad before.

"You're a mean, miserable woman, Rachel Detweiler. I don't know how—or even why—Christian puts up with you." He brushed her aside and stormed off, but not before turning around

"And for the record, I'd kiss a stinkin' pig before I'd kiss you again."

Ouch.

Her eyes pricked as she watched him walk into the woodshop and shut the door in her face. He'd called her mean? He was the cruelest man on earth. She didn't care if she never saw him again. In fact, she'd prefer it.

The sound of a screen door slamming made her turn around. Tobias's younger sister, Elisabeth, approached. Like Tobias, she had blue eyes and blonde hair, along with one of the tiniest waists Rachel had ever seen. When she neared, Rachel could see her eyes were red rimmed from crying.

Rachel met her halfway. "Are you all right?"

Elisabeth nodded. "I'm fine. Just upset over what happened to Moriah. We all are. It's been so hard on her. *Mami* and *Daed* aren't taking it too well either."

Her words caused Rachel's heart to stop. How could she have been so dense? No wonder Tobias was angry with her. She'd been so caught up in thinking about that kiss, so self-centered and defensive, she had forgotten the reason she and her mother had even stopped to visit. His sister's husband had just left her, and instead of trying to offer him comfort, she'd picked another fight.

He was right. She was a miserable person.

"My parents are with Moriah at the Millers," Elisabeth said. "But your *mami* is helping us make some cookies. She said it will keep our mind off of everything. Even Lukas and Stephen are helping, and they hate to cook."

"That's *gut*," Rachel said absently, glancing over her shoulder at the woodshop.

"I've been sent to get you."

Rachel focused on the woodshop for another second, then turned to Elisabeth. "Tell my *mudder* I'll be right there."

The young woman nodded. "I will. Oh, and if you see Tobias, tell him we're making his favorite—oatmeal chocolate chip."

Rachel nodded at Elisabeth and watched her hurry back to the house. But she couldn't follow her inside, not just yet. Not before talking to Tobias one more time and apologizing for being so insensitive. She walked to the woodshop door and placed her hand on the knob, only to hesitate turning it.

Maybe she should leave things be. Tobias was mad at her, but he would get over it. Besides, what did she care if he was angry? He'd been mad at her off and on for years.

But this time was different. He was hurting over his sister, and she'd only made things worse. She had to apologize, at the very least. Taking a deep breath, she opened the door.

He stood in the middle of the shop, sifting his hand through the small pile of wood shavings that lay on a long, tall, tool-nicked table. An unfinished cradle perched next to him, amid millions of tiny flecks of sawdust. The scent of freshly cut wood enveloped her as she breathed in.

"What do you want?" he asked, not looking up.

Rachel looked at his fingers as he continued to push around the shavings. Long, strong fingers attached to a large, calloused hand. The hand of an artist. She'd seen his work before and had grudgingly admitted he had a gift with wood. Always knowing that he had yet another talent had chafed her in the past, but thinking about it now only brought her admiration. Instead of maligning his talent, she should have been appreciating it. Just one more indication of what a rotten person she was when it came to him.

Finally, he glanced at her, his expression lifeless. "What?"

The sawdust made her itch, and she rubbed her nose with her palm. Then she quickly thrust her hands behind her back. "I, um, well, I want to apologize. To you."

He shrugged, then went back to messing with the shavings. "Fine. You apologized. Now leave."

Once again his response triggered a tiny spark inside her, but she pushed it down. He had been right; this wasn't about her. It was about him and his family, a family he obviously deeply cared about. And she needed to show him that she understood.

She didn't stop walking until she was right next to him. "Tobias, I'm really sorry. Especially about your sister. That's a terrible thing to happen to her."

Turning, his gaze met hers, its steeliness softening. "I appreciate that, Rachel. Been hard on her."

"Hard on everyone, I'm sure."

He nodded, his lips flattening in to a thin line. "All my life I've been taught that fighting is wrong, that hitting another person, no matter what, is forbidden. But right now I could hurt Levi Miller with my bare hands for what he's done to Moriah."

"No one would blame you if you did."

"Yes, they would." He let out a flat chuckle. "You know they would." With a flick of his hand he swept the wood shavings off the table. They floated and shimmered to the floor.

She couldn't argue with him, because what he was saying was true. "So what are you going to do?"

"Nothing. There's nothing I can do. Moriah moved back home yesterday. I guess things will go back to the way they were before she was married."

Yet they both knew things would never be the same. Not for his sister . . . and not for them. Their kiss had changed that.

They stood together in silence for a moment, Tobias staring at the mess on the shop floor in front of him. "Guess I better clean it up."

"I'll do it." Rachel quickly went to the back of the shop and found the broom. Without looking at Tobias, she started sweeping the shavings into a small pile.

He let out a breath. "I'm sorry for what I said, Rachel. You know. About kissing the pig. That was uncalled for."

"I deserved it." She glanced around the shop. "Where's the dustpan?"

"Hang on." He disappeared into the back of the shop, then came out with a large metal dustpan. Lowering into a crouch, he placed it on the floor and she swept the debris into it. "No one deserves to be insulted like that," he continued. "I should watch my mouth."

At his mention of the word *mouth,* they both looked at each other. She saw his gaze focus on her lips, then dart away. "Finished?" he finally asked, staring down at the floor.

"*Ya.*"

He picked up the dustpan and deposited the shavings into a metal trash can, then leaned it against the can before taking the broom from her grasp. "*Danki.*"

"Don't mention it. By the way, I just saw your sister before I came in here. Everyone else is inside baking cookies. Elisabeth said they're making your favorite—oatmeal chocolate chip."

"Those are her favorite." Tobias's lips quirked in a half smile. "She thinks everyone should like what she does. That way she always gets what she wants."

"Really? That's an interesting way to look at things."

"Annoying, but that's Elisabeth."

"So what is your favorite cookie?"

"Peanut butter. With little chunks of peanuts sticking out. Actually anything with nuts is good."

Rachel regarded him for a moment. "What do you think of pecan pie?"

"Love it. Why?"

"Just wondering."

"Well, I doubt there's pie in the house, but the cookies should be good. Believe me, I've never met a cookie I didn't like."

"We should probably go get some then. I promised Elisabeth I'd come inside. I'm sure *Mami*'s wondering where I ran off to."

"Yeah, we should go. It's a little chilly in here anyway."

As they walked out of the shop, Rachel glanced at the buggy again. "Can it be fixed?"

Tobias nodded. "My cousin works on buggies. He's coming out tomorrow after work to take a look at it. The axle's broken and the wheels are bent, but the rest of it's in good shape. Shouldn't be too much trouble to fix."

"That's good."

They headed toward the house, but Rachel suddenly stopped in her tracks.

He turned around. "What is it?"

They had just put their differences aside for once, and now she was on the verge of throwing everything off-kilter. But she couldn't go inside without knowing if he truly meant what he said a few moments ago. "Tobias . . . do you really think I'm a horrible person?"

His head tilted to the right, regret coloring his features. "Rachel, I'm sorry. My mouth again. Keeps saying things it shouldn't."

"Even when it's the truth?"

He scrubbed his face with the palm of his hand before regarding her again. "You asked me, so I'm gonna be honest. You're always angry with me, Rachel. Most times I feel like anything I do or say will make you mad at me. I'll admit, sometimes I egg you on. But other times, well, it's hard to be around you."

His admission cut deeply, even as she realized his words were true. She was resentful of him, and she didn't understand why. Not completely anyway.

"Hey, let's drop it." Tobias smiled and waved his hand toward the house. "No need for all of us to be depressed. We better get some cookies before everyone else eats them all."

Rachel sighed. Leave it to a man to think of his stomach above all else. But in all honesty she knew Tobias was creating a diversion, and she was grateful for it. He had enough to deal with right now. He had made his observation, and neither of them were interested in pursuing the conversation any further.

Yet she knew she'd be thinking about what he said for a very long time.

Chapter 9

The first few days after Moriah returned home, her family had given her the space she needed. They treated her nearly the same as they had before she married. Her parents didn't ask many questions, which she appreciated. Her brothers were a bit kinder than before, and her sisters were less inquisitive, especially Elisabeth. They all knew about the baby, but naturally their excitement was tempered by the circumstances.

When Moriah accepted that she couldn't spend the rest of her life in her bedroom, mourning what she had lost, she busied herself in a flurry of activity. She helped her family with their chores and practically took over all the cooking duties for her mother. She brought lunch out to her father, Tobias, and Luke in the woodshop, and occasionally she helped with customer orders. A few young wives in the church had new babies, and she sewed several outfits for each one. Since she'd always wanted to learn to knit, she bought an instruction book, needles, and several skeins of pale yellow yarn. By the end of the day, she was usually exhausted.

After three weeks of busyness, she still felt lost and confused. At night, the hardest time for her, sleep was always elusive. She tried mentally repeating Scripture, but that didn't help. Instead, she laid in her single bed, tossing and turning, thinking about Levi, mulling over regrets, asking God why this had happened to her. She was still no closer to an answer. Her future looked bleak and lonely. She could never remarry. Her child would never know his or her father. Or even have a father. Yes, her family had rallied around her, and they would always be there for her. But they couldn't fill the emptiness she felt when she saw other couples, or stop the sadness she felt knowing she would never have another child.

At times she couldn't bear to even look at her own family because doing so brought pain and regret. For years the Bylers had spent every Thursday evening engrossed in a family activity—playing a board game, reading the Bible or other stories aloud, or singing hymns together. But even during those family evenings, she felt like an outsider. She would never have the experience of sitting next to her husband, sharing the Bible with their children, as her parents did. Her siblings would all marry and have families of their own. They wouldn't be looked on by the rest of the community with pity or, even worse, as an outcast. Her dreams of a large family and a loving husband were shattered.

So she did the only thing she could do. She survived and put her focus on her baby. She was powerless to bring Levi back; he had made his decision and there was nothing she could do about it. And while she knew the pain of his rejection and the loneliness filling her soul wouldn't heal quickly, she had to at least try to have as normal a life as possible, for the sake of her child. Her babe would never feel abandoned or betrayed. She would make sure of it.

When the third week of April arrived, Moriah was busier than ever. The Bylers were hosting church that Sunday, and her family members were deep in the throes of preparations. Their house had a large basement where the service would be held. The furniture and wood floors needed to be dusted, cleaned, and polished. Even though there would be a potluck meal after the service, the Bylers still needed to provide a good portion of the food. Moriah had the task of preparing the apple crumb pies.

That Wednesday morning she finished rolling out the last pie crust on the kitchen table, then placed it in a metal pie pan. With her fingers she crimped the edges, then stepped back from the table. Twelve crusts, ready to be filled, then baked later on in the afternoon when her mother came back from the market and her sisters were home from school. Elisabeth and Ruthie would make the crumb topping out of flour, cinnamon, sugar, and butter and sprinkle it on the homemade apple pie filling Moriah had prepared the day before.

As she washed her hands under the cold water, a yawn escaped. Her mother said fatigue was normal in the beginning of pregnancy, but Moriah knew that wasn't the only reason for her exhaustion.

She dried her hands and went to the linen closet, where she found a basket filled with old, clean rags. Selecting a large one, she set to the task of dusting every exposed space in the house. She had just started on one of the end tables when she heard a knock on the door.

"Just a minute." She tucked the rag in the pocket of her white apron and answered the door. Her eyes widened. "Gabriel?"

"Hi." He glanced down for a moment, shifting from one foot to the other. Then he looked back up. "I was driving by, and I thought I'd see if your horses needed any shoes."

"Our horses are fine, but that's thoughtful of you to stop by."

"Oh," he said, shoving his hands in his pockets. "All right then."

When he didn't turn around and leave, she asked, "Is there anything else I can do for you, Gabriel?"

"*Nee.* Nothing else." He paused, looking more unsure than she had ever seen him. "Well, I was also wondering how you're doing."

Ah, so that was his real reason for stopping by. He came to check on her. She was both surprised and touched. "I'm doing all right," she said with a small smile. "As well as expected, I guess."

"*Gut.* Glad to hear it." He rocked back and forth on his heels.

A gust of wind swirled around them, cutting through her dress and chilling her skin. He didn't seem in any hurry to leave, so she asked, "Would you like to come in for a minute?"

He hesitated, then nodded. "If you don't mind."

"*Nee.* I don't mind at all. I'm glad to see you." Gabriel's expression relaxed. He seemed relieved by her welcome. Although she saw him and his *daed* at church, their paths never crossed any other time. She didn't realize until this moment how much she had missed them both.

Once inside, he slipped off his black hat, then ran his hand through his brown hair. "Cold spring day."

"*Ya.* Would you like something to drink? I've got coffee, and there are a few cookies left over from lunch."

"*Danki,* but I'm fine. Had a big meal with *Daed. Frau* Stoltzfus brought over a couple casseroles last night." His head dipped down a tiny bit as he looked at her directly. "Everything okay with the baby?"

She smiled. He'd asked the question so tentatively, yet with genuine concern. "So far everything is going well."

"Do you know when he's due?"

"She—or he—is due in November."

His lips curved into a small smile. "A harvest baby. That sounds nice." He rubbed his smooth chin for a moment. "Have you heard anything from Levi?"

Without warning, the sting of tears sprang to her eyes. She didn't think she had any left. "*Nee,*" she said softly. "Have you?"

His expression became downcast as he shook his head. Then he glanced at her and winced. "I'm sorry, Moriah. I shouldn't have asked you about him. I didn't mean to upset you."

"It's okay." She brought her fingers to her eyes and rubbed them, trying to send the threatening tears away. When she looked at him, spots danced in front of her eyes, then quickly faded as his kind face came into clear view.

"I better go." He put his hat back on and opened the door. Before he walked out, he turned around and faced her again. "I know I don't have the right to offer, but if you ever need anything, Moriah, just ask."

"*Danki,* Gabriel. I appreciate that." As she watched him step out onto the porch, she added, "Say hello to your *daed* for me."

"I will." He hurried to his buggy, untethered the horse, and jumped in the driver's seat. Moments later he pulled away.

Slowly she shut the door, her thoughts confused. She shouldn't be that surprised by Gabriel's visit, since they were still technically family because of the baby. But he didn't have to stop by and check up on her, or even ask about the baby. He knew that her family would take good care of them both. Still, she was glad he did.

"I'm fine, Moriah." Ruth crossed her arms over her chest as she lay in her bed, propped up by several soft pillows. "I don habe a code."

Moriah placed a bed tray laden with warm turkey noodle soup, orange juice, and two cherry-flavored cough drops. Normally their *mami* had forbidden food in the bedrooms, but she always made an exception for a sick child. "*Ya,* Ruthie, I'm afraid you do."

"I shood habe gone to school today," she said, ignoring Moriah's words and the tray in front of her.

"You should eat your soup. That will help you feel better. Besides, you love turkey noodle soup."

"Not hungry." Ruth turned her head and stared out her small bedroom window. She was the only child that had her own room, a tiny area up in the attic. It would get almost unbearably hot in the summer and frigid cold in the winter, but Ruth loved having a space to call her very own. Except for today. Nothing would make her happy. Not only wasn't she feeling well, but she hated to miss school.

Moriah sat down next to her and tucked a strand of Ruth's dishwater-blonde hair behind her small ear. Her sister had her hair pinned up, but she wasn't wearing her *kapp*. "Ruthie, please eat a little bit of the soup. And have a sip of the orange juice as well. As soon as you feel better you can go back to school."

Ruth didn't respond right away. When she finally faced Moriah, she sighed. "Okay," she said, sounding like she had cotton balls stuffed up her nose. "Thig mebbe I can go to school tomorrow?"

"We'll see. It's up to *Mami,* of course."

"But you wood send me, woodn't you?"

With a smile, Moriah rose from Ruth's bed. "If you were better, I would." She had never met a child so enthralled with school. School had been a necessary part of life, and Moriah had done well in her studies. But she had never cultivated a love for education like her youngest sibling did. After this school year, Ruth would only have two more years left, and Moriah could only imagine how hard it will be on her sister to leave school for good after the eighth grade.

Bringing the spoon up to her mouth, Ruth blew on the pale brown liquid. One thin noodle hung limply over the side of the utensil. "You don habe to stay," she said, then sipped her soup.

"Let me know when you're done then."

Ruth nodded. "I'll probly read a book after that."

"And hopefully get some sleep."

Her sister smiled, her brown eyes red-rimmed from watering. "I will. I promise."

Giving her a nod, Moriah then turned around and went downstairs to the kitchen. When she inhaled the scent of the turkey noodle soup, her belly growled. The nausea had subsided over the past couple weeks. It was the first week of May, and she was almost three months along. Grateful that her morning sickness had been short-lived, she picked up a small white bowl from inside a cabinet and walked over to the soup pot simmering on the stove. Just as she was spooning the steaming soup, she heard the sound of a car pulling in the driveway. Assuming it was one of her *daed*'s customers, she sat down at the table. Folding her hands and closing her eyes, she started to say grace. Before she finished the prayer, someone burst through the front door.

"Moriah! Moriah!"

The voice sounded like Gabriel. What was he doing? She jumped up from her chair and almost ran into him as he dashed into the kitchen. A knot suddenly formed in her throat. Something was horribly wrong. One look at Gabriel's stricken face told her as much. "What happened? What's wrong?"

"There isn't much time, Moriah. We have to leave. Now."

"Leave? What are you talking about?"

Gabriel took her by the arm. "I'll tell you in the car—"

"Car? Where are we going?"

Facing her, he held on to her shoulders. "Moriah, it's Levi."

Hope replaced the dread inside her for a split instant. "You saw Levi? Has he come back?"

"*Nee,*" he said, guiding her to the door. "He's in the hospital."

Gabe hated hospitals. He hated the chemical smell, the unnatural glow of fluorescent lighting, the unending and repetitive questions people asked you while refusing to answer your own. But more than anything he hated the pain and the sadness that permeated the brick building. The last time he'd been in a hospital, his mother was being treated for cancer. Hospitals held nothing but bad memories for him.

And now he was in the middle of another horrible nightmare. He'd received a phone call from the call box early that morning. The caller had identified herself as a "hospital representative." He had no idea how they'd found his number, but he hadn't cared once they told him what had happened to Levi. A three-car accident on Interstate 90. That was all he knew, because that was all they would tell him.

Now, three hours later, he, his *daed,* and Moriah were sitting in the emergency room's visitor area at University Hospital, waiting to hear about Levi. Technically he was still in the *bann,* but nothing would have kept them away from him, not when they weren't sure how injured he truly was. The church used the *bann* as a corrective measure, as a means for bringing the erring person into repentance and back to the Amish. And even though Gabe, his father, and Moriah were expected to limit their interactions with Levi, they'd all agreed seeing him now was worth any chastising they might receive.

Gabe glanced at his father's ashen face as he sat next to Moriah. He could only imagine the memories this place held for him. First his wife. Now his son.

Then he looked at Moriah. Her eyes were dry, her expression stoic. But she had shredded the tissue in her hands to bits. This couldn't be good for her or the baby. Hadn't she suffered enough? Not only had her husband left her, but now she had to wait and see if he was dead or alive.

Gabe closed his eyes at the morbid thought. Levi couldn't die. That was impossible. Regardless of what his brother had done, Gabe still loved him. He couldn't bear to lose him.

Jumping up from his seat, he said, "I'm going to find out what's taking so long. We should have heard something by now."

"*Nee,*" John said, holding up his hand. "Give them time to do their job, Gabriel. I'm sure they'll tell us what's happened to Levi when they can."

Gabe was amazed at his father's composure. Then he remembered the pillar of strength he'd been during his mother's illness. Other than his reaction to Levi's leaving, he never showed much emotional weakness. Gabriel admired him for that and wished he had a fraction of the inner strength both his father and Moriah possessed.

While he heeded his father and didn't approach the woman at the front desk, he couldn't sit still and wait either. Instead he walked over to the window and stared outside into the parking lot. Not a horse or buggy in sight. Just lots of cars. Lots and lots of cars.

Suddenly he became aware that he was being watched. He turned and saw a young woman staring at him. He looked out the window again, ignoring her. He was used to being stared at, especially when he ventured outside of Middlefield. The Yankees there were used to the Amish way of life, but this woman likely had never even seen an Amish man before.

"Mrs. Miller?"

He spun around at the sound of Moriah's name. A trim man wearing a white coat stood at the doorway of the waiting room, a stethoscope around his neck. Gabe assumed he was the doctor.

Moriah rose from her chair. "Yes?"

"Can I speak with you privately?"

Although the room wasn't crowded, there were a few people sitting in the chairs, watching TV, thumbing through magazines, or dozing off. Dread pooled in Gabe's belly as he crossed the room to stand next to Moriah. From the doctor's bleak expression, he could tell the news wouldn't be good.

"This is my h-husband's brother," Moriah said. Gabe didn't miss how she stumbled over the word. "And his father. Whatever you have to say to me, you should also say to them."

The doctor nodded, then gestured for them to follow him into the hallway, a few feet down from the receptionist. The area allowed more privacy than the waiting room.

"The car accident your husband was in was extremely serious, Mrs. Miller. He's suffered massive internal injuries, along with a concussion. I'm not going to sugarcoat this for you." He paused and looked at each of them, then returned his attention to Moriah. "We're concerned about the amount of blood he's lost. We're giving him transfusions, but he's lost a great deal."

"What does that mean?" Moriah asked.

"It means that his situation is very, very grave. He needs to have surgery to repair the damage to his organs. You must sign a consent form in order for us to proceed. The faster we get him into surgery, the better his chances are of recovery."

Gabe's blood turned to ice. Chance of recovery? No, he couldn't have heard the doctor correctly.

"The nurse will be out with the paperwork. Will you sign the form, Mrs. Miller?"

Moriah nodded.

As the doctor turned to walk away, a tall, distinguished man in a black suit barged into the emergency room area. "Where is my daughter?" he bellowed, dashing up to the glassed-in receptionist area.

The red-haired woman seated behind the counter slid open the glass window. "May I help you?" she asked, her voice calm and detached.

"I want to know where my daughter is! I demand to see her right now!"

The ruckus caught Gabe's attention. When he took a good look at the older gentleman, his mouth dropped open. Robert Johnston, owner of Johnston's Farms.

"Sir, if you'll kindly have a seat—"

"I will not have a seat! I get this phone call that my daughter's been in some sort of accident, but you people won't tell me anything, and you expect me to have a seat?"

"What's your daughter's name, sir?"

"Taylor Johnston."

"I'll see what I can find out." The receptionist shut the glass window.

Robert Johnston started to pace in front of the waiting room entrance. Gabe glanced down at Moriah, who was staring at the man. He didn't know if she had made the connection yet or not. His father, on the other hand, did. John's worried gaze met Gabe's.

"Mrs. Miller? Here are the forms the doctor needs to you to sign."

Gabe hadn't even heard the nurse approach. He looked to see her handing Moriah a clipboard and a pen. Moriah barely scanned the documents, then signed her name and handed them back to the nurse.

"Thank you. Mr. Miller is being prepped for surgery, which is on the second floor. Just take the elevator down the hall, then turn left. There will be a receptionist in the waiting room area, just tell her who you're waiting for." The nurse placed her hand on Moriah's forearm. "We're doing all we can for your husband, Mrs. Miller."

"Thank you," Moriah whispered.

To his left, Gabe heard the glass window sliding open again. "Mr. Johnston?"

Mr. Johnston stopped pacing and strode up to the counter. "What have you found out?"

"Your daughter is going to be fine."

The man slumped against the window. "Thank God."

"The nurse said you could see her. I'll let you in."

The faint sound of a buzzer filled the air as a set of brown double doors opened near the entrance of the emergency room. Mr. Johnston disappeared through the doors, and they softly closed behind him.

"Gabriel," John said.

Turning, Gabe answered, "*Ya*?"

"We need to go upstairs. Moriah, are you ready?"

She nodded again. The color had seeped from her face, fear and confusion present in her blue eyes.

He followed her and his *daed* to the elevator. Once they arrived at the surgery waiting room, he told Moriah and his father to go sit down. "I'll let the woman know we're here."

After he gave the receptionist the information she needed, he turned to see his *daed* and Moriah seated next to each other, holding hands, both obviously deep in prayer. As he waited for them to finish, he walked over to a pale-blue wall. The décor of the room, from the comfortable chairs to the peaceful paintings of country scenery, were meant to invoke serenity, but inside Gabe felt anything but calm. He struggled to wrap his mind around what had happened. A car accident. Obviously Levi had been with Taylor. She would be okay, but Levi was struggling for his life. Of course he was glad that she hadn't been seriously injured . . . He needed to push her out of his mind. He had to think about Levi. He had to pray for his brother. Taking off his hat, he leaned his head against the wall, closed his eyes, and started to pray.

Moments later he felt the light touch of a hand on his arm. Opening his eyes, he looked down to see Moriah standing beside him.

"Are you okay?" Her luminous eyes, less haunted than when they had been in the emergency room, gazed up at him. Worry lines still etched her features, but she took the time to ask about his well-being. How could anyone expect him not to love such a caring woman?

"*Ya,*" he managed, slipping his black hat back on his head. "How are you doing?"

She shrugged. He noticed she hadn't moved her hand. He hoped she never would.

"Levi will make it, Gabriel," she said, her voice hitching slightly on the last word. "I have faith that he will."

Unable to stop himself, Gabe covered her hand with his own, drawing strength and comfort from her touch. "Then I have faith he will too."

Moriah touched her hand to her forehead, as if applying pressure would relieve the throbbing inside her head. Five hours had passed since they had first arrived at the hospital, and Levi was still in surgery. There had been no word about his condition, but she clung to her hope that he would pull through. She had spoken very little to Gabe and his father. All three of them had been mired in their own thoughts. She had never realized a hospital could be such a lonely place, even when you were surrounded by people. Even when you were with your family.

Finally, a doctor entered the waiting room, one she had never seen before. He wore a green short-sleeved shirt, green drawstring pants, and a white, brimless cap on his head. Striding to the reception area, he said a few words to the dark-skinned woman seated behind the desk who pointed toward Moriah. The doctor nodded, then walked over to her.

"Mrs. Miller? I'm Dr. Whitman. I'm the surgeon who operated on your husband."

Her chest tightened as she stood. "How is he?"

"I'm happy to say he's doing as well as can be expected. We believe the surgery to be a success. It was touch and go there for a while, but he's a strong young man."

Gabriel and John stood on each side of her. As the relief shot through her body, she felt limp, like a rag doll. "Can we see him now?" Gabriel asked as he put his arm around her shoulders.

Dr. Whitman shook his head. "He's in recovery right now. It will be a couple hours before we release him to intensive care. After two or three days we hope to transfer him to a regular floor. Once he's fully recovered, he'll be able to go home."

"Praise the Lord," John whispered. "Praise the Lord."

With a smile the doctor said, "This is the kind of news we enjoy giving. Feel free to go down to the cafeteria and grab some supper. Mr. Miller won't be in his room until around seven."

John reached out for the doctor's hand. "Thank you so much, Dr. Whitman." His voice was raspy with emotion. "Thank you, thank you."

"You're welcome. I'll go back and check on him. We can go over his progress in the morning." He nodded and left the waiting room.

Still feeling weak, Moriah leaned against Gabriel, grateful for his strong support. Levi made it. She vowed not to leave his side until he was well enough to come home. Their home. Surely he would realize that he didn't belong in the Yankees' world. He belonged with his family. With her and their child.

"I don't ever want to see this room again," John said, wiping his eyes with the back of his hand. He grinned. "Let's go get something to eat. Suddenly, I'm starving!"

Gabriel smiled in response. "Me too." Then he removed his arm from her shoulders and looked at her.

"You were right," he said softly. "He's gonna be okay."

"Thanks to God," Moriah said. "All thanks be to God."

Chapter 10

Moriah felt the touch of a hand on her shoulder. Her eyes flickered open. She shifted her body in the green vinyl-backed chair and lazily looked up. Gabriel was standing next to her, gazing down with concern. When she fully awakened, she jolted upright, remembering where she was. Levi's intensive care room. "Is he awake?"

"*Nee.*" Gabriel dropped his hand. "The nurse said he was up a little while ago."

"Why didn't they wake me?" she said, dismayed.

"He wasn't conscious for very long. Besides, they knew you needed the rest. I'm glad they let you sleep."

She rose from her chair and smoothed her white apron. The fabric was wrinkled, as was her light-green dress. The rest of her was probably a mess too. "What time is it?"

"Almost five a.m. There's a visitors' waiting room down the hall. *Daed* is asleep on the couch in there. I wanted to check and see how you were doing. And Levi."

Moriah looked down at her husband as he lay on the hospital bed. Wires, endless wires were attached to his body, which in turn were connected to blinking, illuminated machines and dangling bags of fluid and blood. He lay flat on his back, a white sheet draped over his lower body. She touched her mouth with her fingertips, trying to stem the tirade of sorrow and pity that coursed through her. His face was almost unrecognizable from the swelling around his eyes and mouth. A bandage encircled his head, covering his brow. The nurses had assured her that he wasn't in pain; the medication pump ensured that. But she didn't see how.

No one had any concrete details about the accident, but she didn't really care right now. Her complete focus was on being there for her husband. If she had failed him before, she refused to fail him now, especially when he needed her so much.

"Are you hungry?" Gabriel asked. "We can go downstairs and get some breakfast."

"I don't want to leave him."

"Moriah, he couldn't be in better hands. Nothing will happen to him." He moved to stand alongside her. "You've been in here all night. You need to take a break."

She watched Levi for a moment, not moving until she detected the slight rise and fall of his chest. Gabriel was right, of course. The nurses and doctors wouldn't let anything happen to Levi. Turning, she nodded. "Let me freshen up first."

"I'll meet you in the waiting room." Gabriel took one more look at his brother, then left.

Levi's arms lay limply against his sides. She slipped her hand in his and squeezed. "I'll be right back," she whispered, then reluctantly let go. Exiting his small room, she made her way to the restroom, which was just around the corner. Once she was inside the single washroom, she closed the door, then locked it.

Facing the mirror, she sighed at her reflection. Her *kapp* was askew, and there were dark circles under eyes. The inside of her mouth felt pasty, and her shoulders ached. Reaching up, she pulled the bobby pins from her *kapp* and placed it on the side of the sink. She smoothed her hair the best she could, then replaced her *kapp*, tucking the ribbons inside the front bodice of her dress. After splashing her cheeks with cold water, she felt a little better, and more fully awake.

After breakfast she would call her mother and let her know how Levi was faring. Her father had a cell phone in the woodshop, which he used only for business purposes. However, Moriah doubted he would mind if she called. She'd also see if maybe Elisabeth or one of her brothers could hire a taxi and bring her a fresh change of clothes. With Ruth being sick, she didn't want her mother to have to make the trip, and she had no idea how long she would be at the hospital with Levi. Not that the time mattered to her. She wasn't leaving him until he was able to come home. Everything that had happened between them—his rejection of her and his faith—none of that mattered now. Not only had she already forgiven him, she would forget. They had a second chance now, a new opportunity to work on their marriage, and soon a new baby to love and cherish. Glancing at the mirror one last time, she smiled. For the first time in what seemed like forever, she had something to look forward to.

Gabe rocked back and forth on his heels and slipped his hands in his pockets as he waited for Moriah. He considered waking his father, then decided against it. Neither of them had slept much in the waiting room. It wouldn't hurt to let his *daed* get more rest. He'd bring him a muffin and coffee from the cafeteria when they came back.

The hallway was empty, save for the one stocky nurse wearing bright-pink pants and a multicolored top who passed by. He thought about how exhausted Moriah had looked when he had awakened her, and naturally, he was concerned. But he knew she was relieved that Levi would be okay; they were all happy about that.

But what did Moriah think would happen after his brother healed? Gabe wondered if he would come back to Middlefield. His girlfriend, Taylor, hadn't shown up to ask about him. Granted she had been in the accident, but from the emergency room receptionist's account, she was going to be okay. If she loved him, wouldn't she be there for him? Like Moriah was now?

He sighed and leaned against the wall. If anything this should show Levi where his responsibility, and his life, truly was. In Middlefield, with the Amish, with his family. Gabe believed his brother and Moriah could work things out, especially knowing Moriah's forgiving and tender nature. Hopefully his brother wouldn't be so stupid this time.

The outer doors to the intensive care unit opened, and Moriah stepped out. Gabe's breath hitched, as it always did when he saw her. She had straightened up her *kapp*, and her cheeks held a rosy glow, one he hadn't seen since before Levi left. Heavens, she was beautiful, even after all she'd been through.

He suddenly had second thoughts about not asking his *daed* to join them. Being alone with Moriah, even in a public place, wasn't a great idea right now.

But he restrained his reaction and the feelings accompanying it. He buried them deep down, further than he ever had before, keeping his injured brother at the forefront of his mind. "Ready?" he asked, glad for the noncommittal tone of his voice.

"*Ya.* I am hungry. Or should I say *mei boppli* is. I'm eating for two after all." She gave him a sweet smile.

And, despite everything he tried to do to prevent it, he smiled back.

"That hit the spot."

Moriah watched as Gabriel leaned back in his chair, his hands clasped over his flat stomach, covering the bottom part of the straps of his suspenders.

"I should hope so," she said good-naturedly, eyeing the remnants of the huge meal he'd consumed—scrambled eggs, bacon, sausage links, fried potatoes, a biscuit, and two cups of coffee. Her breakfast of maple-and-brown-sugar oatmeal paled in comparison.

"Sure you don't want anything else?" he said. "The food here isn't half-bad. Not like your cooking, of course."

She blushed. "*Danki.* I enjoy cooking."

"I enjoy eating what you cook." He straightened, suddenly appearing flustered. "I mean, I enjoyed what you used to cook . . . before Levi—oh forget it, you know what I mean."

"I do." She smiled. "I'm looking forward to cooking for you all again."

"I hope that's exactly what happens."

"You hope?" Moriah looked at him, uncertainty puncturing her bubble of hope. "You don't think he's coming back?"

He held up his hand. "*Nee, nee.* That's not what I meant. Only that it will take time for him to heal."

She paused before responding, looking at him for a long moment. While his words said one thing, the doubt flickering in his eyes said another. But she wouldn't let Gabriel's reservations about Levi distract her from making sure that her husband and her marriage were fully restored. "We should get back," she said, pushing away from the table.

"*Ya.*"

"I need to call *Mami* first. She'll want to know how Levi is faring. I also need some clothes, and Levi will probably want some of his things too once he's feeling better."

"I tell you what," Gabriel said, rising from his chair. He picked up the small Styrofoam container that held a blueberry muffin for John. "Don't worry about calling your *mudder*. I'll take a taxi back to Middlefield and visit her myself. Let me know what you need and what I should bring for Levi, and I'll make sure it's done."

"You don't have to do that—"

"Moriah, I don't mind. I have to head back and check on the shop anyway. I left Aaron in charge. I'm sure everything's fine, but he hasn't worked for us very long, so I need to check up on him."

"All right," she said as they walked out of the cafeteria together. A sense of eagerness enveloped her at the thought of seeing Levi again. Maybe he would be awake by the time they got back. If not, then surely he would be sometime today. She wanted to be there when it happened.

They exited the elevator on the second floor and walked down the hallway to the intensive care unit. When they stopped by the waiting room, it was empty. "*Daed* must be with Levi," Gabriel said. Turning the corner, he pressed a large silver disk, which opened the ICU's double doors. They stepped into the unit and walked to Levi's room.

Moriah's breath caught when she looked through the glass that formed one wall of Levi's room. John was seated beside Levi, holding his hand . . . and Levi's eyes were open. Tears clouded her vision, and she barely saw John motion for her and Gabriel to come in.

Once inside, John gestured for Moriah to sit in his chair. She did so, then stared at her husband. She almost couldn't believe he was finally awake. Filled with gratitude, she couldn't speak.

"Hi," he said, his voice barely audible.

"Oh, Levi." She took his hand and held it. He didn't squeeze back, but she didn't care. The tears fell down her cheeks.

"Moriah . . . please." He looked at her, his eyes barely open due to the bruising. "Don't."

"I'm sorry." She briskly wiped at her cheeks and smiled.

"That's better." He turned his gaze from hers and looked at Gabriel. "Glad you're here."

Moriah glanced over her shoulder at Gabriel, who was swallowing hard. He moved to the opposite side of the bed so that they surrounded Levi.

"Don't try to talk too much," she said to him. "There's plenty of time for that."

Levi shook his head slightly, and she could see it took a lot of effort for him to do so. "Moriah, I want you to know . . . I'm sorry."

She grasped his hand in both of hers, then kissed his scratched up knuckles. "It's all right, Levi."

"*Nee*, it's not. I don't deserve you. I never did."

"Don't say things like that."

He closed his eyes and didn't respond.

A moment later John said, "I think he's fallen asleep again." He put his hand on Moriah's shoulder. "We should let him rest."

She nodded, then rose from her chair. Taking one last look at her husband, she said, "Don't worry, Levi. I'll be back." Then she turned and John led her out of the room.

Gabe lingered behind. He shook his head as he watched Moriah leave. Despite everything Levi had put her through, she was still tender with him, reassuring him that she would come back. Gabe marveled at her once again.

"Gabe?"

He looked down at Levi, surprised to see him awake again and his gaze intense. That had to be a good sign. "*Ya, bruder*?"

"Promise me something." Levi licked his dry lips.

Bending down closer so he could hear his brother's weak voice, he said, "Anything, Levi. Whatever you want me to do."

Levi's eyes drooped. "Take care of her . . . Take care of Moriah."

Gabe started to respond but saw that Levi had drifted off to sleep once again. Of course he would take care of Moriah. He would as much as she would allow—or as much as Levi would allow after he came back home.

Turning, he left Levi and went to the waiting room, not wanting to disturb his brother. Moriah and his father were seated on the couch, their expressions more peaceful than he had seen in a long time. He expelled a long breath. Everything would be okay. He truly believed that.

"Have a seat, *sohn*," John said, gesturing to the chair opposite the cushioned sofa. "How's Levi?"

Gabe lowered himself into the plush, light-green upholstered seat. "He fell asleep again."

"Not surprised. He's been through a lot, but he's on the mend now." Reaching toward Moriah, John patted her hand, and she smiled in return.

Closing his eyes, Gabe settled back in the chair. It was pretty comfortable, and he suddenly became drowsy. He'd catch a short nap, then make arrangements to go back to Middlefield. He wondered how Aaron was doing at the shop. Hopefully they hadn't had too much business.

"Mrs. Miller?"

Gabe's eyes flew open at the sound of a male voice. He looked up through sleepy eyes to see a doctor, this one unfamiliar to him. The troubled expression on the man's face made Gabe bolt upright.

"Yes?" Moriah said, rising from the couch.

She also looked sleepy, and Gabe assumed she had taken a nap while he had been asleep. He glanced up at the clock on the wall. A little over an hour had passed since he'd left Levi.

The doctor walked into the room. He seemed younger than the surgeon who had operated on Levi. Adjusting his rimless glasses on the bridge of his nose, he cleared his throat. "I'm sorry, Mrs. Miller."

"Sorry?" Moriah's voice cracked. "Sorry for what?"

"We did all we could."

A metallic taste coated Gabe's mouth. What was he talking about?

"We're not sure what happened, but we suspect a clot went to his lung." The doctor paused to give her time to absorb what he'd said. "This isn't something we can predict, or plan for. Sometimes it just happens. I'm truly sorry for your loss."

"My loss?" Moriah raised her hands to her lips. "He's gone? Levi's gone?"

"Moriah," John's voice, filled with grief, reached Gabe's ears.

"*Nee, nee.* He can't be gone. He was fine; that other doctor said so. I just saw him!" She turned an accusing glare at Gabe. "You said he was asleep!"

His legs started to shake. "He was when I left." He faced the doctor, the full meaning of the situation hitting him like a steel rod to his gut. "He was fine when I left."

"Mr. Miller, it happened so suddenly, only moments ago. I don't know what else to tell you. Your brother is gone."

His body felt numb. Levi, dead? It wasn't possible. Yet one look at the doctor's expression confirmed the truth.

"*Nee,*" Moriah moaned. She walked to the glass window and put her hand on it. Sobs wracked her body. "He can't be gone. Not when I finally have him back."

Gabe, consumed with his own pain, came up behind her and wrapped his arms around her. She turned and leaned her head against his shoulder, her tears wetting his shirt, her body shaking against his. Unable to control his own grief, he pulled her tightly against him, and they both cried in each other's arms.

Chapter 11

"Gabe, you don't have to do this." Tobias put his hand on Gabe's shoulder. "The fellas and I will handle it."

"I know you will. Let me help you anyway."

Tobias shrugged, sorrow reflected in his blue eyes. He handed Gabe a shovel, then stepped back.

Gabe choked back his tears as he thrust his shovel into the nearby pile of dirt that had been dug out of the ground the day before. He tossed the first heap of soil onto his brother's grave.

The funeral service had ended a short time ago, and everyone but four of Levi's friends, who had served as pallbearers along with Tobias and Luke, had left for the house. The six men had stayed behind to bury Levi. The Byler family was at his house, preparing refreshments for anyone who wanted to pay their respects. John and Moriah had gone back with them, but Gabe had chosen to stay and help finish the burial.

The men worked quickly—too quickly for Gabe's liking. When the last shovelful of dirt was tamped down across Levi's grave, Gabe experienced pain so wrenching it threatened to double him over. He knelt beside the fresh soil. His brother, his twin—gone forever.

Regrets flooded over him. He had given up on Levi too easily. He should have gone out to Gates Mills more often, worked harder to convince him to come home. Instead he had written him off, letting his anger over his treatment of Moriah supercede everything else.

Now there was nothing he could do. There was no turning back time, no making up for mistakes. Levi was gone, and a part of Gabe had gone with him.

"We're heading back to your house," Tobias said, hunkering down next to Gabe. "Take your time. I'll tell them you'll be along in a bit."

He turned to Moriah's brother and nodded. "*Danki,*" he said, his voice sounding gravelly and strange.

Alone at the graveside, Gabe looked at the small, square headstones on all the graves in the cemetery. Each one was the same size and shape, plain and unadorned. Just like Levi's would be. Details of the accident had slowly surfaced in the aftermath of Levi's death, and over the past three days, their family had been able to piece together what had happened. Taylor had been driving her fancy sports car, with Levi in the passenger seat. They had been sideswiped by a semitruck and sent careening across the berm into oncoming traffic, with Levi receiving the bulk of the injuries. While the surgery had initially been a success, he had indeed died from a blood clot.

Gabe dug his hands into the earth and squeezed. At least when Levi had been with the Yankees, there was always the slim hope they would see him again. Now that hope was gone. Yet even through his grief, he couldn't be angry with God. Levi had made his choices, just as Gabe had made the decision to write off his brother. He couldn't blame God for the mistakes they had both made. He could only try to find a way to heal from them.

The one thing he could take comfort from was that during the breakfast he had shared with Moriah in the hospital, Levi had spoken to their father and asked him for forgiveness, explaining he wanted to come back to the church. Although Levi hadn't repented publicly in the church, under the circumstances the bishop and ministers had accepted that as repentance. Levi would be with his people from now on.

He let the dirt sift through his fingers as he stared at the small, plain, square concrete marker that poked out of the ground. Through the blur of his tears he remembered the last words Levi said to him. "I promise, *bruder*," Gabe croaked. "I promise I will spend the rest of my life taking care of Moriah." He stood, then slowly made his way to his buggy and climbed inside. Taking one last look at Levi's final resting place, he chirruped to his horse and headed back home.

Moriah instantly came to his mind, and he wondered how he could possibly keep the promise he had made. She had just lost her husband—twice. No one would expect her to turn around and accept someone else, especially her former brother-in-law.

But he had given his brother his word, and he would honor it. He had always stood by a promise, and firmly believed that a man should stand by what he says. Gabe would see to it that Moriah and her child would be cared for. He would do everything in his power to make that happen.

He pulled into the front of his house, and took in the numerous buggies that filled the driveway and spilled out onto the yard. He'd have to park close to his neighbor's house, but he didn't care. He took comfort in the support the community offered Moriah and his father. They would need it. They would all need it.

"*Danki.* Thanks for coming." Moriah said. She'd repeated those words so many times they reverberated in her head. Her body and mind both felt numb. Eventually she would appreciate the outpouring of support from everyone, but right now she just wanted to be alone.

"You've been on your feet all day." Her mother came up beside her and put her arm around her shoulders. "I know you're exhausted, so don't try to tell me that you're not. Have you eaten anything?"

"*Nee.*"

The low hum of the conversation dropped as the front door opened. Gabe entered, his complexion gray, his eyes red. He was the last to arrive, and she suspected he had spent some time alone at Levi's grave. She'd heard the twin bond was stronger than that between other siblings. If Gabe's visage was any indication, it was true.

Their gazes met as he made his way across the room. He thanked several people along the way as they gave him their sympathies, but he kept moving toward Moriah and didn't stop until he was right in front of her.

"I'll go check on the sandwiches," Emma said, stepping to the side. "Sarah said she was going to make some more. She could probably use the help. And please, try to eat something."

"I will."

When Emma disappeared, Gabe asked, "How are you holding up?"

Moriah shrugged. "Best I can. You?"

"Same thing. Have you seen *Daed*?"

"He's in the *dawdi haus* with some of his friends. The company started to overwhelm him, I think."

"I should go see how he is." But Gabe didn't move. Instead, he looked at her, biting his bottom lip. "I don't want to leave you alone, but I need to check on *Daed*."

She offered him a weak smile. "Gabriel, this house is full of people. I'm hardly alone."

He looked sheepish. "Right. Didn't think about that." He gave her one last look, then turned and headed to see his father.

Moriah scanned the room, taking in all the friends and family who were giving their support. But despite their presence, despite reassuring Gabriel that he wasn't deserting her, she had been wrong. She'd never felt more alone in her life.

Gabe sat in the old handhewn rocker his grandfather had made over fifty years ago, watching the glowing coals of the woodstove. The sun had set hours ago, but he couldn't sleep. He had decided to stay in the *dawdi haus* with his father, who'd retired soon after their company had left. He remained partly to keep an eye on *Daed*, and partly because he couldn't bear to stay alone in the main house.

Now he rocked in the chair, trying to settle the turmoil inside him. Memories of his brother continually surfaced in his mind. He remembered the tire swing their father had hung on the huge oak tree in their backyard. Every fall he and Levi would rake the leaves into a big pile and then compete to see who could swing higher before letting go and landing in the soft, musty leaves. He could still see the look of triumph on Levi's face every time he won. The memory brought a fresh wave of pain, added another layer of regret.

How was he supposed to survive this?

The sound of his father's shuffling footsteps caused him to sit up straight. He wiped his wet eyes with his hand as John entered the room.

"You shouldn't be sitting here in the dark, Gabriel." He turned on the gas lamp.

"And you should be resting." Gabe shot up from his chair and went to his father, who waved him off.

"I've been resting." John lowered himself onto the couch, then patted the seat next to him. "Let's talk. We haven't done that in quite awhile."

Gabe sat next to him, then leaned forward and rested his elbows on his knees, letting his loosely clasped hands dangle between them. He tilted his head and looked at his father. "You surprise me," he admitted.

"How so?"

"The way you're handling all of this. I remember when Levi left . . . how hard it was on you."

"This is hard too, Gabriel. Very hard. My son died. I won't see him until I get to heaven, God willing. But even though it breaks my heart, I can find some peace in that." He looked at Gabe intently. "When Levi left, he turned his back on the church. That burden was almost too great to bear."

"But you did."

"I only seemed to. You can't live stewing in grief forever. I learned that when your *mami* died. A person's got to move on, live his life following God's lead. But that didn't mean I didn't spend every night on my knees praying for my boy."

Gabe stared down at the polished wood floor. "I should have done that. I should have done more."

John patted him on the back. "Don't let regrets tear you up inside, Gabriel. Levi wouldn't want that."

Lifting his head, Gabe said, "No, he wouldn't."

"Keep remembering that Levi came back to God. I have no doubt he would have come back to us too."

"How can you be so sure he came back to God?"

"Because of what he said. He asked my forgiveness—our forgiveness. He had already been forgiven by the Lord. I truly believe that."

To his surprise, Gabe did find comfort in his father's words. To know that his brother had made things right with the Lord brought a semblance of peace to his soul.

"There's something else troubling you," John said.

Gabe's head jerked in his father's direction. "How did you know?"

"Most of the time you're hard to read, but tonight you're an open book. Levi said something to you. Is that what's bothering you?"

"*Ya.*" Gabe sat back and settled himself more firmly on the couch. "He asked me to take care of Moriah and the baby. But I don't understand why."

"Probably because he knows you're the best man for her."

Gabe sat forward, gaping at John. "What do you mean?"

"I know you love her. I suspect Levi knew that too. And for some reason you've chosen to keep that a secret from her."

"She was in love with my brother, *Daed*. And I thought he loved her. I didn't want to cause any trouble for them."

"But what about you? Did you plan to spend the rest of your life pining for your brother's wife?"

"Of course not! I would have found someone else . . . eventually." But he knew the words were a lie. He had never wanted to be with anyone else. "That doesn't matter now. I promised Levi I'd be there for Moriah, but I don't know how that's possible."

"Why not?"

His father must have lost his mind. "*Daed,* she's newly widowed. She was married to my brother, who is my identical twin. I'll just be a reminder of what she's lost."

"Then you'll just have to convince her otherwise." John yawned. "Pray about it, Gabriel. With God, anything is possible. Even what seems impossible." He stood. "I'm more worn out than I thought. I'm going to bed, and I suggest you do the same."

Gabe nodded. He waited a little while longer after John left before heading to his room. He stripped down to his long johns and climbed into bed, sliding between the cold sheets. Both his father and his brother had known about his feelings for Moriah. So much for keeping them hidden. Suddenly, a thought occurred to him, causing him to sit upright.

Did Moriah know?

He panicked for a moment, then calmed down. She couldn't possibly know how he felt. If she did he would have known, or at least sensed it. She would have kept her distance from him, something he continually failed to do.

Lying back down, he decided to take his *daed*'s advice and pray about it. He couldn't fulfill his promise to Levi without some divine intervention.

Chapter 12

Moriah perused the bolts of soft pastel fabric neatly lined up in rows in her cousin's fabric store. She had decided to make a baby quilt, even though she had done little quilting before. Her sewing consisted of making clothing, mostly her own and baby clothes.

After selecting a combination of pale blue, green, and yellow, she picked up a couple spools of thread and a packet of needles, then went to the front of the store to check out. The store was empty this afternoon, and her cousin Mary was sitting behind the cutting table engrossed in a book.

"Find what you need?" Mary set her book down and picked up a pair of shears from a box near the table.

Moriah set the bolts of fabric down. "*Ya.* I need a yard of each."

"Okay." Mary took the fabric and started to measure it out, talking as she worked. "How have you been doing?"

"I'm all right. Keep myself busy."

"I've been meaning to get over to see you," Mary said, not looking up. She slid the sharp scissors down the width of the blue fabric, separating it from the bolt. "I'm sorry, but things have been real hectic here lately." A flush appeared on her face as she glanced at Moriah. "Except for today. For some reason it's really slow. Could be because it's a nice summer day. June is always one of the best months, I think."

Moriah nodded. "That's all right. You can stop by anytime." She'd had few visitors since Levi's death almost a month ago. At first that had been fine with her; she had appreciated the time alone. But now she wished for some company other than her immediate family. And of course Gabriel. He had been paying visits to her on a regular basis. She assured him everything was all right with the baby, but he still insisted on visiting every other day. She wasn't sure what to make of that.

"*Danki,*" Mary said, putting the last yard of cloth in a white plastic bag. "I will."

Once outside, she put her bag in the buggy and began to step inside when a sharp pain zigzagged across her abdomen. Instinctively she put her hand on her stomach, and the spasm soon subsided. The door to the shop behind her opened, and Mary came rushing to her side.

"Are you all right? I saw you through the window. What happened?"

Moriah straightened, expecting to feel another spiky twinge and was relieved when she didn't. "I don't know," she said. "I just had this sudden pain, and now it's gone."

Mary's expression relaxed. "I wouldn't worry about it too much. I got those with my children every once in a while. But if it keeps happening, make sure you let someone know. Are you using a midwife?"

"*Ya.*"

"Next time you see her you might want to mention it. Now, go on home, have some tea, and unwind."

"*Danki*. I'll do that."

As she headed home, Moriah tried to stem her worry. Despite her cousin's reassurances, she couldn't help but be concerned. Her baby was everything to her. She couldn't bear if something happened to her child. Not when she had lost everything else.

Rachel plopped down on her bed and opened one of the new books she'd purchased from the gift shop at the restaurant. She didn't read many novels, but this one looked kind of interesting and featured Amish characters. And a romance. "Might as well get some romance somewhere," she mumbled as she turned to the first chapter. "It's not like I've got any in my life." If she was lucky, she might also learn a thing or two.

Very little time elapsed before she put the book down. Her mind had wandered too much, and she'd ended up reading the second page three times, only to realize she still didn't know what it was about. Shoving the book aside, she flipped over and lay on her stomach, resting her chin on top of her clasped hands. An unsettled feeling came over her.

Christian had been gone about two months now. The Monday after the buggy incident with Tobias, he'd called the restaurant using a neighbor's phone and told her he decided to stay in Charm for a couple more weeks and work on his aunt's farm. He wasn't any more specific than that about his return. Even though he had written her a couple of very brief letters, she felt their relationship was spinning in circles again. How were they ever going to get to know each other better if they spent all of their time apart?

She hated to admit that a part of her was glad he hadn't come back right away. She wasn't sure how she was going to face him after kissing Tobias.

But it was only one teeny, tiny kiss, and that's all it would ever be. Never mind that it was a kiss she still relived in her mind, nearly every night in her dreams.

A glance at the clock told her it was 1:00 p.m. Yesterday she and her mother had tended both the flower and the vegetable garden, and the lawn didn't need mowing or edging either. The day was too nice to spend inside. Scrambling off her bed, she fixed her *kapp* and straightened the white ribbons. She had to find something productive to do or she'd go crazy.

As she made her way downstairs, a thought occurred to her. She would visit Moriah Miller. She hadn't seen her since Levi had passed away a few weeks ago. What a tragedy. The circumstances surrounding his death had been so sad; her heart had gone out to Moriah.

A stab of guilt pricked at her. She should have visited Moriah long before now. Although their mothers were close friends, she and Moriah had never been. During visits to the Bylers', Rachel often played outside with Tobias and his brothers, while Moriah had preferred to be inside with her mother.

The thought that Tobias might be there, and that she might run into him, crossed her mind, but she shoved it out of the way. She wasn't going there to see him; she was lending her support to Moriah. But if she did happen to catch a glimpse of him . . .

Good grief, she was hopeless.

She rushed downstairs and headed for the kitchen. Warm summer sunlight streamed through the open window, illuminating the kitchen. Rachel enjoyed the warmer months of the year. They used the gas lamps and woodstoves less, and the windows were wide open, letting in fresh air. Her mother sat at the kitchen table, sorting through index cards of recipes.

"Where are you off to?" Sarah asked, examining a dog-eared card.

"I thought I'd visit Moriah Miller today."

Sarah put the card down and smiled. "I think that's a wonderful idea. I know Emma's been worried about her." She clucked her tongue. "Poor thing. She's such a sweet girl, and has been through so much."

Rachel nodded. "I won't be gone long, just a couple of hours."

Sarah picked up another card. "Let her know my prayers are with her."

"I will."

Half an hour later Rachel pulled her buggy into the Bylers' driveway. As she maneuvered her horse to the parking area next to the woodshop, she saw Emma leaving her house.

"Hello, Rachel!" Emma walked down the porch steps and met Rachel at her buggy. "What brings you by?"

"I came to visit Moriah. Is she home?"

"Oh, you just missed her. She's at the Millers'." Her expression sobered. "She said something about cleaning their house and making some meals for Gabriel and John. I tried to talk her out of it."

"Why?"

"She's been working hard lately, especially since Levi's death." Emma crossed her thin arms over her chest and sighed. "I don't want to see anything happen to her or the *boppli*."

"I'll be glad to help her, *Frau* Byler."

"That would be wonderful, Rachel. I'm sure she wouldn't mind if you stop over there for a bit. In fact, I think she'd be delighted."

"*Danki.* I'll do that."

A little while later she arrived at the Millers', eager to help Moriah. After tethering her horse, she caught sight of her brother emptying a barrel of trash into a small dumpster behind the shop. If she had seen him infrequently before he had started working for Gabriel, now she saw him even less. He left before she awakened, and always went to the job on foot, which was a good three-mile walk. So far he'd managed to keep the job for a couple months, something he never would have been able to do when he was using drugs.

Still, despite this positive aspect of his life, she felt more disconnected from him than ever. He was more reticent lately. Before his arrest, he and their father had shouting matches, with Aaron's anger verging on physical violence. Yet since his return he had been a model son, albeit a nearly silent one. She'd considered talking to him once, not just words in passing but a real conversation. But Aaron was even less approachable now than he'd been when he first came home, and she wasn't sure what she should say to him. So she didn't say anything.

As if he sensed someone watching him, Aaron glanced at her over his shoulder. He gave her an imperceptible nod, as if she were no more familiar than a stranger, and went back in the shop.

His emotional distance stung. Suddenly, an overwhelming sense of rejection consumed her. Everyone wanted to keep their distance from her—her brother, Christian, even Tobias had been cursorily polite to her the few times she had seen him. What was wrong with her? "Rachel? Is that you?"

At the sound of Moriah's voice, she swallowed her pain. Angling her body a quarter turn, she saw Moriah standing on the front porch several feet from the shop. Mustering up what she hoped was a decent smile, Rachel waved to her. "Hi!" she said, a little too brightly.

Moriah didn't seem to notice. "Are you here to see your brother?"

"*Nee.* Actually, I came to see you."

Moriah's face lit up. "Then come on in. I just made some tea."

"Sounds great." Rachel gave her a real smile this time, Moriah's warm welcome chasing away some of the despair she'd felt a moment earlier.

Moriah held the door open for her, and Rachel walked in. "Come on back to the kitchen. We can visit in there."

Rachel had never been inside the Millers' house before. There had never really been an opportunity, as Gabriel and Levi's parents had been much older than her own folks, and she hadn't spoken too much to the twins while they were growing up. She took in the tidy front room, with its sparse furnishings and small wood fireplace. She noticed the Millers still had a woodstove. Her own family had purchased a propane stove a couple years ago, when the church leaders had agreed to allow some propane-powered appliances in the home.

Following Moriah to the back of the house, she inhaled the scent of chicken stew cooking on the stove. "Smells wonderful," Rachel said.

"Would you like some?"

"*Nee,* I'm not really hungry. But *danki* for offering."

"I thought I'd surprise Gabriel and John when they come in

from work. I'm sure they're getting tired of casseroles all the time." Moriah retrieved two mugs from a kitchen cabinet, then lifted the tea kettle off the woodstove and poured the hot amber liquid into the cups.

"That's thoughtful of you. I'm sure they'll appreciate it."

Rachel accepted her mug of tea but didn't drink it right away. Instead she sat down at the kitchen table and observed Moriah, who was rolling out biscuit dough on the floured countertop. The rolling pin suddenly slipped out of her hands, hit the floor, and rolled underneath the table.

"I got it." Rachel bent down and retrieved the rolling pin. As she went to the sink to wash it, she saw Moriah rub her temple with her fingertips. "Are you okay?"

Moriah nodded and handed Rachel a clean, dry towel. "*Ya.* I'm fine. *Danki* for washing that."

"You're welcome." Rachel saw dark circles of fatigue underneath Moriah's eyes. Now she understood why Emma was concerned. "How about if I finish up the biscuits?"

"*Nee,* I can do them." She took the rolling pin from Rachel and applied the wood cylinder to the dough. "I'm almost done anyway."

"Is there anything else I can do to help?"

Moriah shook her head, then turned and gestured toward the kitchen table. "Please, enjoy your tea."

Rachel hesitated, but then finally sat down. She sipped the lemon-flavored tea, which had cooled to the perfect temperature. But before long an odd uneasiness came over her. In the past, though their conversations were infrequent, she and Moriah would talk about their siblings or funny things that happened to them during their families' visits together. Yet so much had happened this past year, especially to Moriah, that for the first time, she didn't know what to say.

Moriah seemed engrossed in cutting out biscuits and averse to accepting help. She also didn't seem interested in making conversation. Rachel watched as Moriah wiped her brow with the back of her hand, her fatigue even more noticeable now. She should offer to help again, but it was common knowledge that Rachel wasn't a very good cook—unlike Moriah, who could make a delicious meal out of the most sparse of ingredients.

Moriah had also experienced things Rachel hadn't—marriage, pregnancy, and unfortunately, the death of her husband. Should she bring up any of those subjects? One thing she didn't want to do was discuss Tobias, especially with his sister.

After a few more minutes of silence, Moriah turned. "How is your tea?"

"Delicious." Rachel could detect the sadness in Moriah's eyes, coupled with loneliness. Rachel couldn't imagine the turmoil churning inside the young woman. She also felt powerless to help her.

Moriah gave her a small smile, then turned to place the last biscuit on a metal cookie sheet. She opened the hot oven and put the biscuits inside. As she closed the oven door she said, "From what I gather your brother has been a big help to Gabriel and John in the shop. He's a really hard worker."

Rachel frowned slightly. Not exactly who she wanted to talk about, but at this point she was glad to talk about anything. She lifted her tea and took a sip then set it down again. "He seems to have straightened himself out."

"I don't know what they would do without him," Moriah added. "Since Levi . . ." A shadow passed over her face, but she quickly smiled again to cover it before turning around to wash her hands in the sink. "I have noticed that he doesn't say much, though. He seems to like to keep to himself."

"No kidding," Rachel muttered. Then she looked at Moriah. "Don't get me wrong. I'm glad you're all happy with him. I just hope he doesn't go back to his old ways."

"Why do you think he would?"

Rachel shrugged, cupping her hands around her mug.

"Do you think he will fail?"

Rachel's eyes widened. "I hope not. But Aaron was a drug addict and he spent time in jail. I'm just saying that it's easy to fall back into old habits. But I didn't say I wanted him to fail."

"I'm sorry, Rachel. I didn't mean to upset you."

With a sigh, Rachel said, "No, I'm sorry. I shouldn't be so sensitive. And I shouldn't have said that about Aaron. I know he's been trying really hard to change his life." She shook the coffee mug, swirling the liquid inside. "To tell you the truth, I don't know what's going on with him. We haven't talked much since he came home. Actually, we haven't talked at all. Sorry, I don't mean to complain."

Moriah stretched her arm across the table and covered Rachel's hand with her own. "That's all right, I don't mind hearing about it. Trust me, we all have our problems."

Guilt churned within Rachel. Her own problems were petty compared to how Moriah had suffered.

Moriah squeezed her hand. "I'll pray for you, Rachel. And for Aaron."

Rachel glanced down at their hands. When was the last time she had prayed for her brother? She couldn't remember. And perhaps that was part of the problem. Lately she had focused all of her prayers on her own concerns—her doubts about Christian, her mixed-up feelings about Tobias. She silently vowed to put Aaron at the top of her prayer list from now on.

"*Danki,*" Rachel said. "I appreciate you praying for him."

"I'm glad to do it. I haven't been praying much at all lately, and you've reminded me how important it is to keep up that personal communion with God." She removed her hand and sat back in the chair. "I'm really glad you came today."

"Me too." Rachel grinned, then sniffed the air. Her stomach growled. "Maybe I'll have some of that chicken stew after all."

With a long pair of tongs, Gabe removed a red-hot horseshoe from the burning forge and set it aside to cool. Some smiths plunged their hot shoes into cold water, but that made the iron brittle and would require a horse to be shoed more often. John had preferred to let his shoes cool on their own, and Gabe had always followed suit. He only cooled off metal by dunking when he made decorative ironwork. His forehead dripping from the heat of the forge and scorching metal, he wiped the sweat off his brow with the back of his gloved hand, knowing he had probably smeared black soot all over his forehead.

While the metal cooled, Gabe tallied how many more shoes he had to make before the day was up. Nineteen. Tomorrow he needed to spend the day applying those shoes to several horses. While he was busy cleaning out hooves and filing the shoes so they would fit snugly, Aaron would work on making a simple iron sconce. Since his father had decided to add fancy ironwork, such as sconces and lantern hangers, to their inventory last year, he and Gabe had taught Aaron how to make a couple of plain styles. He turned out to be a quick study.

Turning around to grab another metal bar, he saw Aaron across the shop, struggling to pick up a heavy load of rods. As was the young man's way, he never asked for help, but this time Gabe could see he really needed it. Putting his iron down, Gabe passed by John, who was filing the rough edges of one of the shoes, and went to assist Aaron.

"Thanks," Aaron said in his trademark quiet tone once they'd moved the rods.

"No problem. Don't be afraid to ask for help, Aaron. You don't have to carry the load yourself."

Aaron nodded in return, but didn't say anything, merely went back to work. Gabe watched him for a moment, wondering what was going on inside the kid's head. He'd been a mystery ever since he'd hired him. But he couldn't complain about Aaron's work ethic at all—sometimes he worked harder than Levi ever had. Then again, they had all been working extra hard since Levi's death. Keeping busy helped stave off a bit of the grief.

One thing he could say for Aaron, he was a thorough employee. He'd been able to find the file that was missing off the pegboard, although he didn't tell Gabe where he'd found it. He just put it back on its peg and went back to work. Gabe didn't care, as long as he had his tool back.

Suddenly the sound of a loud crash caused Gabe to spin around. John, who had moved over by the forge, was reaching out to steady himself. Gabe watched in horror as his father's hand landed on the super-heated side of the forge. The rancid smell of burning flesh permeated the air.

"*Daed!*" Gabe ran over to John, who was holding his burned hand against his chest. Although he didn't utter a sound, agony contorted his features.

He looked at the red flesh of his *daed*'s hand, which was now bubbling with blisters. "You've got to see a doctor."

John sucked in his breath. "I . . . don't need . . . a . . . doctor." John started to sway, and Gabe put a supporting arm around his shoulders. "Just . . . take . . . me inside."

"*Nee*—"

"Don't argue! Help . . . me inside!"

Surprised at his father's sudden burst of energy and convinced by the stubborn look in his eyes, Gabe did as he was told. He led John into the kitchen, where he was surprised to see Moriah talking to Rachel Detweiler.

"Good heavens, what happened?" Moriah said, jumping out of her chair when they entered the room.

"He burned his hand on the forge," Gabriel said, easing his father into another chair at the table. John's complexion had suddenly turned gray, adding to Gabe's worry. "I want to take him to the hospital, but he refuses to go."

"Don't . . . need . . . to," John said, still holding his hand against his chest.

"Now's not the time to be mulish," Gabe said, losing his patience. "It'll only take me a second to call for a ride—"

"He's right, Gabriel." Moriah brought over a clean towel and laid it on the table. Gently she took John's wrist and positioned it on the towel, taking care not to let his burned palm touch the terry cloth fabric. "It will take too long to get him to the emergency room. We need to take care of it here."

"I know . . . what to do . . . anyway," John said, his breathing becoming steadier. He looked at Moriah. "Up in the cabinet . . . second to the right . . . there's salve."

"Rachel," Moriah said. "Help him hold his hand. Be careful

not to touch the burn. There doesn't seem to be any damage on the back, so he can lightly rest it against the towel. Just make sure his hand doesn't move."

With a nod Rachel did as Moriah requested.

Gabe watched with fascination—and a bit of awe—as his father directed the women in tending his burn. True to his word, he knew exactly what to do and instructed Moriah on how to wrap his hand with gauze from the first aid kit he always kept on hand, even when he and Levi were growing up. Moriah seemed to know where everything was in the kit. Gabe surmised she had probably found it and kept it stocked while she and Levi were married.

"That's better," John said, once his hand was securely wrapped. Some of the color had returned to his face. "Now, I need a cup of tea. The nighttime blend, Moriah. And make it strong."

"Do you want a pain reliever?" She rinsed out the kettle and filled it with fresh water.

He shook his head. "The salve is doing the trick."

Gabe plopped down at the table, the tension draining from his neck as he realized his father was going to be all right. "I still wish you would have let me take you to the doctor."

"And miss being nursed by the two prettiest ladies around?" John cracked a smile, albeit a faint one. "*Nee.* Not a chance."

Gabe grinned back. His father's smiles had been so rare lately, ever since Levi had died. It was nice to see him lighthearted, even if he was in pain. "What were you doing by the forge?"

John sobered. "I thought I'd help you with the shoes. I know how many you have to finish off today. Didn't count on tripping over my own two feet." He glanced down at his bandaged hand, his expression filling with melancholy once again.

Not wanting to add to his father's frustration and guilt, Gabe patted him on the back. "I appreciate the help, *Daed.* And you're right, I do have a lot of shoes to make today."

"Then you should get back to it, don't you think?"

"You don't need me anymore?"

John looked up and shook his head, not quite as somber as before. "I've got these two, remember?"

Gabe looked at Rachel, who smiled at him. He didn't know her very well, but he would have to tell her later how much he appreciated her helping his father.

Moriah poured John his cup of tea, then went over to Gabe. "We'll make sure he's okay," she said. "If there's a problem, I'll come get you."

"I don't want you do go to any trouble—"

"It's no trouble," she said, smiling at him.

Dear God in heaven, what a beautiful smile she had. "I didn't realize you were here. Or Rachel."

"I thought you and John might like something different to eat, so I stopped by to make some chicken stew. There's enough for at least two days. I also thought I'd straighten up a little bit around here."

Her generosity touched him. He knew it had to be difficult for her to be here, surrounded by painful memories. Yet she had set aside her own grief to help them out. Although he wished more than anything her motives were driven by something other than a sense of duty to her late husband's family, he knew it wasn't true. "It smells wonderful," he said, breathing in deeply. And it did. She was an excellent cook. "But you don't have to go to all this trouble."

"I don't mind. We're family, remember?"

How could he forget? "Right. Family." Just not the kind of family he wished they could be. As he gazed at her, he noticed a smudge of flour on her temples. He fought the urge to wipe it away. "You look tired," he said softly. "Don't worry about the house. I plan to clean it up this weekend. Besides, you know us bachelors. A little dust doesn't get us too riled up."

Her grin grew wider. "Don't worry about me. Or the house. Just get back to work. Rachel and I will take care of everything here." She stepped toward him and shepherded him toward the door, giving him no recourse but to leave.

A few moments later he entered the shop, the faint acrid scent of his father's burned hand still hanging in the air. He glanced at the forge and gave a quick prayer of thanks that his *daed*'s injury hadn't been worse. Gearing himself up for the rest of the afternoon's hard labor, he looked around the shop for Aaron. When he didn't see the young man, he headed for the back room. The cashbox was open, and Aaron was shoving something into his pocket.

What was he doing with the money? Instantly suspicious, Gabe asked, "What's going on here?"

Aaron slammed down the metal lid of the box. "You had a customer a few minutes ago. Came and picked up two of the sconces."

"What was his name?"

Aaron's complexion reddened. "I forgot. He needed change, and I had enough in my pocket. I was just paying myself back."

"Why didn't you get the cashbox and give him change from that?"

A guilty look crossed his face. "I—I didn't think about it at the time. He seemed in a hurry."

Gabe regarded him for a moment. He hadn't heard a car pull up in front of the shop while he had been inside with his *daed*, nor had he heard a car pull away. Granted, he hadn't shown Aaron how to use the cashbox either, although that was pretty simple and didn't need any training. He could visualize Aaron digging in his pocket for change while trying to appease an impatient customer. Most of their customers, including outlanders, were fine, polite people. But every once in a while they'd get a rude one, and Gabe would respond as humbly as he could, as was the Amish way.

Gabe took the box from Aaron and opened the lid. "How much do you need?"

"I already got it." Aaron stared down at the floor.

Shutting the box with a click, Gabe then opened the drawer of his father's battered desk and put the box back in its usual place. "We need to get back to work. *Daed* will be out of commission for a while, so I need you to help me with the shoes."

Aaron looked up with surprise. "What do you need me to do?"

For the rest of the afternoon Gabe and Aaron worked at completing the horseshoe order. They finished well after sundown. Gabe offered to drive Aaron home, but the younger man refused, saying he'd rather walk. Although the walk wasn't all that far, he figured Aaron had to be exhausted. Still, he declined Gabe's second offer to take him home and left the shop carrying a small, blue cooler that served as his lunchbox, a lone form disappearing into the darkness.

Dog-tired, Gabe dragged himself across the yard and into the kitchen, his stomach growling like a pack of wolves with a fresh kill. A small bubble of happiness burst inside when he saw a plate of food, covered with foil, warming on top of the woodstove. The scent of chicken stew, apples, and spices filled his nostrils and made his stomach growl. He tore off the foil, picked up the plate, then sat down and shoveled the food into his mouth. Once he finished eating, he would check on his father. Right now he had to tame the beast in his belly.

Just as he put the last mouthful of apple brown Betty into his mouth, Moriah walked into the room. He was surprised to see she was still here. She looked as equally surprised to see him in the kitchen.

"I see you found supper," she said, walking to the table. She picked up his dishes and took them over to the sink.

"You don't have to do that." Gabe tried to take a glass from her hand, but she moved it out of his reach.

"Nonsense. I'll just give them a quick wash before I leave."

He picked up a dishtowel off the rack that hung near the sink. "Then I'll dry."

"*Danki*. I hate the drying part." She handed him a wet dish.

"How's *Daed* doing?"

"He's sleeping in his old room. He wanted to go back to the *dawdi haus,* but I wouldn't let him."

"Good idea."

"He seemed fine, though."

"Because of your *gut* care."

"Well, not just me. Rachel helped out too. He's a tough one, I'll say that for him."

"*Ya*. He's tough all right. He's been through a lot." Taking the fork Moriah offered him, he added, "We all have."

She nodded and remained silent for a few moments, the only sound in the kitchen the clinking of the dishes in the sink. After Gabe had wiped the last dish, she turned to him. "I haven't thanked you properly for checking up on me the past couple of weeks. But like I told your *daed,* it's not necessary."

"I know I don't have to." He turned and faced her. "Moriah, don't you understand? I want to."

Chapter 13

Speech abandoned Moriah when she heard Gabriel's words. He wanted to check up on her? Why would he want to do that? She could understand him dropping by once or twice, but he had come to see her at least three times a week since Levi had died. A faint tingling sensation rushed through her as he continued to hold her gaze, his chestnut-colored eyes filled with an emotion she couldn't comprehend. Then it disappeared.

Gabriel cleared his throat as he turned away from her. "Uh, well, that didn't take long," he said, putting away the last dish. "Chores go by a lot faster when there are four hands working instead of two."

"That they do." She watched his profile for a moment, but exhaustion had been dogging her for the past hour or so. She didn't have the strength to try to figure him out. Instead, she turned around and surveyed the kitchen, making sure everything was neat and tidy. She and Rachel had ignored his plea to not to clean anything, and between the two of them, the Millers now had a spotless house, an accomplishment that deeply satisfied her. Rachel had been a great help, and Moriah was very glad she had stopped by to visit. She truly liked the young woman, and hoped they could become closer friends.

When she was satisfied that everything the kitchen was in tip-top shape, she said, "There's coffee cake for tomorrow's breakfast; it's wrapped in foil in the pantry. And there are some sandwiches for lunch. I put the chicken stew in the cooler; you can reheat that for supper tomorrow."

"Wow." Gabriel's brows lifted as he grinned. "*Danki,* Moriah. Sounds like you were busy today."

"I like staying busy. It . . . helps."

His eyes met hers for a brief moment, and they both looked away. "I know. I've taken on more jobs than ever since Levi . . . since he passed. Although I wonder if that was a mistake. *Daed* might not have hurt his hand if he hadn't felt he had to help me out."

"Not everything is your fault, Gabriel."

He frowned. "I know that."

"Sometimes I wonder if you do. Is that why you've been coming by so often? Out of a sense of guilt? Or do you just feel obligated?" She was too tired to worry about the edge in her voice. She didn't want to be someone's obligation, especially not Gabriel's. Obviously he had more than enough to do. He didn't need to waste time driving out to see her.

"*Nee.*" His smile faded and his forehead furrowed with consternation. "Look, I just told you I wanted to see you. But if you don't want me coming around . . . I don't want to be a bother, Moriah."

Remorse pricked at her, and she closed her eyes for a moment. She shouldn't have spoken to him that way. He'd been nothing but kind to her, and this was how she repaid him, by hurting his feelings. "I'm sorry. I really do appreciate you thinking of me. It's nice to know someone cares."

His eyes suddenly softened, and she found herself transfixed by them. "I do care," he said.

"Because we're family. And friends. At least I'd like to think we are."

"We are. But that's not the only reason—"

Before he could finish his sentence, she was assaulted by a stab of pain similar to the one she had experienced that morning. She bent over and tried to catch her breath.

"Moriah?" Gabriel immediately came to her side, his arm around her shoulders, his body bent in a similar shape to hers. "What's wrong?"

"I don't know." The pain subsided, disappearing almost as quickly as it came. When she didn't feel anything else, she slowly straightened.

"What, is it a cramp or something?"

"Maybe."

"Here, sit down." He guided her over to a chair and held it out for her. "Do you need to put your feet up?"

"My feet are fine." Actually, she felt completely fine now, at least physically. But the alarm she'd felt earlier that day multiplied tenfold. However, she wouldn't let Gabriel know. He looked worried enough as it was.

"Has this been happening a lot?"

"Only one other time." She didn't feel the need to tell him when.

He knelt down beside her. "Do you want a glass of water? Maybe some crackers or something? You shouldn't have worked so hard today."

She found his hovering slightly amusing. And a little surprising. He'd been so aloof during the time she and Levi had been together. And even though they'd grieved together at the hospital and funeral, their subsequent visits had been awkward—at least she thought so, with Gabe saying very little when he stopped by. But she was carrying his niece or nephew; of course he'd be concerned.

"I didn't work that hard," she said, trying to reassure him. "And the pain is gone." All of a sudden she felt another sensation, one she had never felt before. Excited and without thinking about it, she grabbed his hand and placed it on her belly. "Can you feel that?"

His hand twitched and he grinned. "Wow."

She nodded, thrilled with the movement she felt inside her. Then she looked down at her hand covering his, and another familiar feeling intruded on the happy moment. Sorrow. Levi should be here, feeling his baby's light movements. He should be sharing this moment with her, not Gabriel.

But she hid her emotions for Gabriel's sake. His face shone with joy. She wouldn't destroy that for him. They both had so little to rejoice about, and had lost so much—she a husband, him a brother. She had become adept at burying her feelings, shoving them deep down inside until she thought they were completely gone, but even then they often appeared when she least expected it, like now. Yet she suppressed them again, not only for his sake, but also for her own.

"*Danki*."

His soft voice interrupted her thoughts.

"For what?"

"For sharing this with me." He slipped his hand out from beneath hers and stood up. "That was pretty special."

She smiled, amazed at how affected he seemed to be. "I'm glad you were here to share it. Although I wish . . ."

"I know." His expression dimmed. "I wish he was here too."

Not wanting to dwell on their mutual sadness, she rose from her seat. "I really have to get home. I'm sure *Mami* is starting to worry about me." She smoothed the front of her apron.

"I'm taking you home."

"That's not necessary."

"*Ya,* it's necessary. What if you have another pain? Plus it's dark and you could get into an accident."

"I've driven in the dark before," she said, a little impatiently. What did he think she was, some frail flower whose stem would snap off in a light breeze? Her parents and siblings seemed to think so. Even Rachel had earlier in the day. But anyone can drop a rolling pin. That didn't mean she wasn't capable of doing anything for herself. "I'm not helpless."

"I'm not saying you are. Remember what happened to Tobias a couple months ago? I won't let you risk yourself or the baby because some Yankee doesn't know how to drive a car."

She recalled the buggy accident, remembering how lucky Tobias and Rachel had been, considering her brother had sustained only a bump on the head. They could have been seriously hurt . . . or worse. She couldn't bear the thought of anything happening to her baby. "All right. You've convinced me."

"*Gut.* I'm glad you've come to your senses." He winked at her, a gesture similar to what Levi used to do when he would tease her, yet somehow completely different. Then again, why wouldn't it be? Even though they looked nearly exactly alike, as she was so often reminded, Gabriel was nothing like his brother.

Gabriel grabbed his summer hat, made of tightly woven straw, and plopped it on his head. He opened the door for her, and they walked into the balmy night air. He opened the buggy door on the passenger side and helped her in, then untied his horse and jumped beside Moriah on the seat. Within minutes they started toward her house.

Once the buggy was in motion, she leaned back in the seat. Fatigue instantly overcame her, and she closed her eyes. Only for a moment. She just needed a minute of rest.

"Moriah."

Feeling the pressure of someone touching her shoulder, her eyes flew open.

"We're here," Gabriel said.

"Already?" She tried to stifle a yawn, but didn't quite succeed.

"*Ya,* sleepyhead."

"How long have I been asleep?"

"Since I pulled out of the driveway." He smiled.

"Really?" She opened the buggy door, and he was at her side before she could step on the ground. "*Danki,*" she said, then yawned again. "Sorry. I don't know why I'm so tired."

"My guess is you're working too hard."

She ignored his words. "Come on inside. I'll get *Daed* or one of my brothers to drive you back home."

"*Nee*. I'll walk. It's not that far."

"It's too dark to walk."

He stuck his hand in his coat pocket and pulled out a flashlight. "I always come prepared."

She grinned. "Why am I not surprised?"

"Go on in the house. I'll put up your horse."

"Are you sure?"

"*Ya*. Just promise me one thing?"

"What's that?"

"You'll tell the midwife about these pains you're having."

"Don't worry. I will."

"Oh, and one other thing." He looked at her intently and took a step forward. "Consider this fair warning. I'll be checking in on you—whether you like it or not. And don't think it's because I have to. Remember, I want to." He gazed at her for a moment, then nodded. With that he stepped away and led the horse toward the barn.

She had half a mind to go after him and tell him not to bother, but she was too tired. Although he kept insisting he wanted to see her, she wished he wouldn't, and somehow she had to convince him not to. The last thing she wanted to be was a burden on him. He already had plenty of those to bear.

"I can't see that anything's wrong." Rebekkah Fisher, Moriah's midwife, lifted her hands from Moriah's slightly protruding abdomen. Her mother had insisted on fetching her when Moriah told her about the pains she'd been having. "How often have you felt the pain?"

"Just a few times. Twice the other day, in the morning when I was at Mary's fabric store, and in the evening at the Millers'. Then once yesterday. I haven't had any today."

Rebekkah rubbed one of her chubby fingers across her lips. "Hmm. You're perfectly healthy, except you look tired. Are you getting enough rest?"

Moriah sat up in her bed and nodded, cringing inwardly for being untruthful. She clasped her hands together and put them in her lap. She hadn't had a good night's sleep in a very long time, despite her fatigue. Working hard during the day hadn't made sleeping any easier.

Rebekkah eyed her skeptically. "I guess I'll have to take your word for it. Are you napping at all?"

"*Nee.*"

"Then I'm prescribing at least one nap a day. If you can't sleep, then just lie down and relax. Thirty minutes every day. I also want you to lie down if you feel any pain."

"I'll make sure she does," Emma chimed in, moving to stand next to the midwife. She looked at her daughter. "I'm not one to say I told you so—"

"Since when?"

Emma smirked. "Very funny, *dochder*. Hopefully you'll listen to your midwife. You haven't listened to me very well. I've only had six children, you know."

"I know." Moriah rose from her bed. "*Danki* to you both for caring. I really appreciate it. But I'm okay, really." She went to her closet and pulled out one of her long white aprons, then slipped it over her head, making sure she didn't disturb her *kapp*.

"I'm glad you're feeling *gut*." Rebekkah gathered her black leather satchel and slung the strap over her plump shoulder. She gave Moriah a stern look. "I'll be back in a couple of weeks for another checkup. However, if the pains become worse or more frequent, let me know. God forbid, but it could be something serious, and we'll have to take care of it right away. In the meantime, get some rest."

"I will."

"Would you like to stay for some coffee?" Emma offered.

"I'd love to, but I have another appointment."

"All right then. Let me see you out."

When Emma and Rebekkah disappeared downstairs, Moriah

went over to the window and looked outside. The sun was trying its best to pierce through the stubborn cloud cover, casting thin beams of light before disappearing completely behind a blanket of gray. Rain threatened, filling the air with sticky humidity. She glanced down at the ground below and looked at the vegetable garden situated in front of the house. Along with her mother and sisters she had planted several rows of tomatoes, corn, cucumbers, carrots, sweet peppers, and green beans. Yesterday she had pulled every weed out of the soft dirt. Today she would turn her attention to the flower beds that bordered the house, and planned to work outside as long as the rain held off.

Outside Rebekkah steered her buggy out of the Byler's driveway. Just has she left, another buggy drove up, slowed, and turned in. She immediately recognized the driver.

Gabriel.

Her hand went to her *kapp,* making sure it was secure and no loose strands of hair had released from it. She also glanced down at her dress and made sure her apron was straight.

Suddenly she stopped her movements. Why did she care what she looked like in front of Gabriel? Especially when she needed to tell him she didn't want him stopping by anymore.

She exhaled a long breath as she saw him get out of the buggy and head toward the house, taking long, confident strides. From the vantage point of her bedroom, his face was obscured by his straw hat, but she could make out his broad shoulders, his muscled arms straining against the sleeves of his shirt. Her belly started swirling, and she placed a hand against it. Something other than the baby had caused the sensation. She chalked it up to nerves, even though she'd never been nervous around Gabriel. Confused, yes. But not anxious. Yet she'd never been in this situation with him before.

"Moriah!" Emma called from downstairs. "You have a visitor."

She took another deep breath, then went downstairs and entered the front room. He was standing by the sofa next to the window. Quickly he removed his hat and held it in his hands. "Hi, Moriah," he said softly.

Again, the tickle appeared in her belly.

"Would you care for something to drink?" Emma walked into the room. "I've just made some lemonade. It's refreshing on such a sticky day."

"*Nee,*" Moriah said.

"*Ya,*" Gabriel said at the same time. He glanced at Moriah, wariness creeping into his eyes.

Emma looked at both of them, then said, "One lemonade it is. Please, Gabriel. Feel free to sit down." She shot Moriah a perplexed look before retreating into the kitchen.

Gabriel didn't move. "Do you want me to sit down?"

"Gabriel, I . . . listen, I don't mind if you stay. But I was serious about you not needing to come by so often."

"I know."

His answer surprised her. "Then why did you come?"

"Because I told you I would."

"Moriah!" Emma's voice sounded from the kitchen. "Tell Gabriel I made fresh apple cake! Come in here and I'll cut you both a piece."

"Apple cake?" His eyebrow lifted. "Now, how can I resist an offer like that?"

As Gabe followed Moriah to the Bylers' kitchen, he inhaled the sweet cinnamon scent of Emma's apple cake. And while he was more than happy to partake of the delicious dessert, having the opportunity to spend more time with Moriah was a thousand times more satisfying.

"*Willkum,*" Emma said, gesturing to an empty seat at the table. "I'm glad you could stay."

He glanced at Moriah and wondered if she would add anything to her mother's statement. She didn't, so he waited as her mother slid a fork beneath a plump slice of the cake and lifted it from the baking pan. A fat layer of white frosting topped the piece that Emma placed on a dish.

He accepted it with a smile, but he kept his emotions in check. He found it easier to do than in the past, mostly because they didn't torture him as much. He'd come to a decision about Moriah. Even though she seemed resistant, he would continue to check in on her, to make sure she was all right. He would also find opportunities to spend time with her, like they did the other night and were currently doing. They had been good friends in the past, and he wanted to renew that friendship. And who knew, maybe the friendship would turn into something more, and he could fulfill his brother's dying wish to care for Moriah.

Which was also Gabe's deepest desire.

"So how is your *daed* doing, Gabe?" Moriah asked.

"His recovery is slow, but he's going to be okay. I still think he should see a doctor, but he won't listen to me."

"Recovery?" Emma asked.

"Didn't Moriah tell you? He burned his hand on the forge yesterday. She took great care of him."

"Rachel Detweiler was there too," Moriah interjected. "And we didn't do much, just bandaged his hand. Then we poured tea for him and made some apple brown betty. That's his favorite dessert."

"Good thing she was there. *Daed* can be stubborn, and I don't do well with medical stuff. I faint at the sight of blood."

She turned to him, surprise registering on her face. "You do not. I know this for a fact."

He looked at her. "How?"

"First grade. I cut my finger on one of those sharp rocks in the school yard. You took a handkerchief out of your pocket and wrapped it around my finger to stop the bleeding while Levi ran and got the teacher."

"I didn't know about this," Emma said. "Dear me, I hope it was clean."

"Don't worry, *Mami,* it was." She directed her attention back to Gabe. "You didn't pass out then, and I doubt you'd pass out now."

"I'm surprised you remembered that," he said. He had forgotten all about the incident.

"How could I forget? The teacher didn't have any bandages, so I had to spend the rest of the day with a huge white finger. You must have wrapped that thing around it about five times." She laughed. "Even then you were a nice guy."

Gabe smiled. She'd never complimented him before, not in any meaningful way. To hear her words and to see her laugh were like a warm balm on his heart.

"I think I'll take the rest of the cake out to the men." Emma rose from her chair. "Those four have the biggest appetites I've ever seen. Gabriel, can I get you anything else?"

"*Nee,*" he said. "I'm fine. The cake is delicious, *Frau* Byler."

"*Danki,* Gabriel. I'm glad you're enjoying it. Moriah, I'm going to Mary's fabric store after I give this to your father and brothers. Do you need anything?"

"*Nee*. I was just there the other day."

After Emma left, Gabe looked at Moriah, who had grown serious again. She picked at her cake, lifting a bit of frosting on the tine of her fork. "You're not hungry?" he asked.

"Not too much."

"Was that Rebekkah Fisher I saw leaving a little while ago?"

Moriah nodded.

A tiny thread of panic wound through him. "Did she say everything was okay?"

She looked up at him. "*Ya*. The baby is fine. Rebekkah wants me to get more rest."

Gabe shoved a bite of the cake in his mouth. "Sounds like good advice," he said after he swallowed.

"I get plenty of sleep."

"I don't think so."

Her head popped up, and from the surprised expression on her face, he regretted being so blunt. But he couldn't figure out why she wasn't telling the truth. "Moriah, anyone can see you're tired."

She set her fork down and looked at him squarely, a spark of irritation in her eyes. "What about you, Gabriel? How are *you* sleeping at night?"

Her question rendered him speechless for a moment. He hadn't expected her to be so straightforward in return. "Not so well. Which is why I understand, Moriah."

"You understand?" Her eyes grew moist, and her voice shook. "You understand what's it's like to lose your husband, not once, but twice? To know that he'll never be here to share in the birth of his child?"

His chest tightened. "You know I don't. But I loved him too, Moriah. He could make me so angry sometimes, especially when he . . . when he left. But that doesn't mean I don't wish almost every minute of the day that he was back. That I don't live with regrets. That I don't want more than anything to do things over. A lot of things." He closed his eyes, blocking his own tears. He'd never verbalized the thoughts that had jumbled through his mind on so many sleepless nights since Levi's death.

"Me too," she said, reaching for his hand. Tears dripped down her face. "I can't help but wonder why God took him away from me." She looked at him. "From us."

"I've asked that question so many times." Her touch eased the pain in his heart. "We can't understand God's ways. We can only trust that His plans are for *gut*."

"I don't know how any *gut* can come from this." She withdrew her hand from him and stood, then picked up their plates and put them next to the sink. He could see her wiping her tears with the back of her hands, and when she turned around, her eyes were dry. "*Danki* for coming by, Gabriel."

Dismissed. But he wasn't about to leave so easily. He walked over to her. "Don't push me away, Moriah. Let me help you."

"I don't need your help." She looked up at him. "If you're worried about not being able to see the baby, you don't have to be. You and John will always have a place in my child's life."

"I'm glad to know that, but that's not why I'm here. Moriah, I would be here even if there was no baby. I'm here because I want to be. I'm here because I care."

"But why?" Her lower lip started to tremble. "Why do you care?"

"Because I—"

A knock sounded on the front door. Inwardly he groaned. He had been about to reveal his heart, to tell her why he cared so much. Now she was moving away from him, and he no longer had the chance.

He followed her as she went to the front door and answered it. "Hello," she said to the visitor as he came up behind her.

His eyes grew wide with shock as he saw the woman standing on the Bylers' front porch. Taylor Johnston. Levi's lover.

Chapter 14

"Joseph, I promise you, there is something going on between the two of them."

Tobias stuffed the last bite of apple cake in his mouth and tried not to eavesdrop on his parents. It was difficult not to, as his mother wasn't exactly whispering. If he didn't have to finish sanding the dresser drawers, he would have gone to the other side of the shop and let them have their privacy. But he wanted to get these drawers stained before the day's end, and he wouldn't be able to do that if he didn't get busy sanding.

The grit of the sandpaper against the rough wood made a good amount of noise, but he could still hear his parents' discussion.

"I think you're overreacting, Em," Joseph said.

"I'm not overreacting. You weren't in there when they were talking. You didn't see the way he looks at her. I can't believe I didn't notice before."

"Maybe because there's nothing to notice."

"Joseph, I know what I saw. That young man's got feelings for Moriah. No wonder he's been dropping by so often."

"You said he was just being courteous, and you liked his thoughtfulness."

"That's what I thought. Now I'm not so sure. What should we do?"

"I don't see as we have to do anything."

"I just don't know if she's ready for this. After everything she's been through and with her being pregnant, she's very vulnerable right now."

"This is Gabe Miller we're talking about here. He's a good man. Always has been."

"That's what we thought about Levi. And look how that turned out."

"Gabe and Levi are different people. You know that. Good boys, both of them, but different."

Tobias flipped over the drawer and started sanding the wood on the underside. The movement must have alerted his parents, because they lowered their voices, much to his relief. The less he knew about Moriah's situation with Gabe, the better off he would be. She was his sister and he cared about her, but that stuff was off limits, in his opinion.

Though she could do worse than Gabe. A lot worse. He had a good reputation and was well liked by nearly everyone in the community. But as his mother pointed out, Levi had been as well, and what he had done to Moriah was inexcusable. Who was to say Gabe wouldn't do the same thing?

With a shake of his head, he returned his attention to the job at hand. He had more important things to think about than Moriah and Gabe. Like getting this dresser done. And like thinking about Rachel Detweiler. Confound it, he couldn't get that girl out of his mind. Especially the kiss she'd given him the night of the buggy crash. Her lips had been so soft, the kiss so whisper light, his senses reeled just thinking about it. He could tell she felt guilty over it, as she had made a point to remind him that she was Christian Weaver's girlfriend. But she wasn't the only one feeling guilty about that night. Even though she'd been the one who kissed him, he had been thinking about doing the same thing. She'd just beat him to it.

He'd mentally kicked himself more than a few times for betraying Christian. What kind of person was he to like another guy's girl? And why did that girl have to be Rachel Detweiler? He'd spent most of his life disliking her. Now all he could think about was kissing her again.

"You keep sanding the wood like that you're going to rub a hole in it."

Tobias looked up to see his father's stern expression. His mother was gone and he hadn't even heard her leave. "Sorry, *Daed*. Guess I got distracted."

"Pay attention next time." Joseph took another look at the dresser, then walked away.

Blowing the large buildup of wood dust off the bookshelf, he turned it on its side and began sanding the top, forcing himself to focus. Even when Rachel wasn't anywhere near him, she still made him forget his head.

Moriah opened the door and stared into the green eyes of a stranger. She didn't recognize the Yankee woman who stood before her.

The visitor's gaze turned from Moriah to Gabriel, and Moriah watched the green eyes widen, then the woman's body begin to sway back and forth as if she were about to faint.

"Levi?" she said.

Confused, Moriah wondered how she knew Levi. But quickly, the woman's expression changed from shock to disappointment. "His brother," she said.

Moriah spun around. So Gabriel knew this woman too? "What's going on?"

"I knew your late husband," she said. "May I come in?"

Gabriel took a step forward until he was standing next to Moriah. "I don't know if that's a *gut* idea, Ms. Johnston."

Johnston? "As in Johnston's Farms?" Moriah regarded her again. The woman's platform heels made her several inches taller than Moriah. Her luxuriant red hair hung in loose waves around her shoulders. She had vibrant green eyes and full, red-painted lips. Perfect skin and a flawless figure, as her tight, white, short-sleeved shirt and blue jeans showed. Moriah felt dwarfed by her presence, and didn't doubt for a minute that she came from a family of great wealth.

"Yes. My father owns Johnston's Farms. Where Levi used to work." She held out her hand to Moriah. "I'm Taylor Johnston. "

Still confused, she glanced at Gabriel briefly before inviting her inside. His expression remained guarded, and Moriah wondered what he had against this woman. "Please, sit down. Can I get you anything? Lemonade? Water?"

She shook her head. "I'm fine. I won't take up too much of your time." She cast a look at Gabriel, then turned her attention to Moriah again. "Can we speak in private?"

Moriah looked at Gabriel. Apparently he wasn't thrilled with the idea, but Taylor seemed unnerved by his presence. "Gabriel, do you mind?"

He hesitated, saying, "It might be better if I stay."

Moriah still felt unnerved by their unfinished conversation moments earlier, so she said, "I'll be fine, Gabriel. *Danki.*"

He sighed. "Let me just grab my hat. I left it in the kitchen."

While he was gone, Moriah motioned for Taylor to sit on the couch. "Are you sure I can't get you anything?"

"I'm sure." Taylor scanned the room. "So this is where Levi used to live?"

"*Nee.* This is my parents' house."

"Oh. I just assumed . . . when I stopped at the blacksmith shop, Mr. Miller said I could find you here. I thought you were still living in the same house."

"I moved back here after Levi . . . left."

Taylor's cheeks reddened. "I see."

Gabriel emerged from the kitchen. He looked at Moriah once more, the emotion she'd seen during their encounter in the kitchen still vivid in his expression. She had asked him why he cared about her, and when she saw the intensity of his gaze, the darkening of his brown eyes, she felt new emotions stir within her, which both thrilled and terrified her. Clearly she'd had a momentary lapse of reason, more than likely due to fatigue. Still, even though she could rationalize her feelings, she didn't want to explore them any further. She refused to hope for anything other than a healthy baby.

"All right," he said. "I'll be back by in a couple of days."

It was on the tip of her tongue to protest his visits yet again, but she wouldn't argue in front of Taylor. Instead she barely nodded, a gesture that caused Gabriel to emit a small smile. She'd have to set him straight the next time.

He nodded toward Taylor, then left. Moriah thought she saw Taylor visibly relax once Gabriel was gone, and Moriah knew she was relieved to see him leave too.

"How do you know my brother-in-law?" Moriah asked.

"We met once," Taylor responded, staring down at her hands. "He came out to the farm."

"Oh."

She looked up. "I'm so very, very sorry."

"Thank you. Levi's death has been hard on all of us."

Taylor picked at her index finger with her thumb. "No, I mean I'm sorry for what I did to you and Levi."

Everything seemed to slow down around Moriah, as if her life had been permanently yoked to a leaden, unmovable force. "What did you do?" Her voice sounded feeble in her ears.

"You mean you don't know?" Taylor's cheeks reddened even deeper. "That your husband and I had an affair?"

Moriah gasped. Taylor's words wrenched her heart. "An affair?"

"It was my fault. Since the accident I've had to face some ugly truths about myself. One of those is that I don't care who I hurt, as long as I get what I want." She paused and looked at Moriah. "What I wanted was your husband. He resisted at first, but I can be persuasive. Very persuasive."

Closing her eyes against the fresh new wave of pain assaulting her, Moriah said, "Why are you telling me this?"

"I honestly thought you knew."

"How would I know?" She opened her eyes. "My husband left me. He didn't explain anything in his letter, only that he was leaving me and his faith. And he didn't want to be Amish anymore.

"Didn't you wonder what made him come to that decision?"

She twisted the ends of the ties of her prayer *kapp*. "We believe marriage is for life. What God has brought together, no man—or woman—can break apart." She rose from her chair, not wanting to hear anything this woman had to say. Not only had Taylor Johnston taken Levi, for some reason she wanted to push the knife further into Moriah's back. "I think you should leave. Now."

Taylor looked up at her. "Are you pregnant?"

Moriah gripped the ribbons on her *kapp* even more tightly. "*Ya.*"

"With Levi's baby?"

Moriah's eyes narrowed. "*Ya.*"

All along she had thought he left because of something she'd done, and because of his dissatisfaction with the Amish church. Now she knew the real reason. She had disappointed him so deeply on an intimate level he had taken up with another woman. Would there be no end to her pain? To her humiliation? "Please," she whispered, perilously close to tears. "Just go."

"I will, after I tell you why I'm here. Levi and I had been fighting a lot lately, and I could tell he wasn't happy living with me and my father. Then he found out I wasn't pregnant—"

"What?"

"I told him I was pregnant." Taylor stared down at the floor for a moment, then jerked her head up. "Like I said, I've done a lot of soul searching. I was the one driving in the accident, and even though the police said it wasn't my fault, Levi and I had been arguing right before the truck hit us." She licked her lips. "He'd learned that I'd lied to him about being pregnant. We hadn't been together that long, and I didn't like the idea of losing him. So I told him I was pregnant so he would stick around." She paused and looked down again. "And he told me right before the accident that he was coming back to you."

Moriah breathed in sharply. "Why should I believe you?"

"Normally you shouldn't." She sighed. "But you deserve to know the truth. He said he made a terrible mistake by leaving."

Picking up her huge red leather handbag, she stood. "I just wanted you to know he still loved you . . . and still wanted to be Amish. He said leaving you and his faith had been a mistake."

A blend of caustic emotions ran through Moriah. Hearing about Levi's planned return did little to assuage her pain and grief. Still, she understood Taylor's gesture. The woman didn't have to come here and tell the news in person, yet she did. "*Danki*," Moriah managed.

"Don't thank me. I don't deserve it. What I deserve is your hatred."

"That is not our way."

"I've heard that, but I didn't really believe it. Not until now, and now I know he was right." Taylor's green eyes shimmered with tears. "I really am sorry," she said in a thick whisper.

"I know."

Taylor walked past her and out the door. Moriah didn't move—she just stood there in the center of the living room, listening to Taylor's car engine start and pull away. Only when the sound disappeared did she sit down on the couch. Her movements were still slow as she tried to process what Taylor had said.

Someone knocked on the front door, but she didn't move to answer it. She didn't want to see anyone else. She couldn't take another blow.

Gabe knocked on the wooden screen door again, more firmly this time. Maybe Moriah was in the back of the house or upstairs where she couldn't hear him, which was why she wasn't answering the door.

Halfway down her street, Gabe had realized it was a mistake

to leave Moriah alone with Taylor. He'd hurriedly turned his buggy around. What had he been thinking? He should have stood his ground, or at least stayed in another room. But Moriah had been insistent that he leave. Her tone of voice had been polite, but he saw it in her eyes. She wanted him to go. He supposed his nicked ego had led him to agree to her request. When he pulled in her driveway, he was glad to see Taylor had left.

He knocked for a third time. Drops of water plinked against the roof of the Bylers' porch as a rumble of thunder sounded in the distance. His horse would appreciate the cool shower.

Where was she? Worry shot through him. Lifting his hand to rap on the front door one more time, she finally opened it.

"What do you want?" she said dully.

Gabe discerned instantly that whatever Taylor had said to Moriah had upset her. He'd been afraid of that. Clearly she had been crying. Her eyes were swollen, her nose rosy as if she had been blowing it. "I came to see if you're okay."

"I'm fine." She moved to shut the door.

He laid his palm on the frame, preventing the screen door from closing. "I can see you're not."

"Leave me alone, Gabriel." She sounded on the verge of sobbing.

No way was he going to leave now. He pushed against the door with his hand, gently, but with enough force to show her he wasn't going anywhere. "What did Taylor say to you?"

Moriah looked at him, her eyes consumed with defeat, then turned and walked away.

A knot formed in his gut as he followed her inside. The air felt heavy, sticky, as the sky darkened and rain pelted harder outside. Sweat broke out on his forehead. He took off his hat and laid it on the table. Her back was still to him, and despite the hot July temperature, she hugged her shoulders. "Moriah, I can't help you if you won't talk to me."

Whirling around, she said, "Did you know? Did you know about her and Levi?" Before he could answer she added, "Never mind. I can tell by your face that you did."

"I'm sorry, Moriah." Gabe took a step toward her. If only he could pull her in his arms. He could soothe her, explain why he didn't tell her.

But she moved away from him. "You knew, and you didn't say anything." She sniffed and wiped her nose with the tissue in her hand. "You lied to me."

He shook his head, trying to close the distance between them. "*Nee,* Moriah. I didn't lie to you."

"You weren't completely honest. That's the same thing."

Raking his hand through his hair, he said, "I couldn't tell you. What *gut* would it have done? I didn't want you to hurt any more than you already were." He dipped his head so he could look directly at her. "I wanted to protect you."

Her shoulders slumped, and he could see the strength drain from her. She gazed at him with weepy blue eyes, eyes that he had fallen in love with more than six years ago. "What else are you hiding from me, Gabriel? What other secrets do you have? Or will I have to wait until someone else dies to find out?"

He froze, as if her words had been a physical blow. "That's not fair, Moriah."

She took a deep breath and closed her eyes. "I know. I'm sorry."

"*Nee,* I'm sorry." A flash of lightning lit up the sky. "You're right. I haven't been honest with you. Not completely. And you have a right to know why."

His somber countenance stunned Moriah. She'd never seen him so serious, even when he had told her about Levi leaving her. Dread pooled inside her, and she wished she hadn't questioned him. Hadn't she had enough?

"There is something I need to tell you," Gabriel said. "It's something I should have told you a long time ago." He gestured to the sofa. "Can we sit down?"

She nodded, knowing they had both come too far in this conversation to turn back now. Outside a boom of thunder shook the house, much the same way her life had been rocked to the core. They sat down together, and she could see the sheen of perspiration on his forehead. The room had become unbearably hot and humid, the afternoon thunderstorm doing little to cool things down.

"Moriah, I only want you to be happy. You have to believe that. Everything I've done has been driven by that desire."

The irony of his statement struck her. She'd never been so miserable in her life.

"Remember when we were in school, the day you and I first walked home together?"

She nodded. "Levi was sick and stayed home. We were in fifth grade."

"Sixth. We took the long way home. Remember how we talked about everything?"

"We even went and sat by the creek for a while. Just talking."

"I got in trouble for being late." He grinned, but the expression was tempered with solemnity. "That's when I knew."

"Knew what? Gabriel, what does this have to do with anything?"

"It has to do with everything." He swallowed, his Adam's apple bobbing up and down. "I—Moriah, I love you." He let out a long breath.

"I know," she said wearily. "I love you too. You're my husband's brother, and the uncle to my child. Of course I love you."

He shook his head, his brown hair flopping against his ears. "*Nee,* you don't understand. I *love* you. Not like a *schwester.*" He took her hand in his. "I love you like a man loves a woman. Like a husband loves his wife."

When his gaze locked with hers, her heart stopped beating. She could see that his words were true. It was evident in his eyes. As he looked at her with such warmth and love, she wanted to weep. It was obvious in the way he held her hand, gently, almost reverently, like he never wanted to let her go. "Gabriel," she said, almost unable to form his name. "I . . . I . . ."

"Shhh." He brushed the top of her hand with his thumb. "Let me finish. I wanted to tell you, but I was afraid. Afraid you'd reject me, or laugh in my face."

"I would never have laughed at you."

"I know that now. But my twelve-year-old heart didn't. Then by the time I had found my courage, you were in love with Levi, and he loved you. I didn't want to stand in the way of that. So I kept my feelings to myself. At least I tried."

Moriah felt like a fool. How could she have been so oblivious to everything? Memories flooded her mind—how reticent Gabriel had become shortly after she and Levi were together. How kind he'd been to her after Levi left. How he had been so attentive to her since his brother's death, so loyal . . .

So loving.

"Did anyone else know?" she asked. "Did Levi know?"

"I didn't think so. I had tried so hard to keep it inside and thought I had. But the day I went to Johnston's Farms, I found out Levi did know. And that leads me to the second thing I need to say."

"There's more?" Her mind and emotions were swirling in a cauldron of confusion.

"In the hospital, Levi asked me to take care of you."

She jerked her hand out of his and stood up. "What?"

He stood and faced her. "He made me promise that I would take care of you."

"Why would he do that? He loved me and wanted to come home. Taylor told me."

Both surprised and elated to hear this news, Gabe asked, "She did? What else did she say?"

"That he was coming back to me . . . to home . . . to the Amish."

Gabriel smiled. "*Daed* was right. Levi had come back to God. And he was coming back to you."

"So why would he tell you to take care of me?"

"Because he knew he wouldn't make it. He knew I loved you, and he knew I would take care of you." Gabriel went to her and covered her shoulders with his large palms. "And he was right. Moriah, my love for you hasn't changed. It's only grown stronger over the years. I would care for you, and for this child"—he nodded at her tummy—"for the rest of my life."

Moriah couldn't speak. She couldn't think, and she didn't know what to feel. It was all too much to take in at once—too many secrets, too much betrayal. Too much confusion. She wrenched herself from his grasp. "Leave, Gabriel."

"*Nee*. I don't think you should be alone."

"I *want* to be alone." She looked up at him, a vortex of anger growing inside her. Anger at Levi for leaving, for dying, for putting her through all this. And anger at Gabriel for not telling her the truth about her husband or about his feelings. The blade of their betrayal cut at her heart and her soul. "Get out," she said, clenching her hands together.

"Moriah, please."

"I said leave!"

"What's going on here?" Tobias stood in the doorway of the front room, his clothes damp from the rain outside. Obviously he had entered the house from the kitchen and she hadn't heard him come in. "Moriah," her brother said. "Is everything all right?"

"*Nee,*" she said, unable to hold back the flood of hot tears any longer. "It's not all right. I don't know if things will ever be right again!" With that she flew out of the room and headed for her bedroom upstairs, far away from Gabriel Miller.

"What did you do to her?" Tobias entered the room, anger sparking in his blue eyes.

Gabe didn't blame him for being upset. He wanted to kick himself for upsetting Moriah. He'd gone about it all wrong, he could see that now. He told her too much, too soon. Now he wondered if she'd ever speak to him again. "I made a mistake," he told her brother. "A huge mistake."

Tobias stared at him for a moment, his hardened expression softening a bit. "You want to tell me what's going on?"

Gabe started to say no, but then changed his mind. He needed someone in the Byler family to know his side of the story.

Maybe he would have an ally in Tobias. "I told your sister I loved her."

Tobias sucked in his breath. "*Ach.* That *was* a mistake, Gabe. What did you do that for?"

"You don't seem surprised."

He shrugged. "I heard *Mami* talking to *Daed* about it." Then he let out a small chuckle. "What can I say? *Mei schwester* is loveable."

The tension drained from Gabe's body at Tobias's levity, though Gabe also knew Tobias meant it. "That she is."

"I don't know what to tell you, Gabe. Feelings are funny things. You can't always choose who you love. Sometimes love chooses you, whether you want it to or not."

"You sound like the voice of experience."

"Eh, maybe. Let's just say I've learned a few things lately."

Gabe went to the table to get his hat, then nodded good-bye to Tobias. When he stepped out on the front porch, he saw that the rain had stopped. A bright rainbow arched in the sky for a brief moment, only to disappear behind the clouds.

A sign. Perhaps the flood of pain they'd all gone through would soon come to an end. At least he hoped.

Chapter 15

As Rachel pulled her buggy up to Eli Yoder's barn, she could hear the hum of talking and laughter coming from the front part of the large white building. She hadn't attended a Sunday night singing in a long time, since she and Christian had started dating. But Christian hadn't returned from Charm yet, and it was the middle of summer. Maybe this was his way of telling her that their relationship was over.

Surprisingly, she was only mildly irritated with him and actually felt more than a small amount of relief. Truth be told, Christian hadn't been on her mind much lately. Not as much as Tobias had. She still couldn't get him out of her thoughts, and she couldn't help but look for him at church on Sundays even though they'd rarely said more than a couple words to each other. She seemed to pine for him more and more.

Her feelings didn't make sense. Christian was the perfect man for her, at least in theory. The other day she had taken out a sheet of paper and divided it down the middle, creating two columns. One she labeled Christian, the other Tobias, and from there she proceeded to list their positive points. Christian's list dwarfed

Tobias's, even with Christian being gone for so long. Logically she should be in love with him, not Tobias.

Love? The prospect of her loving Tobias was preposterous. And thrilling. And ridiculous. And dreamy.

She groaned. Even her thoughts were contradictory and confusing.

After tying up her horse to the hitching post, she jumped down from her buggy. The sun had started to dip in the horizon. The Yoders had set up a volleyball net and several young people were deeply involved in a game. She half expected to see Tobias in the midst of the action, and she was disappointed when she realized he wasn't there.

"C'mon, Rachel!" One of the girls yelled from the other side of the net. "We need you on our team."

Rachel shook her head. Normally she would have jumped at the chance to play, but she didn't feel like it tonight. "Maybe next time."

The girl shrugged, and the game resumed.

She walked into the barn, and several more friends greeted her. The scent of hay hung in the air, and against the wall she saw a table laden with cookies, potato chips, and peach and blueberry fry pies. She looked around the room and saw three of her girlfriends standing in the corner of the room, whispering and laughing. She started over toward them, eager to find out what was so funny.

Halfway to her destination, someone tapped her on the shoulder. Turning around, she was surprised to see Tobias Byler standing behind her.

"Hi, Rachel," he said in a soft voice.

"Tobias." A tingling sensation coursed through her stomach.

"Can I talk to you for a minute?" he asked, glancing at the door behind them. "Privately?"

She surveyed the large expansive barn, which had been cleaned especially for tonight's gathering. Square bales of hay were pushed against the wall, their sweet, dusty smell overpowering the scent of horses. The bales were used as seats, but there were also about a dozen or so chairs spread out in the room, a few of them already filled with people talking and laughing. Since she had arrived early, there weren't too many people inside. "We can't talk here?"

"I'd rather not."

His serious expression alarmed her, so she agreed. "Where should we go?"

"Just outside."

"All right."

When they reached the outside, they didn't stray too far from the barn. They had just enough privacy to be hidden from everyone else, but not so much that they wouldn't be discovered if someone walked to the back of the building. A waist-high, white fence surrounded the property. She turned around and leaned against it, looking up at him.

Without much fanfare he said, "I just wanted to tell you that I appreciated you visiting Moriah a couple weeks ago."

She lifted her brows. "How did you know about that?"

"She told me." He looked out over the pasture, where a small herd of black and white cows were feasting on the tender blades. The tangy scent of freshly mown grass drifted through the evening air. The *clip-clop* of a horse and buggy sounded in the distance. "My sister has been through a lot, you know. We're all pretty worried about her." Clearing his throat, he continued, "I'm glad you were able to be a friend. She needs as much support as she can get."

His appreciation elicited a smile. It hadn't been much of a sacrifice on her part, just a simple visit to an old, if not close, friend. But to hear Tobias talk, to see the mix of gratitude in his eyes, made her feel like she'd done something amazing.

"I'm glad I could spend some time with her." Rachel tried to keep the emotions bubbling underneath the surface from shining through her voice. "She's a *gut* listener."

"*Ya.* She is." He tilted his head at her. "How's Christian doing?" he asked, turning from her and leaning his back against the fence.

"I wouldn't know," she said, suddenly forgetting her practiced response for that very same question.

Surprise flickered in his eyes. "You haven't heard from him?"

"*Nee,* not much anyway. But I'm sure he's having a marvelous time with his aunt and uncle in Charm."

"Have you been down there to visit him?"

"What's with all the questions?"

"I'm just asking. Making conversation."

"Well, I don't want to talk about Christian." A warm breeze swirled around them, lifting up the ribbons of her *kapp.* She pressed them down. "Especially not with you."

"Suit yourself. I just thought *maedel* always liked to talk about their beaus. And I've been told I'm a good listener." He gave her a crafty look. "If you ever want to talk."

She didn't understand his sudden interest. She also didn't like the way his sly smile made her feel. All tingly and giddy inside. Actually she didn't mind the feeling; she just didn't appreciate that Tobias was the cause of it. "I'm a very private person. I'm not like the other *maedel.*"

He turned and faced her, his grin fading. "You're right," he said softly. "You are different from the other *maedel*. It's what I like about you."

Rachel's mouth almost dropped open. Did Tobias just admit he liked her? She gazed directly at him, noticing the short blond whiskers on his chin. He noticed, and his lips parted into a grin, one that made her heart melt like ice on a summer day. This couldn't be real; it couldn't be happening. The urge to touch his cheek with her palm almost overwhelmed her as his gaze held her in a gentle caress. "You like me?" she whispered.

He looked away from her, his expression a mix of surprise and confusion. For the first time she saw past his charming, careless façade; he was fighting to put it back in place. "I . . . I—"

"Rachel?"

She swirled around at the sound of her name and saw Christian standing behind her.

Tobias had never been jealous a day in his life. But when he saw Rachel run up to Christian, he turned green.

"Christian!" she exclaimed, going to him, but stopping short of throwing herself in his arms. Instead she put her hands on her hips. "You have a lot of nerve showing up here after all this time."

Christian, to his credit, appeared contrite. "Rachel, I'm so sorry. I wanted to come back earlier, but my uncle's injury was very serious. He came close to breaking his back, so they needed me to stay there until he could heal."

"And you couldn't tell me this in a letter?"

Tobias hid a grin. For once someone else was on the receiving end of her ire. And with good reason. Christian should have never been away from her for this long without giving her more of an explanation.

"I'm not much of a letter writer. To be honest, I was exhausted. I know I should have called and written more, but I kept thinking he would recover and I could come home soon. But it took longer than we all thought. He's still not a hundred percent, but I couldn't be away from home any longer."

"Oh, Christian, I'm so sorry." She took her hands off her hips and walked toward him.

Tobias's good humor disintegrated. He didn't like the soft way Rachel was talking to Christian, or the moony expression on Christian's face. Tobias cleared his throat and they broke apart, Rachel turning around and giving him an annoyed look.

Christian peeked past her shoulder. "Hello, Tobias. Nice to see you." He strode toward him and held out his hand. "It's *gut* to be back home."

"I'm sure it is." He shook Christian's hand, guilt striking him. He had no right to be jealous. Christian and Rachel had been courting long before Tobias had understood his true feelings for Rachel. Christian was his friend, and he had been so close to betraying that friendship by telling Rachel how he felt. He'd already let it slip that he liked her, and she seemed shocked by the revelation. He could only imagine how she would react if he told her how much he really cared about her.

Christian leaned forward, lowering his voice. "Hey, do mind if I have a few moments alone with my girl?"

Another wave of jealousy rose within Tobias, but he shoved it down. "Sure." He shrugged in the most nonchalant way he could muster, then looked at Rachel. "I promised Carol Mullet I'd sit beside her during the singing anyway."

Pain flashed in her eyes, and for the second time in five minutes, he wanted to kick himself. He'd made no such promise, even though he knew that Carol had liked him for a long time and probably wouldn't mind one bit if he sat next to her. He'd lashed out from his own envy and had hurt Rachel in the process, all because he couldn't handle how she made him feel—irritated, excited, interested, and most of all, confused.

Pulling down the brim of his straw hat, he headed inside the barn, needing to get away from both of them. He stood in the doorway and immediately saw Carol standing next to the refreshment table. She gave him a small wave and then smiled, her gray eyes shining behind her wire-rimmed glasses. Carol was a nice enough girl. Maybe he would sit with her after all. Perhaps she could help him forget about Rachel, who was now off limits since Christian had returned. He walked over to her and gave her his most charming grin.

"I missed you so much, Rachel."

Rachel pulled her gaze from Tobias's retreating form. "What?"

"I missed you." Christian smiled, more animated than she'd ever seen him. "I hated being apart from you for so long."

"Me too," she said absently. Why had Tobias promised to sit with Carol Mullet? Did he like her? If he did, then what kind of game was he playing, telling Rachel he liked her when he really liked someone else? Or did he just enjoy teasing them both?

"Rachel? Are you listening to me?"

She blinked and looked at Christian's face. "*Ya,* I'm listening to you." Irritation sparked her voice. "I'm standing right here, aren't I?"

Christian's smile faded. "I know you're mad at me, and you have every right to be. I should have called more, written more." He took a step toward her. "I promise, I'll make it up to you."

The sound of hymn-singing wafted over to them. Glancing around, she saw that the teens playing volleyball had already gone inside the barn. She and Christian were alone.

"I did a lot of thinking while I was gone," Christian said. He reached out and took Rachel's hand.

She jumped, surprised at the gesture. "Christian, what are you—"

"Shhh." He put his finger on her lips, and her eyes widened. "We need to talk."

Moving her mouth from his hand, she said, "I don't really think this is a *gut* ti—"

"I think we should get married this November."

"What?"

"Get married. I've thought about you every day while I was gone. It was like a part of me was missing without you. I believe God was telling me that we were meant to be together. Forever."

"But, Christian, doesn't this seem sudden?"

"I know it does, but I've been doing a lot of thinking while I was gone. When my uncle got hurt, it took a toll on my aunt. She thought she'd lost him. You should have seen how she took care of him while he was laid up."

Rachel couldn't believe his words. "You want to get married so I can take care of you?"

"*Nee*, it's not just that. I also heard about Levi." His expression sobered. "Life's too short, Rachel. And I don't see any reason why we should wait any longer to get married. You never know what might happen."

"But, Christian, you just got back. I need some time."

He took a step back, disappointment darkening his features. "Are you saying you don't want to marry me, Rachel?"

"*Nee*, I'm not saying that—" Before she could finish, he bent toward her and kissed her lightly on the mouth.

"You've made me so happy, Rachel. I know you'll be a *wunderbaar frau*."

Wife? Had she somehow agreed to marriage and didn't realize it? She didn't recognize the man in front of her. She'd never seen him so excited, so exuberant. It was as if he was a completely different person. And now she was going to marry him?

She didn't even know him anymore.

"Let's go inside," he said, putting his hand on the back of her waist as if he already possessed her. "The singing's started."

In a daze she walked with him to the barn. Thirty or so young people were sitting on wooden chairs, some in groups, some in pairs, surrounded by bales of fresh hay. When they stepped inside she expected him to drop his hand, but he didn't. Her cheeks turned red as she realized he'd all but shouted to their friends that she and Christian were more than just courting. Her gaze landed on the floor, wishing she could turn around and tell Christian that she needed to think about his proposal. When she looked up, she spied Tobias.

He was sitting next to Carol Mullet. Very close to her. She looked as if she would pop with glee. Glancing up from the hymnal, his gaze caught hers for a split moment, then he looked at Carol and smiled.

So that was it. The feelings she had for him were definitely one-sided. Good thing she found out now, before she had *really* started liking him. She should have known better anyway. Tobias Byler was only interested in himself. Soon Carol would realize that, just as Rachel had. Her initial analysis had been right—Christian was far superior than Tobias could ever hope to be. He wouldn't toy with her emotions, wouldn't make her feel like a fool. She didn't need to think about Christian's proposal any more. She had already made up her mind.

"Ready?" Christian whispered in her ear as he led her into the barn.

She turned to Christian and smiled. At least she tried to, but the burning lump in her throat made it difficult. Fortunately he didn't seem to notice. "*Ya*. I'm ready."

"Moriah, I think it's clean enough."

From her position on the kitchen floor, Moriah looked up at her mother. Emma crossed her arms, a stern expression on her face. Moriah turned her attention back to the spot she was scrubbing with a soapy rag. Sweat dripped from her brow onto the floor. "I just need to get this spot up," she said.

Emma crouched down and took the rag out of her daughter's hand. "I said, it's clean enough."

Unwilling to argue with her mother, Moriah moved to rise from the floor. The baby had grown quite a bit in the past month, swelling her belly and making her feel off balance. Emma reached out and helped her to her feet.

"You have no business scrubbing the floor," Emma chided. "Not when I can do it. Or Elisabeth and Ruth."

"You have enough work to do," Moriah said, wiping her slick forehead. August heat filtered through the house. "I'm only trying to do my share."

"You're doing more than your share. Sit down, Moriah." Emma gestured toward the kitchen table. "I'll bring you something to drink."

"*Nee,* I can get it."

"I said sit down. No arguments."

Moriah dutifully sat. Her mother returned with a cold glass of water, filled with ice cubes from the outside gas freezer. "Drink this. It will help cool you off."

The water felt refreshing sliding down her parched throat. She hadn't realized how thirsty she was. She had been so focused on getting the stain up from the floor, scrubbing and scrubbing until her hand ached. But it was no use. The stain had set in. Just as sorrow and loneliness had settled into her soul.

"I'm worried about you, Moriah. Your *daed* is too." Emma sat down, her own face rosy from the heat of the day. "You're working even harder at your chores than before, and you've been so quiet the past few weeks. You haven't even wanted to stay for dinner after the church services." She laid her hand on Moriah's forearm. "Please, *dochder,* tell me what's going on."

Moriah looked away. She didn't want to talk about her tumultuous feelings, not when she'd been trying so hard to cast them away. Levi's affair haunted her while Gabriel's declaration of love confused her. He had said he would take care of her for the rest of his life. That Levi asked him to do so. But she hadn't been good enough for Levi. What if she wasn't enough for Gabriel? What if she would never be enough for any man? She didn't want to find out. She couldn't go through this pain again.

"Moriah, honey, please. Talk to me. Is this about Gabriel?"

She jerked her head. "What makes you say that?"

"He used to visit all the time. I notice he hasn't been here in a while."

"He's busy."

Emma sighed. "I'm sure he is, but he always found time for you before."

"He must have realized I wasn't worth it."

"Now where is that coming from?"

Moriah rose from her chair. The truth was, Gabriel had come around, several times, but she had sent him away. She hadn't seen him for nearly three weeks now, except at church, where she avoided him. Evading him was easier than seeing the yearning in his eyes. "I'm going to take a nap, *Mami*." Without waiting for her mother to respond, she left the kitchen and went upstairs, glad that Elisabeth was at her babysitting job so she could have their room to herself.

She lay down on her side and stared at the wall on the opposite side of the room. The bedroom was sweltering hot, but she didn't care. Her baby moved, and she put her hand over her belly. The babe's active movements were the only thing that brought her joy anymore. But even that was tempered by the knowledge that the baby would never know his or her father.

Next to her bed was a Bible, but she didn't pick it up. She hadn't read the book in weeks, not since the day Taylor had visited, that same day Gabriel had revealed his secret. Her prayer life had always been strong, but she couldn't bring herself to pray. What good would it do? She didn't even know what to pray for anymore. All her hopes and dreams had been shattered, and she didn't trust her own judgment. How could she, when she had completely believed in Levi's fickle devotion, but had never noticed Gabriel's love?

There was one thing she had decided on. After the baby was born, she would get a job to support herself and the child. Her parents would always have a place for her, but she didn't want to depend on them anymore either. She would never marry. She would never put her trust in love again.

Flipping over on her back, she closed her eyes, tired of the thoughts assaulting her, tired of feeling empty. Finally, she succumbed to her weariness.

Gabe stood in front of the blazing forge until his face felt like it was on fire. He welcomed the burning as it heated his cheeks, threatening to sear the skin. Only until he couldn't stand it anymore did he step back, his face tingling as his flesh cooled.

If only his resentment could be as easily extinguished.

Even though the shop didn't officially open for another hour, he came out here to think, to try to figure out what he should do. He hadn't seen her in nearly a month, and he was dying inside. Telling her he loved her had broken a dam of yearning inside him, one he couldn't repair.

Leaning against one of his work tables, he hung his head. "What did you expect?" he said aloud to the empty shop. "Her to fall in love with you?"

No, he hadn't expected it. But he had hoped for it.

He loved her so much—still did—but now it was even more difficult to hide that love than it had been before. When she had been married to Levi, when he hadn't confessed his feelings aloud, he could push them down. But now that she knew, his love increased each time he caught a glimpse of her, and it was compounded by the fact that she was still out of his reach.

Picking up a rod of iron, he held it in the fiery flame of the forge, watching it grow red hot. As the rod heated, so did Gabe's emotions. Yanking the rod prematurely out of the forge, he tossed it in the water bath and threw off his gloves.

"You're up awful early."

Gabe answered his father, but didn't turn around. "*Ya.* Thought I'd get a head start."

"By ruining that piece of metal?"

With a sigh Gabe said, "Sorry."

John came up beside him. "I'm not bothered about that, *sohn.* I'm worried about you."

"Don't be. I'm fine."

"That's what everyone says, especially when they're the exact opposite. I know your heart is hurt over Moriah, especially after you told her how you feel about her, but she needs time, Gabriel."

"*Ya.*" Gabe said, but the bitterness seeped through his voice.

"You can't force her into your life, *sohn.*"

"I'm not forcing anything!"

"You don't think telling her about Levi's request might make her feel pressured?"

"I didn't have a choice." He tossed his hat on the work table and hung his head. "She was upset with me about not coming forward about Levi's affair. She asked me if I had any more secrets." He glanced up. "I had to be honest with her. I wanted her to know I would never give up on her, that I would always care for her. I wouldn't be like . . ."

"Like Levi?"

"I would never hurt her, *Daed*."

"She's already hurting, Gabriel. You both are."

"Even more reason for me to make her understand how much I love her."

"You can try. But you need to prepare your heart. Be ready to accept that you may never have her. God may have chosen another husband for Moriah."

Just the thought of it made Gabe's stomach twist in knots. If that happened he didn't think he could take it. He would never abandon his father, but how could he live with seeing her married to someone else again? "I thought you were on my side."

John put his hand on Gabe's shoulder. "I am. I always will be, no matter what. But sometimes, despite our best intentions, certain things aren't meant to be. And if you think you're letting Levi down, don't. If he were here now, he wouldn't let this go on."

"If it wasn't for me, he might be here now." Gabe sat in a chair and let his head drop in his hands.

As he sat down beside him, John asked, "What do you mean?"

"If I had told her how I felt a long time ago things would be different."

"You can't know that for sure. Moriah might have gone on to marry Levi no matter what you told her. Remember, God always has a plan."

"But what kind of plan is this? Levi's dead; Moriah's pregnant, left to raise her baby alone."

"Her family will help her. We'll all help her."

"You know what I mean. That child needs a father."

John stroked his beard for a long time. "What's the real reason you want to marry Moriah?"

"You know why. I love her. I love her more than anything."

He patted him on the shoulder. "Spend some time in prayer, Gabriel. Seek God through this. And above all, remember that sometimes the hardest thing to do when we love someone is to let them go."

The door to the shop opened and Aaron walked inside. He glanced at the two men, but didn't say anything. Instead he headed for the back of the shop and put his blue lunch cooler on the cluttered desk.

"Remember what I said." John stepped away. "Take it to God, Gabriel." He went to the front of the shop and flipped the Closed sign to Open.

Gabe worked steadily throughout the day, but his mind was consumed with Moriah and his father's words. He didn't have to pray about his reasons for wanting to marry Moriah. He loved her, and he wanted to spend the rest of his life with her. The thought of living without her made him weep. If that wasn't love, then he didn't know what was. But he did need to pray for her, for both of them. Only God could see them through this. Other than that, the only thing he was sure about was that he'd do whatever he could in his power to make her happy. Even if that meant staying away from her forever.

Chapter 16

"Tobias, what is your problem?"

Tobias looked at his brother Lukas, whose tanned complexion was florid with anger. Lukas tossed the piece of molding on the table in front of him. "This is the third time you've measured this wrong. It doesn't fit, and now I've cut too much off. If we don't get this armoire finished, *Daed* will have our heads."

"Sorry. I'll do it right this time."

"You better." Lukas was the most skilled woodworker in the Byler family, even better than their father. They all had natural talent, but Lukas's passion for the craft surpassed them all. As serious about work as he was about life, he brooked no careless mistakes from his brothers. He turned around and headed back to the opposite end of the long work table, where he had been gluing and nailing the molding on the side of the large piece of furniture.

Respect for Lukas's skill, combined with his own irritation at his lapse of attention, kept him from arguing with his brother. Instead he stalked to the very back of the shop where they stored the wood and selected another long piece of cherry molding. The wood was beautiful, as this particular Yankee customer wanted the best and had no problem paying for it. Lukas was right; if they screwed this job up, they would be losing a valuable customer, something that would upset their normally placid father.

He carried the molding back to the table and took out his tape measure. He intended to apply singular focus to his task, but as it had been happening all day, Rachel entered his thoughts. She was marrying Christian. Even though they hadn't announced it, everyone knew. Rachel's mother had been giddy with excitement, and he had over heard her and his *mami* talking about wedding plans a couple times during the church dinners. But the most telling sign had been the change in Christian. Before he had left for Charm, he had been a simple guy, not one to show too much emotion. Now, you never saw him without a smile. Of course who could blame him? If Tobias was marrying Rachel, he'd be walking around with a goofy grin too.

But Rachel's reaction confused him. She didn't act like a woman in love, at least how he thought one should be acting. He remembered how happy his sister had been when she and Levi had gotten engaged. Granted, that wasn't the best example, considering how their marriage ended, but at the time Moriah had been very much in love with Levi, and everyone could see it. Kind of like they all could tell with Christian. Yet Rachel had seemed more resigned than anything else. Resigned and apathetic.

Or maybe that was wishful thinking on his part. He hated the idea of her and Christian together, but there was nothing he could do about it. Declaring his feelings for her now would complicate everything. And Tobias hated complications. He liked being Amish in part because he enjoyed the simplicity and ease of life. Not that he didn't work hard, because he did. But he appreciated knowing what was around the next curve. With Rachel, he sure wouldn't have that. Better to let Christian deal with her temper, her need to always have the last word, her competitive nature.

Lucky Christian.

"Tobias, the molding?" Lukas shouted at him. "I need it now."

Shoving Rachel and Christian out of his mind, he ran the tape measure across the length of the molding and made the appropriate tick marks. Double-checking his work so he wouldn't experience Lukas's wrath, he took the molding to his brother, who put it up against the armoire. Nodding, he gave Tobias a half smile of approval.

At least someone was satisfied.

Gabe's palms grew damp as he pulled his buggy into the Bylers' driveway. It had been over a month since he'd seen Moriah, and he couldn't stand it anymore. He had spent every night on his knees, asking for God's guidance. The only thing that came to his mind clearly was that he needed to see her, but he didn't know if that was God's direction or his own overriding desires. Eventually he decided to take action, which had led him to try to visit her again.

He parked the buggy and stepped onto the driveway. His hat shielded his eyes from the glare of the bright sun. September had brought slightly cooler temperatures, mostly at night. Soon the harvest would begin. He had planted a small garden, and together he and his father would can the tomatoes, green beans, and beets the ground had yielded. Maybe one day he and Moriah would plant a garden for their own family, but he didn't dare dwell on that prospect for very long.

The door to the wood shop opened, and Gabe turned to his

right in time to see Tobias come outside. His light-blue shirt and dark pants were covered in sawdust. When he saw Gabe, he held up his hand and waved.

Gabe shoved his hands in his pockets and walked over to him. Tobias brushed off some of the dust from his black suspenders, but he was still covered in the fine wood powder. "Hello, Tobias."

"Nice to see you, Gabe."

"*Wie geht's?*"

"Fine, everything's fine. Just taking a break. You here to see Moriah?"

"*Ya.* Is she home?"

Tobias nodded, his welcoming expression growing sober. "She is. I don't know if she'll want to see you, though."

Gabe had expected as much. "Are you saying I should leave?"

"*Nee.* I'm not saying that at all. In fact, I'd be happy if you could talk to her. Maybe you can cheer her up a bit."

"I don't know. I really messed things up."

"Gabe, you didn't abandon her. You're still here. I don't think you're messing up at all." Tobias started toward the house, then motioned for Gabe to follow. "I'll tell her you want to see her."

"*Danki,*" Gabe said, grateful to have Tobias in his corner. He stood by the back door while Tobias walked into the kitchen. A few moments later he came outside, shaking his head. "She doesn't want to talk right now. I'm sorry."

Gabe nodded, drawing in his lips. "I'm not surprised."

Tobias looked irritated. "For the life of me, I'll never understand women. They do the opposite of what's good for them."

Suspecting he wasn't just referring to Moriah, Gabe said, "Having some lady troubles yourself?"

"Am I ever. Sometimes I wonder why I even bother."

"Because they're worth it." He said the words not only to convince Tobias but also to convince himself. "Listen, I don't know what you're up against, but let me give you a little advice. If love is within your reach, do everything you can to grab it. Don't let her get away." He looked up at the Bylers' house. "You'll only live to regret it."

Tobias cocked his head to the side. "That is good advice."

"Given from experience."

"I know." He smiled. "It's gonna take Moriah some time, Gabe, but I think she'll eventually realize she needs you. Don't give up on her."

Gabe looked at him. "I don't intend to."

"I think your wedding dress is coming along very well." Sarah carefully folded a small pleat in the waist of the dress and stitched it in place. "Don't you think so?"

Rachel stared at the dress in progress. They had cut the dress out of a lovely light-blue fabric a few days ago, and with both of them working on it, it was almost completed. She pushed her needle through the hem of the dress, only to stab her finger. "Ow."

"I told you to use a thimble." Sarah continued to sew, a shiny silver thimble on the middle finger of her left hand.

"They always slip off."

"That's because you're not used to using them. I'm afraid I waited too long to teach you to sew."

"I wasn't exactly eager to learn."

"True. You took to sewing like you took to cooking."

"Not very well." Rachel put her injured finger to her mouth.

"I wouldn't say that. You're adequate." Sarah smiled. "You'll have lots of practice after you and Christian are married. Good heavens, I can't believe the wedding is only six weeks away. We have so much more to do!" Sarah sighed with contentment and folded another pleat.

Rachel wished she could share her mother's enthusiasm about her upcoming nuptials. She also wished she could share her future husband's. Christian's excitement had yet to wane, and all their conversations now centered on their marriage. He had already decided where they would live, in his parents' *dawdi haus* until they found a home of their own. There were a couple of houses for sale in West Farmington, which wasn't too far from their families. They had already looked at one together. Rachel had hated it.

More than once they talked about children. Christian wanted a large family, at least eight kids. Rachel wasn't sure how practical that would be, considering how expensive it was to raise so many children. When she pointed that out, he gave his standard reply: God will provide. While she truly believed this, she still worried how they would make ends meet once they were married.

She was starting to think they had rushed things. As the wedding date neared, she became more and more anxious, and not in a good way. She'd even started dreaming about the ceremony. More than once she had awakened in a cold sweat when the groom in her dreams hadn't been Christian. It had been Tobias.

"Is Christian coming by today?" Sarah asked, snipping the blue thread.

"*Ya.*"

Sarah put down her needle. "You don't sound very excited."

"I see him almost every day now," Rachel said. "I guess the excitement has worn off."

Her mother gave her a dubious look, then picked up a spool of thread. "It's normal for brides to be nervous, Rachel. I was terrified when I married your father."

"You were?" She'd never heard her mother admit this before.

"*Ach,* I was. Like you and Christian, we didn't court long. And though I knew I loved him, I was still scared."

"How did you know you loved him?"

"Let's see. I'll have to think about that. We've been married almost thirty years now." She fingered one of the ribbons on her white *kapp,* and Rachel could suddenly imagine her mother as a young girl newly in love. "I thought your father was one of the most exciting men I'd ever met."

"Really?"

"*Ya.* He was so charming, quick with a joke, but very kind. I remember one afternoon he came by to help my *daed* with the harvest, and one of my cats had just died. He stopped working to sit with me. I cried like a baby over that pet, and when I was done I felt foolish. I was eighteen years old at the time, a year younger than you, and I was far too old to be crying like that. But Emmanuel never teased me about that. Instead he put his arm around my shoulders and I leaned against him. That's when I knew I would love this man for the rest of my life."

Rachel's sighed. "What a romantic story. I never knew *Daed* had it in him."

Sarah chuckled. "Your *daed* has a side he never shows you *kinder.*" She reached out and touched Rachel's hand. "Marriage isn't easy, Rachel. It takes hard work. But the rewards and blessings are many. We couldn't be prouder of our *kinder.*"

"Even Aaron?"

"Even Aaron." Tears sprang to her eyes. "Aaron has had a rough time of it, to be sure. But he's changed. God is doing a *gut* work in him, I can see that. Hopefully one day you'll see that too."

Her father suddenly came in the kitchen, covered in dirt from working in the barn. Sarah held up her hand and stopped him from taking another step. "Emmanuel! Off with those boots."

He grumbled as he pulled them off and set them outside the door. "Can I come in now?" he said, pulling off his hat, revealing the bald spot on the top of his head that had grown larger with age.

"*Ya*. Now you can come in." Sarah turned back to her sewing as he went to the cabinet to get a plastic cup. He took it to the sink and filled it with water from the tap.

Rachel regarded her parents for a moment. They weren't overly demonstrative with their affections, as was the Amish way. But she had never doubted that they loved each other. For the first time she thought about how their relationship had weathered raising six children, especially Aaron's drug abuse. She tried to imagine herself and Christian thirty years from now.

For some reason, she couldn't.

"Christian's coming," her father said, looking out the window. "That boy's like clockwork with his visits, isn't he?"

"*Ya*," Rachel said, still unsettled by her lack of clarity regarding her future with Christian.

"There's someone coming behind him too. You expecting someone else?"

Rachel rose from her chair and started toward the window. "*Nee*. Only Christian."

"Then who's that?"

She recognized the vehicle right away.

Tobias.

Tobias wanted to throw up. Never had his stomach been so twisted up. For the past two days he thought about his conversation with Gabe Miller. He watched as Gabe stopped by their house and kept trying to visit Moriah, even though she refused to see him. The man said he wasn't giving up on her, and he was as good as his word.

But Gabe's visits weren't the only thing that had gotten Tobias thinking. Gabe's admonishment to grab love when it's right in front of you had echoed in Tobias's mind. He could see how miserable both Gabe and his sister were. How her marriage to Levi had been a mistake, and how both of them were living with regrets.

Tobias didn't want to live that way. He didn't want to regret letting Rachel go, even if he wasn't sure he ever had her in the first place.

He'd never been a man of risk, always playing things safe. Today, he would take the biggest risk of his life. If he didn't vomit first.

He pulled his buggy beside Christian's. He'd been hoping Christian wouldn't be here, but now he had second thoughts. Now he could talk to them both at the same time and hopefully make them both understand why he had to do this.

Christian jumped out of the buggy and walked toward Tobias. "Hello," he said, sporting that crazy lovesick grin he'd had on his face since returning from Charm. "What brings you by?"

His stomach coiled into another knot. He truly understood what Gabe had gone through, being in love with Moriah but not wanting to hurt his brother Levi. Tobias didn't want to hurt Christian, and for a split second, he thought about turning around and going straight back home. But he had come this far. There was no turning back now.

"I'm here to see Rachel," he said to Christian.

"Oh? What about?"

Tobias didn't like the possessive way Christian asked the question, as if Rachel were already his wife. "I just need to talk to her."

"Can it wait 'til later? We were planning to go look at another house this afternoon. I think she'll like this one, and the price is right."

"*Nee.* It can't wait." He looked past Christian to see Rachel coming out of the house. His stomach twisted again, but not with nerves this time. Good heavens, she was so beautiful. Fair-haired Rachel, with sharp blue eyes and tongue to match, along with a fiery temper that he loved to spark. He couldn't let her marry Christian. Not without a fight first.

"Tobias, what do you want?"

He could see she was annoyed with him, probably over the way he had treated her at the singing in August, where he had purposely flirted with Carol Mullet in front of her. Looking back on that now, he realized how immature he'd been. If he had only been honest with himself, and honest with Christian, then maybe Rachel would be his right now. Instead someone's heart would soon be broken.

He hoped it wouldn't be his.

"I need to talk to you, Rachel." He looked at Christian. "There's something you both need to hear."

Rachel couldn't imagine what Tobias had to say. He seemed uneasy. Disconcerted, as if he were about to jump out of his own skin. Instead of his usual relaxed stance, his hands were thrust deeply inside the pockets of his trousers, and his full lips were pressed tightly together.

Christian moved to stand next to Rachel. He put one hand on the back of her waist, which had been his habit whenever they were in public together. As if he were branding her as his own. The more he did it, the less she appreciated the symbolism. "What is it that you want to tell us?"

He took a deep breath and looked at Rachel. "I wanted to tell you I'm sorry. I acted like a *dummkopf* at the singing last month. I apologize."

She didn't know what to say. That had happened almost three weeks ago, and she hadn't thought about it since. Well, not too often anyway. Okay, more than she wanted to admit, but still, she had assumed he'd forgotten all about the incident by now.

Christian looked confused. "What are you talking about?" He glanced at Rachel.

Tobias held her gaze, and she could barely breathe. His eyes were filled with something she'd never seen before, an emotion that made her run hot and cold at the same time.

"Did I miss something?" Christian said.

She ignored him. How could she be expected to pay attention to Christian with Tobias looking at her like that?

Tobias moved toward her. "Rachel, I'm sorry for every dumb thing I've ever said to you. For all the stupid things I've done. I promise, things will be different from now on."

"How?" She could barely speak, her mouth had gone dry.

He took another step. "Trust me. I promise you, they will."

"Will someone please tell me what's going on here?"

Tobias glanced at Christian. "I need to apologize to you, friend."

"Apologize?"

"For what I'm about to say." He looked back to Rachel and leaned toward her. "You can't marry Christian, Rachel."

Her eyes grew wide at his unexpected words. "Why?"

"Because. I want you to marry me."

Rachel literally could not speak. She tried to form words, any words, but nothing came out of her mouth. Tobias asking her to marry him rendered her speechless.

Christian, however, was not. "I don't know what you're up to, Byler. If this is a joke, it isn't funny."

"It's not a joke. I'm sorry, Christian, but I'm in love with her."

"You're what?" Finally finding her voice, she had to fight to keep from swaying sideways. "What did you just say?"

"I love you, Rachel. I should have told you that night at the Yoders', but I chickened out. I should have asked you to marry me that night, but I didn't. I made a mistake, and I'm trying to fix it."

"Wait a minute." She held up her hands and took a step back. "You made a mistake by not asking me to marry you?"

"*Ya.* Because if I had, you wouldn't be with him." He gestured to Christian, who was glaring at him with open hostility. "Look, I'm not doing this to hurt you. You're my friend."

"Some friend. You're trying to steal my girl."

"I'm not trying to steal her." He faced Rachel. "I'm giving her another choice. Rachel, tell me you don't love me. Tell me you love Christian, and that you want to marry him. If I hear those words, I'll walk away right now, and I'll never bother you again. I promise."

Rachel looked at him, then at Christian. She didn't say anything for a long moment.

"Rachel?" Christian dropped his arm from her waist. "Tell him. Tell him you love me."

Turning, she faced Christian. "Do you love me?"

Christian gaped. "Of course I do. Why would you even ask?"

"Because you've never told me. I've never heard you say the words."

"Of course I've said them." He frowned. "Haven't I?"

She shook her head. "*Nee.* You haven't. And I need to hear them."

He lowered his voice. "I love you. I'll tell you that for the rest of our lives if you need me to."

"Why? Why do you love me? Better yet, why do you want to marry me?"

Christian backed away. "Wait a minute, why am I the one being questioned here? You should be asking Tobias this. *Nee,* you should be telling him to leave."

"I can't. Not until I have my answer." Her heart thrummed in her chest, threatening to explode.

"You already know why I want to marry you, Rachel. We've talked about this."

"We've talked about where we'll live, and how many children we'll have. But we've never talked about us, Christian. We've never shared our feelings." Her body shook with emotion. "I've never said I love you either. I don't think you even noticed."

Christian's eyes hooded. "Rachel . . . what are you saying?"

"I'm saying I can't marry you, Christian. Things don't feel right between us. They never have."

"Is this because of him?" Christian pointed at Tobias.

"*Nee.*"

"Then you don't love him?"

She gazed at Tobias. Handsome, charming, unpredictable Tobias. He drove her crazy, and she knew he always would. Yet she couldn't imagine living without him.

His mouth curved in smile, one that promised a life of passion, consternation, and love.

"*Ya,*" she said. "I love him." Then she turned to Christian. "I'm sorry. I really am."

"That's how you really feel?"

Rachel nodded. "*Ya.*"

Christian shook his head, his shoulders slumping. "I guess there's nothing more for me to say." Without looking at either of them, he spun around and went to his buggy. Tobias and Rachel moved out of the way as he turned the vehicle around. When he pulled up alongside them, he stopped. "I do care for you, Rachel. I just want you to know that."

"I know. I care for you too."

"But that's not enough, is it?"

"*Nee.* It's not enough."

He looked at Tobias, his eyes narrowing. "If you ever hurt her, you'll have me to deal with."

"I understand."

Christian slapped the reins on the horse's flanks and drove off. Rachel turned to Tobias, apprehension suddenly filling her. "Did you mean what you said?"

"About loving you? *Ya.*" He leaned in closer. "About marrying you? Absolutely. I love you, Rachel. I know my past actions have shown otherwise. All I'm asking for is a chance to prove how much I want to be your husband. To fall asleep with you at night and wake up with you in the morning. To be with you for the rest of our lives . . . until death do us part."

His words etched themselves on her heart. That was what she needed to hear, and they were words Christian would have never been able to say, not with the sincerity and love Tobias had. Oh, how much she loved this man, more than she ever thought possible. More than anything she wanted to fall into his arms and accept his proposal. But she couldn't resist holding him off a little longer.

"Well, I do have a wedding dress that's almost finished." She tapped her chin with her finger. "Getting married to you would be the practical thing to do, since *Mami* and *Daed* have made so many preparations already."

"I just told you how much I love you and you're talking about being practical?"

"I can't help it. I'm a practical woman."

"And I've never done anything practical in my life."

Rachel grinned. "It's never too late to start." She took his hand, surprised by her boldness, yet the gesture felt completely natural. "I can't wait to marry you, Tobias Byler."

"Because it's practical?" Even though the words were said in a teasing way, she could see the faint glimmer of worry in his eyes.

"*Nee.*" She squeezed his hand, happy to see the joy suddenly reflected in his expression. "I can't wait to marry you . . . because I love you."

Chapter 17

Gabe stood on Moriah's front porch, hesitating to knock. Frankly, her rejection had started to wear on him, and he wondered if he should heed his father's advice and let her go. But something inside him refused to give up, not yet.

"Father God," he whispered. "Please, let her open the door to me. Help me to reach her. I can't do this without you." Bolstered by his prayer, he rapped on the frame of the screen door. Emma answered right away.

"Gabriel," she said through the screen. Although Emma hadn't always been home when Gabe stopped by, he knew she was aware of his frequent visits. Still, she didn't seem annoyed with his persistence. Quite the opposite. "It's *gut* to see you. *Wie geht's?*"

"*Gut, danki.* Is Moriah home?" His standard question, which was always met with Moriah's standard answer—she was too busy to have visitors. He fully expected to hear those same words from Emma.

"*Ya,* she is." Emma opened the door and stepped outside on the front porch. "Rebekkah put Moriah on bedrest this week," Emma said, her voice nearly a whisper.

His heart jumped with apprehension concerning the midwife's decision. "Is she okay? Is the baby all right?"

"The baby is fine. It's Moriah she's worried about. She's not getting enough rest, and she won't listen to anyone when we tell her to take it easy." Emma sighed. "I never knew my *dochder* had such a stubborn streak. Rebekkah told her flat out that if she didn't follow orders, the baby would be in jeopardy. Only then would Moriah listen."

"Maybe I should come back another time," Gabe said, even though he didn't want to leave. This was as close as he'd gotten to her in weeks.

"*Nee*. She's asleep on the couch right now. Go in and sit down, then I'll wake her. I must apologize for her rudeness, Gabriel. You must understand, she hasn't been herself, not for a long time."

"No need to apologize. I only want to talk to her for a moment. I won't bother her too long."

"*Danki*." She smiled. "I know how much you care for her. I was concerned at first. After everything she's endured, I thought the last thing she needed was another suitor, especially so soon. But I can see that this is different. You're different. You're not like . . ."

"My brother?"

Emma nodded.

"You're right, I'm not. Somehow I have to convince Moriah of that."

"I know you will, just as you have convinced me. Come, let's go inside."

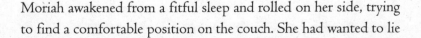

Moriah awakened from a fitful sleep and rolled on her side, trying to find a comfortable position on the couch. She had wanted to lie down upstairs in her room, but the heat of the day coupled with being in the last two months of her pregnancy made the bedroom unbearable. Even though the front room was several degrees cooler, she still felt too warm. Unable to relax, she sat up and started to reach for a magazine to fan herself with when she heard the front screen door close. Emma walked inside, Gabriel Miller following closely behind.

Her body stiffened as a fusion of emotions tumbled through her. Seeing Gabriel standing in front of her, his brown eyes consumed with hope and trepidation, made her realize how much she'd missed him. But the feelings were intrusive. She'd spent the past two months shutting them down. Why did it take him only a few short seconds for him to revive them again?

"Hello, Moriah." His deep voice—soft, gentle—sent a ripple of warmth down her spine, causing her to wince. She didn't need to have this kind of reaction to him. She didn't want to.

"Gabriel, why don't you sit down?"

Moriah looked up at Emma, betrayed. Her mother had known she didn't want to see Gabriel, yet she invited him in. How could she do this to her?

But Emma ignored her as she said, "I'll bring you both a glass of lemonade. Or would you prefer iced tea, Gabriel?"

"Lemonade is fine, *danki*."

As Emma disappeared into the kitchen, Moriah stared down at her lap, fingering the ribbons on her *kapp*. She heard Gabriel clear his throat, but he didn't say anything. An uncomfortable silence stretched between them.

"Moriah?" he finally said. "Will you please look at me?"

After hesitating for a moment, she turned. He had taken off his straw hat, placing it in his lap. He ran his long fingers through his brown hair, and not for the first time she noticed his muscular forearms. "Gabriel, I can't talk to you right now."

"Then when can we talk? Just name the time and place and I'll be there." When she didn't answer him, he added, "You can't keep pushing me away, Moriah."

"I'm not." She gazed at her lap again.

He let out a bitter laugh. "Oh really? Then what do you call refusing to see me?"

"I don't have to see everyone who visits me."

"Moriah, you know that's not fair."

She lifted her head. "Fair? You have no right to talk to me about fairness."

"I reckon I don't." He leaned forward in the chair, an intense expression on his face. "Moriah, I know I've made a mess of things. I should have told you about Levi and Taylor, but at the time I wanted to protect you."

"I don't need protecting. Not anymore."

"I disagree. You're vulnerable right now—"

"I've always been vulnerable, Gabriel. Idealistic. Always seeing the best in people, even when they showed me their worst. And what did it get me? Nothing."

"You have a baby," he said softly.

A stab of remorse ran through her. "*Ya.* I have a baby. And this child means more to me than anything." She looked directly at him. "My baby is all I need, Gabriel. I don't need your concern, or your protection."

Hurt seeped into his eyes. "That's not all I'm offering you, Moriah. I'm offering you my heart. My love."

"I can't accept it."

"Maybe not now, but in time."

She shook her head. "You don't understand. Time won't change anything. It won't change how I feel." She lied, for even now she could feel him melting her defenses with his loving words. "Find someone else. Don't waste your love on me."

"Oh, Moriah." He got off the chair and knelt down beside her on the couch. "I'm not wasting anything, especially my love. I wish there was a way I could make you see how much I want to be with you."

"Because Levi told you to."

"*Nee,* this has nothing to do with Levi. I regret telling you about what he said, but you asked me for honesty, and I wanted to show you that I will never lie to you, or betray you."

She closed her eyes. "You're making promises you can't keep."

He rose. "It's not going to work, Moriah. You can keep me at arm's length, but that won't change the way I feel. I will love you forever. But I can't, and I won't, force you to love me." He picked up his hat and put it back on his head. "It's up to you now, Moriah. All you have to do is say the word and I'll stay. And if you want me to go . . . I'll go."

She couldn't look at him. For if she did she would never be able to utter the words she had to say, for both their sakes. "Good-bye, Gabriel."

He didn't move right away, but then she heard his footsteps on the wooden floor, followed by the bang of the screen door. Only when she heard the faint *clip-clop* of his horse and buggy on their driveway did she let the tears fall.

Emma entered the room, carrying two glasses of lemonade. She took one look at Moriah and set them on the coffee table, then went and sat down next to her. Gathering her daughter in her arms, she said, "What happened?"

But Moriah didn't answer her. She couldn't tell her mother that she had just destroyed her last chance at love. Instead she leaned against her and sobbed.

Later that afternoon, after Moriah had cried herself into a restless sleep, her mother awakened her. "Moriah," she said softly. "You have another visitor."

Her eyelids, heavy with sleep, fluttered open. "Who?"

"John Miller."

Fully awake now, she pushed herself, with some effort, into a sitting position. What was John doing here?

"Do you want me to tell him to come back another time?" She brushed Moriah's forehead with her hand.

Moriah shook her head. "That's all right. I'd like to see him."

A few moments later, John entered the room, his battered straw hat in his hands. Other than at church services, she hadn't seen him in more than two months, and she realized how much she missed him. Even though she had to cut off any chance of a relationship with Gabriel, she couldn't do the same to his father. "Come in," she said. "Have a seat."

John shuffled inside, and then slowly lowered his body down on the chair. "It's *gut* to see you," he said.

"It's *gut* to see you. I've missed you, very much."

"I've missed you too." He looked at the mountainous bulge of her tummy. "How is my grandchild getting along?"

"Fine. Rebekkah said I'm right on schedule with the delivery."

"That's great news. I can't wait to hold him—or her. I remember when Gabriel and Levi were born . . ." He paused, then continued. "What a joyous day that was. Velda and I had never been happier." A smile appeared on his face, crinkling the corners of his eyes. "I'm sure you'll feel the same way too."

She nodded, relying on the joy of her child to block out her pain. "You know you're welcome to see the baby any time you want. And once I'm back on my feet, *Mami* and I will bring the babe over."

"Does that go for Gabriel too?"

Pausing, she said, "I wouldn't keep him from seeing his own kin."

"But you don't want to see him."

Moriah leaned back on the pillow, averting her eyes from John's.

"I thought you two were friends."

"We were."

"You're not treating him like much of a friend. He comes to visit you, you send him away. One of these days he won't be coming back."

"That would be a good thing."

John didn't say anything for a long moment. "I know how he feels about you, Moriah."

Her head jerked in his direction. "You do?"

"*Ya.* And I also know why you don't want to see him. You're scared."

Unbidden, tears welled in her eyes. "Don't I have a right to be?"

"*Ya,* you do. But you can't keep running away from your fear. And ignoring Gabriel isn't going to help matters."

She wiped the moisture from her eyes. "Did he send you over here to talk to me?"

"Absolutely not." John fingered the brim of his hat. "He'd be spittin' mad if he knew I was over here. And I probably shouldn't interfere, but I don't like seeing either one of you stuck on this merry-go-round anymore. Don't shut him out of your life, Moriah. You'll come to regret it if you do."

"But what if I regret letting him in?"

His smile was gentle. "I know you're hurting from what Levi did to you. Everyone understands that, including Gabriel. But that doesn't mean you have cut him out of your life completely."

"He wants so much from me. More than I can give."

"Moriah, for as long as I've known you, you've been a giver. You gave all your heart and soul to my Levi. I loved my boy, but I'm not blind to what he did to you. He ran your well dry, and maybe it's time for you to get filled up. We all have wounds from this, wounds that the Lord needs to heal. Sometimes He heals you Himself." John stood, his movements slightly stiff. "And sometimes, He sends others to bandage us up. One thing I know for sure, you can't be restored on your own." Picking up his hat, he gave her another smile. "Well, guess I've meddled enough for one day. I should be getting back home."

She noticed the fresh scar on his hand, the one he had injured on the forge. "Are you still drinking your tea?"

"Every night. Though I gotta admit, it tasted better when you made it. Maybe someday you won't mind making it for me again." He winked, then turned around and left.

Moriah stared out the window in the front room, mulling over John's words. Was God's hand in this after all? Since Levi's death she had questioned how any of this could be His will. Levi's leaving, his affair, widowed and left to raise a child alone—this was how God showed His love for her?

Then again, how had she shown her love for Him? By shutting Him, and everyone else, out of her life. By refusing to pray, refusing to seek Him in her pain. No wonder she was lonely and miserable.

The family Bible lay on the coffee table in front of her. She picked it up, letting it fall open in the middle. Psalms. She found the High German language a challenge to read, but she muddled through it.

"He healeth the broken hearted, and bindeth up their wounds."

Closing her eyes, she held the Bible against her chest, pouring her soul out to God. Her fear over letting Gabriel into her heart, despite her wanting to let him in. She beseeched the Lord to take away the loneliness and grief, her constant companions. A lump jumped in her throat. "My heart and spirit are broken, Lord," she whispered. "Please, healeth them."

Chapter 18

Moriah folded her hands across her huge belly as she listened to her brother and Rachel exchange wedding vows. Her due date was very near, and she hadn't felt well when she'd awakened. But she wouldn't miss Tobias's wedding for the world.

The entire community had been shocked when Rachel and Tobias had announced their engagement two weeks ago. Everyone but the Detweilers and the Bylers had assumed Rachel would marry Christian. To his credit, Christian didn't say a word against Rachel or Tobias. But he wasn't at the wedding either. Moriah didn't blame him. While she was happy for her brother, who everyone could see was completely in love with his soon-to-be bride, listening to the service was difficult. It was nearly a year to the day she had married Levi.

Her stomach lurched as the baby moved again, and she shifted in her chair. Then a squeezing pain seared across her abdomen. The pains had started yesterday, but they had been sporadic, more uncomfortable than anything else. But this pain was different, more intense. She glanced at her *mami* and *daed,* who were watching the service and beaming at the bride and groom. She didn't want to do anything to disturb their happiness, or her brother's wedding.

Over the past couple weeks she had been engrossed in wedding details, helping her mother and Sarah prepare for today. Yet she had taken time to rest, to read the Bible, and especially to pray.

She still didn't know what to do about Gabriel. She had felt God nudging her to talk to him, but her fear held her back. The few times she had seen him, he had kept his distance, honoring her wishes. She had seen him walk into the Detweilers' home earlier that day, but he had ignored her, instead walking up to Tobias and offering his congratulations right before the ceremony.

He looked so striking in his dark trousers, crisp white shirt, and black vest. He'd removed his black hat, revealing thick locks of chestnut-colored hair. Then he laughed, his smile illuminating his entire face, causing her breath to catch in her throat. An intense longing rose within her, one she had never experienced before, not even with Levi. When he turned from her brother, she inexplicably wished he would make his way to her, just so she could be near him. But he didn't give her a glance as he walked to the back of the room and sat down next to his *daed*.

The bishop pronounced Tobias and Rachel husband and wife, and the two of them turned and faced the congregation. Her brother nearly glowed as he looked down at his beautiful bride, her hand resting lightly on the crook of his arm, a radiant smile lighting up her face. Moriah said a quick prayer of blessing for their union, then another sharp pain stabbed at her midsection. Glancing at her belly, she saw it tighten beneath her gray dress. She winced and looked around, glad no one noticed her discomfort.

Everyone stood and started talking, anticipating the delicious meal to come. Moriah started to rise, but was assaulted by another pain, longer in duration and nearly taking her breath away. When it subsided, she tried to get up again, her protruding belly making her feel awkward and unbalanced, until she felt someone take her elbow and gently help her up.

"*Danki,*" she said, then looked up and gasped.

"You're welcome." Gabriel let go of her arm. "I hope you don't mind, but you looked like you were having a bit of trouble there. Are you feeling all right?"

His kindness amazed her. Even after she had hurt him so deeply, he still cared. "*Ya,*" she said. "I'm fine. The baby is very active today."

"How close are you to delivery?"

"A little over a week, according to Rebekkah."

"I'm excited to meet my new niece or nephew." Doubt crept into his face. "If that's okay with you."

"Of course you can, Gabriel. I would never keep you from seeing the *boppli.*"

Relief washed over his features. "*Danki.*"

His gentleness increased her remorse. She really had been horrible to make him doubt whether he would be a part of Levi's baby's life. She remembered those dark hours when she thought she had been protecting herself from pain. In reality she had not only perpetuated it, but she had spread it on Gabriel too. She had to let him know how sorry she was. "Gabriel, I—"

Her hand went to her belly as another burning wave tore through her. Fortunately this one had been brief, but it had brought tears to her eyes.

"Moriah, something's wrong." Gabriel moved closer to her. "Let me get your *mami.*"

"*Nee,* she's busy with the meal. I'll be all right."

"I don't think so. You're as white as a sheet."

Perspiration broke out on her upper lip. "I don't want to worry my family. This is Tobias's day." She couldn't stand to ruin his wedding.

"Then let me take you home. I'll run and fetch Rebekkah afterward."

Moriah nodded. "All right."

"Where's your cloak?"

She told him where he could find her wrap, and he dashed off to retrieve it. The pain had subsided to nothing, but she was still worried. Her due date was a week away. Certainly she wasn't going into labor now.

Gabriel returned and helped her slip into her cloak. By this time most everyone had moved outside. The day was unusually warm for November, and at the last minute they had moved the meal outdoors. No one had noticed that she and Gabriel had stayed behind, and when he escorted her out to his buggy, she was relieved to see the guests involved in their own activities.

As he helped her into the buggy, another contraction came. He put his arm around her shoulders and she leaned against him, gritting her teeth against the pain. When it subsided, she took a deep breath. "*Ach*. That one hurt."

"What do you need me to do?" he asked, still holding on to her.

"Just take me home."

He assisted her into the seat, then dashed around to the other side of the buggy and jumped in. "Hang on, Moriah. We'll be home in no time."

She nodded, grateful the pain had gone away.

"Do you think you're in labor?"

"*Ya.*" She clutched her belly and exhaled, trying to calm the terror rising inside her. "I don't know if I can do this," she whispered.

Gabriel's hand slipped inside hers. He squeezed it lightly. "You can, Moriah."

Tears fell out of the corners of her eyes. "I'm scared, Gabriel."

"I know you are. But you'll be fine. In a little while you'll have a beautiful *boppli*." His words and touch comforted her.

They made it to her house in quick time. When he pulled into the driveway, another contraction hit, and she waited for it to pass before she got out of the buggy.

Gabriel put his arm around her waist this time and helped her to the house. When she reached the front porch, her water broke.

"Gabriel!" she exclaimed, clutching his *reck*.

He glanced at the ground, unfazed. "It's all right, Moriah. Let's get in the house."

A few moments later he led her to her parents' bedroom, which was the only bedroom on the first floor. She sat down while another contraction, this time stronger, seared through her. Letting out a cry of agony she screamed, "Help me!"

With each of Moriah's cries, Gabriel's anxiety increased. He tried to remain calm for her sake, but inside he could barely keep it together. He hated seeing her like this, consumed with agony as the contractions became stronger and more frequent. When she was able, he laid her back on her parents' bed and brushed her damp brow with the back of his hand.

"I'm going to fetch Rebekkah," he said, amazed by the steadiness of his voice. "I'll be right back."

She clamped her fingers down on his arm. "*Nee!*" He held his breath as another contraction came and went. "Don't leave me, Gabriel. I can't do this alone."

"You won't. Rebekkah will be here to help."

"There's no time." Her gaze bored into his, her eyes holding a desperate combination of pain and fear. "You have to help me."

Gabriel's birthing experience was limited at best. He'd helped a neighbor deliver a calf when he was a teenager, but that in no way compared with this situation. Yet he knew she was right; the speed and the intensity of the contractions filled him with stark panic. He couldn't leave her to have this baby alone.

Yanking off his *reck*, he asked, "What should I do?"

She gripped the sheets as another contraction came. "I don't know!"

That wasn't what he wanted to hear. He flipped off his hat and rolled up his sleeves, his mind frantic. His mouth turned to cotton as he tried to figure out what to do. The next contraction forced her to a halfway sitting position. He could see her knees drop open to the sides underneath her dress. *Dear God in heaven, help me!*

"Moriah?"

Gabe breathed with relief when he heard Lukas's voice coming from the front room. "In here!" he yelled.

Lukas poked his head in the doorway. "*Daed* saw you two leave and he sent me to find out what's going on." His gaze darted from Moriah to Gabe. The color drained from the seventeen-year-old's face. "Is she having the *boppli*?"

"Go get Rebekkah Fisher! Hurry!"

Lukas ran out of the room, and Gabriel continued to hold Moriah's hand. "Rebekkah will be here soon," he said.

She gripped his hand, her face dripping with sweat and red from the pain. "Don't leave me," she said, gasping. "Don't ever leave me, Gabriel."

Without thinking, he lifted her hand to his lips and planted a kiss on the knuckles. "I won't." Her words sparked a tiny flame of hope inside him that she meant something other than him seeing her through the birth. "I'm not going anywhere."

"She's beautiful."

Moriah's eyelids opened at the sound of her mother's voice. She smiled as she saw her baby cradled in Emma's arms, only the very top of her head and face visible underneath the light yellow receiving blanket.

Every fiber of her being hurt, but the dull throb was nothing compared to the relentless pain she'd gone through giving birth. Exhausted, she had fallen asleep soon after she held her new daughter, barely remembering Rebekkah taking the baby out of her arms to wash her tiny body and wrap her in the blanket.

"Perfect in every way." Rebekkah's voice reached Moriah's ears, and she turned to see the midwife standing over her. "You didn't sleep for very long." She smiled. "Would you like to sit up and hold your *boppli*?"

Moriah nodded and allowed Rebekkah to help her to a seated position. The midwife propped pillows behind her back. A clean blanket lay across her lap, and her *kapp* had been removed at some point. The pain of childbirth had been so consuming that she barely remembered what had happened until she'd heard her baby's cry after the final push. Now her arms ached to hold the child she'd been anxious to meet for so long.

"Here she is." Tears welled in Emma's eyes as she passed the swaddled bundle to Moriah. "You should be proud of yourself, *dochder.*"

"*Ya,*" Rebekkah added. "You made my job very easy. By the time I got here the *boppli* was already crowning."

Moriah gazed down into her daughter's face. Her eyes were barely open, but she could make out their bluish-gray color. Her cheeks were round and pink, and her lips were full. Downy brown hair covered her head, the same shade as her father's.

"Do you have a name for the *boppli*?" Rebekkah asked.

"Velda," Moriah replied without hesitation.

Emma put her fingers to her lips. "After Levi and Gabriel's *mudder*?"

She nodded and looked up at her mother. "Velda Anne."

"After my *mudder.*" Tears rolled down her cheeks. "*Danki,* Moriah. And *danki* for my beautiful *grossdochder.*"

Moriah smiled. "Where's Gabriel?"

"He's in the front room." Rebekkah chuckled. "I think you scared about ten years off that man. I'd never come across anyone so happy to see me in my life."

"I couldn't tell." Then again, she had been more than a little preoccupied. Things were starting to come back to her now, and she remembered how he had stayed by her side, holding her hand, giving her words of encouragement until Velda Anne was born. He had still been next to her when she'd fallen asleep. "Has he held the baby yet?"

"*Nee.*" Rebekkah looked at her. "Would you like him to?"

She nodded. "Please. Tell him I want to see him."

Emma went to get Gabriel while Rebekkah made sure Moriah was completely covered. Then she said, "I'll leave you all alone for a few minutes. Velda's asleep, but if she gets cranky, let me know and I'll help you get her fed." She left the room.

Moriah leaned back against the pillow, her baby tucked in her arms. A perfect miracle, she was a gift from God. As she marveled at her daughter, she realized that God had been with her through everything. She had questioned His plan for her life, especially after Levi's betrayal. But now she could see how going through the pain had made her stronger. Over the past few weeks, she had asked the Lord to heal her heart. He had done that not only through her child but through Gabriel as well. Even after she had hurt him, he stood by her.

"Moriah?"

Gabriel stood in the doorway, as if he didn't know whether he should come in or not. His gaze went to Velda Anne, and his smile, coupled with the tenderness in his eyes, touched her.

"Come see your niece," she said, smiling and lifting the baby slightly toward him.

He strode in and stood by the side of the bed, still appearing unsure. She motioned for him to sit next to her, and he did.

"*Danki*," she said, with all the sincerity and gratitude in her heart.

"No need to thank me, I didn't do anything." His brown eyes softened. "You, on the other hand, were incredible."

She blushed, then looked down at her baby. "Do you want to hold her?" He nodded, and she placed Velda Anne in his arms.

"She's beautiful," he said, staring at her. "Emma said you named her after *Mami*."

"*Ya*. I think it suits her."

"I think you're right." Gabriel smiled.

Moriah took a deep breath as an all-consuming wave of peace washed over her. As she watched Gabriel hold her daughter in his strong arms, she understood how right it all was. He had said he would love Levi's child, and she could see that love in his eyes as he gazed at Velda Anne's precious face. He had been by her side through everything, just as he'd promised, never asking for anything in return. He had been her rock through the dark times, and had shared the happiest moment of her life. His belief and love in her had never wavered, a shining example of God's own devotion to His children.

Tears filled her eyes.

"Moriah?" his voice covered her in a gentle caress. "Why are you crying?"

"I'm so sorry, Gabriel. I'm sorry for sending you away, for not trusting in you." She wiped her nose with the top of her index finger.

"Shhh," he said, tucking Velda Anne deeper in the crook of his arm. He reached out and wiped the tears off Moriah's cheek with this thumb. "It's all right."

"*Nee,* it's not."

"Listen to me, Moriah. I won't let you do this. We've all made mistakes, but those are in the past. The time of mourning is over." He pressed a kiss to Velda Anne's forehead, then smiled. "The time of celebrating has begun."

She grinned through her tears. "You're right. We have a lot to celebrate." Consumed with joy, she reached out and took Gabriel's hand.

He squeezed it and smiled, but didn't say anything. He didn't have to. She knew he understood her meaning completely.

Chapter 19

Rachel snuggled Moriah's three-month-old daughter in her arms. She and Tobias were sitting on the Bylers' sofa in the front room while everyone else had gathered in the kitchen. It was Sunday, a day of rest and, in this house, celebration.

"Isn't she adorable, Tobias?"

"*Ya,*" he said, looking at his niece. "Cute." He picked up a copy of *Family Life* magazine from the coffee table and thumbed through it.

"That's all you have to say?"

He cast her a sidelong glance. "What else do you want me to say? She's a *boppli.* They're all cute." He inclined his head and looked at Velda Anne for a moment. "Although I'll admit, she's prettier than most."

"*Ya,* she is. Hopefully we'll have one of our own someday soon."

"Maybe." He gave her a wicked look. "Until then, we'll have fun trying."

"Tobias!" Rachel admonished him, but only halfheartedly. "Your parents could walk in here at any moment."

Instead of behaving himself, he scooted closer to her and nuzzled her neck.

A chill ran through her entire body, and though she didn't want to—she really, *really* didn't want to—she pulled away. "Stop it!"

His sly grin made her toes curl. "Only if you promise we'll continue this later."

Rachel could barely breathe. Being married to Tobias had been everything she ever dreamed of—exciting, unpredictable, at times exasperating, and above all, filled with fun and love. They brought out the best in each other, and even though they hadn't stopped being competitive—she had just beat him in a game of washers last weekend—they also didn't mind losing, as long as it was to each other. They had also started their marriage on solid financial footing. Between what he made working for his father and her tips and pay at the restaurant, they had been able to buy a house last month.

"Let's get out of here," he whispered in her ear.

"You want to go home? We haven't been here that long."

"It's been long enough." He looked down at the baby. "Don't get me wrong, Velda Anne," he said. "I love you, but you're taking up *mei frau*'s attention. She'll tell you herself, I don't share very well."

Rachel laughed. "Fine. Let me take her to Moriah. Then we can tell everyone good-bye."

They walked into the busy kitchen. John Miller was seated at the table with Joseph Byler, the men engaged in a serious conversation. Emma and Ruth were at the opposite end, looking at a devotional book. She didn't see Elisabeth, Lukas, or Stephen, and assumed they had gone upstairs to their room. Finally, she spotted Moriah standing by the kitchen sink, speaking to Gabriel in low tones. The two of them had spent a lot of time together since Velda Anne's birth, and Rachel had never seen Moriah look so content. She smiled as she brought the baby to them.

"Tobias and I are leaving," she said, handing Velda Anne to her mother. "*Danki* for letting me hold her. She's precious."

"You're welcome." Moriah glanced at the baby. "Thank goodness she's asleep. She was up for most of the night."

"And here I thought she was the perfect baby," Rachel quipped.

"She is," Gabriel responded, looking at Velda Anne, then at Moriah. "She is."

Rachel and Tobias said their good-byes and headed for home. She leaned back in the buggy, tucking the warm lap blanket around her.

"You're awful quiet," Tobias said, as he led their buggy down the snow-covered road. There weren't many cars out today, adding to the peace of the Sunday afternoon.

"Just thinking."

"Want to let me in on your thoughts?"

"I was just thinking about Gabriel and Moriah, and how much has changed in the past year. They look happy together, *ya*?"

"*Ya*. I wouldn't mind having Gabe as a *schwoger* some day. He's a *gut* man."

"Do you think they'll get married?"

Tobias shrugged. "Who knows? I may have to warn him that marriage isn't as great as I thought."

"What?" She turned to him, gaping.

He grinned, then chucked her under the chin. "It's even better." Then he winked at her. "Gotcha."

"Tobias, when I get my hands on you—"

"I can't wait to find out."

She laughed, then scooted closer to him, leaning her head against his shoulder, more in love with him than she ever thought possible.

Shortly after Tobias and Rachel had left, everyone moved to the family room except for Moriah and Gabriel. She had transferred Velda Anne to his strong embrace. He never seemed to get enough of holding her. They stood by the sink and looked out the window as dusk descended on the horizon, her mind consumed with thoughts and memories. Velda Anne had taken on the features of Levi, and in essence, Gabriel's features too. But for the past couple weeks, she hadn't dwelled on the past. Instead she had thought and prayed about her future.

At one time she thought she wanted to face it alone, with only her child filling the space in her empty heart. Now she knew how wrong she'd been, how selfish and afraid. There was only one way she wanted to face her future, and only one man she wanted to spend it with.

But had she thrown away that chance?

She gazed up at Gabriel, willing him to look at her. Immediately, as if he sensed her silent pleading, he looked down at her, and smiled. "You look different tonight."

"Do I?"

He turned and faced her, Velda Anne asleep in his arms. "*Ya.*"

"In what way?"

"I can't put my finger on it." He searched her face. "You're just so . . . so . . ."

"*Ya*?"

"Beautiful."

She smiled. "There's a reason for that."

He quirked a brow.

"Because I'm with you."

She heard his breath catch. "Moriah," he whispered, his voice husky. Then he gazed at her. "Are you sure?"

"I'm sure. If you still want me, that is."

"If I still want you?" He groaned. "Moriah, I love you. I would marry you right now if I could. The question is . . . would you marry me if I asked?"

She stared at him for a moment, this man who loved her so deeply she could barely fathom it. Finally, she understood what love was, and she felt it nestle inside her heart. God had taken her brokenness, and through Gabriel's love, had made her whole again. "I would be happy to marry you, Gabriel Miller. *Nee*, I would love to marry you."

Such joy filled his eyes that Moriah felt like she was in a dream. Slowly he leaned forward and pressed his lips against hers, his kiss filling her with promise, with desire, with love.

Velda Anne stirred, breaking them apart. She gazed at her daughter, then looked up at Gabriel. "I love you," she said softly.

"I can't tell you how long I've waited to hear those words." His eyes glistened. "I can barely believe I'm hearing them."

"You can believe them," she said. "Because I'll be saying them to you for the rest of our lives."

Acknowledgments

Writing a novel set in an Amish community and featuring Amish characters was a challenge, one I wouldn't have been able to meet without the help of some very generous people. I'd like to thank Maria Byler and her family for their friendship and willingness to answer my many, many questions about the Middlefield Amish. I also thank Nick Fagan, head of Adult Services at the Middlefield Library for being so helpful and pointing me in the right direction for my research.

A special thank you to my editors, Natalie Hanemann and Jenny Baumgartner. Their invaluable expertise, encouragement, and patience played such a vital part in writing this book. Thanks to my agent, Tamela Hancock Murray, for being my cheerleader for so many years—thanks for not giving up on me! And a big thank you to my friends and fellow authors—Jill Eileen Smith, Tamera Alexander, Maureen Lang, Diana Urban, Edwina Columbia, Deb Raney, and Meredith Efken. Their support and encouragement means so much to me.

Above all, I thank my family—my husband James, my son Mathew and my daughters Sydney and Zoie. I love you all very much.

Reading Group Guide

1. When we meet Gabriel, he is struggling to hide his love for his new sister-in-law, Moriah. He also deals with the guilt of coveting his brother's wife. Have you ever wanted something you couldn't have? How did you handle those feelings?

2. Although Levi grew up in a community that values self-denial and loyalty, he has difficulty denying his impulses. Think back to a time when you were tempted. Did you give into that temptation? What was the result? If not, how did God help you overcome the temptation?

3. When Levi leaves Moriah, she blames herself for his abandonment. Why does she choose to believe she's at fault, instead of Levi? Is there such a thing as a "right" way for her to respond?

4. Rachel resents her brother Aaron. Is it justified? Why or why not?

5. After Levi's death, Gabe believes he gave up on his brother too soon. Do you agree? Is there anything Gabe could have done to convince his twin to come back to Moriah and the Amish?

6. Throughout the story, it's clear that Tobias and Rachel have feelings for each other. Besides Rachel dating Christian, are there any other reasons they didn't reveal how they felt?

7. Gabe loves Moriah, but he isn't honest with her. He doesn't tell her he loves her before she marries Levi, and he doesn't divulge the real reason Levi left. Gabe believes he is protecting Moriah by keeping these secrets. Can you think of some circumstances where hiding the truth might be for the best? Would God approve of that choice?

8. Gabe starts to think that if he had told Moriah he loved her before her marriage, Levi would still be alive. Do you agree with his assumption? Why or why not?

9. As a man of his word, Gabe vows to standby Moriah, even though she pushes him away. How does Gabe's patient faithfulness to Moriah mirror God's faithfulness to us?

10. Romans 7:18 says: ". . . I want to do what is good, but I can't" (NIRV). Despite being a woman of deep faith, in her darkest moment Moriah chooses to drown her misery in work instead of prayer. Why do we often choose the opposite of what's best for us, especially when it comes to seeking God?

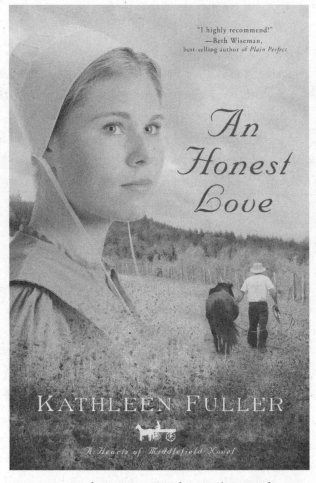